"You're so p[...]"

"You're not bac[...] [...]ry voice.

Nate chuckled. "You're not very good at compliments, are you?"

"I've been told that."

He realized they were standing there, lost in each other's gazes, and making ridiculous small talk when her eyes were saying something else, and he imagined his were doing the same.

He reached out and took her right hand in his. Her fingers were soft although he felt the strength in them. They would have to be strong and supple and efficient to work in an army hospital, especially a forward base. Casualties often came in multiples, and they were usually critical.

Then he took her left one. The fingers were stiff and barely managed to curl slightly along his. His fingers rubbed the long scar on the back of her hand. She tried to pull away, but he pulled her hand up to his lips.

"It's ugly," she said.

"I think it's beautiful. Just like everything about you."

Dear Reader,

I am so delighted to return to magical Covenant Falls, where wounded veterans find a future again with the help of bighearted townspeople and what must be a cupid flying around a certain cabin. That cupid often comes disguised as a dog, in this story an Australian shepherd named Joseph.

I had not intended a miniseries when I wrote my first Home to Covenant Falls book, but the characters in that book wouldn't leave me alone. They wanted their own stories and happy-ever-afters.

In this instance, Nate was flagging me down. He wasn't aware of doing it. After a particularly bad marriage, he has sworn off romance. He doesn't believe in it, even if his two close friends have fallen off the happy bachelorhood wagon. He does not intend to be the next, even when the incoming vet turns out to be a very pretty army nurse haunted by being the only survivor of a terrorist attack that killed her surgical team, including her fiancé.

As in previous cases, it takes a town to heal wounded hearts, this time with the assistance of two wayward camels.

Enjoy!

Patricia Potter

USA TODAY Bestselling Author

PATRICIA POTTER

———

A Soldier's Journey

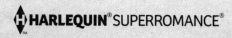

Recycling programs
for this product may
not exist in your area.

ISBN-13: 978-0-373-60954-3

A Soldier's Journey

Copyright © 2016 by Patricia Potter

All rights reserved. Except for use in any review, the reproduction or utilization of this work in whole or in part in any form by any electronic, mechanical or other means, now known or hereinafter invented, including xerography, photocopying and recording, or in any information storage or retrieval system, is forbidden without the written permission of the publisher, Harlequin Enterprises Limited, 225 Duncan Mill Road, Don Mills, Ontario M3B 3K9, Canada.

This is a work of fiction. Names, characters, places and incidents are either the product of the author's imagination or are used fictitiously, and any resemblance to actual persons, living or dead, business establishments, events or locales is entirely coincidental.

This edition published by arrangement with Harlequin Books S.A.

For questions and comments about the quality of this book, please contact us at CustomerService@Harlequin.com.

® and TM are trademarks of Harlequin Enterprises Limited or its corporate affiliates. Trademarks indicated with ® are registered in the United States Patent and Trademark Office, the Canadian Intellectual Property Office and in other countries.

Printed in U.S.A.

Patricia Potter is a bestselling and award-winning author of more than sixty books. Her Western romances and romantic suspense novels have received numerous awards, including *RT Book Reviews'* Storyteller of the Year, its Career Achievement award for Western Historical Romance and Best Hero of the Year. She is a seven-time RITA® Award finalist for RWA and a three-time MAGGIE® Award winner. She is a past president of Romance Writers of America. Patricia is also a passionate animal lover, which is reflected in many of her books but never more so than in her Home to Covenant Falls miniseries. She believes curiosity is the most important trait of any writer, and she's often led far astray when researching a subject.

Books by Patricia Potter

HARLEQUIN SUPERROMANCE

Home to Covenant Falls

The Soldier's Promise
Tempted by the Soldier

HARLEQUIN BLAZE

The Lawman

HARLEQUIN HISTORICAL

Swampfire
Between the Thunder
Samara
Seize the Fire
Chase the Thunder
Dragonfire
The Silver Link
The Abduction

Other titles by this author available in ebook format.

Dedicated to Piya Campaña, my editor,
who seems to know magical ways of her own
to bring out the best of every book.

CHAPTER ONE

HER HEART POUNDED so fast Lieutenant Andy Stuart thought it would burst from her body as she stopped suddenly in the hall of the military hospital.

It couldn't be, but still, she stared at a doctor and nurse whispering to each other in a corner.

Jared. It was Jared. Jared and herself. Joy surged through her. Jared wasn't dead. He wasn't dead! His face. Her face. Together.

She was transfixed. Then the couple moved and Jared's face dissolved into an older, wider face. The woman…

No. Come back.

Confusion filled her and she started to shake.

A nurse approached. "Is anything wrong?"

Yes. Everything. She shook her head.

"Can I help you find someone?"

"No… I know where…" Andy stopped. How could she explain seeing her dead fiancé? How could she explain the joy, then the anger replacing it? *It should have been Jared and me.*

Trembling, she watched as the couple disappeared down the hall. Anger swept through her.

Anger at Jared. Anger at the world in which two people whispered together and *lived*.

"Let me help you," the nurse tried again. "Where are you going?"

Andy directed that fury at the nurse. "It's none of your business," she said and was immediately appalled at herself. She was never rude, particularly to someone who was trying to help. Never until the past seven months.

"I'm sorry, so sorry," she said, then took off for Dr. Payne's office. How could she have thought she saw Jared?

She burst into the reception area, past the receptionist and into his private office. He looked up from his desk, a question in his eyes. She placed herself directly in front of him. "I saw him. I saw Jared. And myself. But it wasn't us. It was strangers, but they had our faces. How could that be?" She was shaking.

Andy hadn't bothered closing the door as she stormed inside. Anger and confusion were too strong.

Dr. Robert Payne calmly got up and closed the door, then sat back down in his chair. "About time," he said.

She stared at him as if he were the crazy one. "A couple," she said. "A nurse and doctor. Whispering to each other in a corner. For a second I thought it was Jared…and me. And then I looked again, and they were strangers. I was so angry. I *am* angry. So damned angry." She wasn't making sense. She knew she wasn't making sense, but she couldn't stop.

Dr. Payne leaned forward. "What you saw isn't that unusual with people who have lost someone they love. Especially given the circumstances."

He paused, then added, "I've been waiting for that anger," he said gently.

Andy paced the floor. "I don't understand."

"You've bottled it all up. You haven't let yourself feel anything. You've just been drifting, indifferent to everything."

"So wanting to hit two innocent people is healthy?"

"You didn't do it, did you?"

"No, but I wanted to."

"It's normal, Andy. It's normal getting angry when you see a happy couple. It's something you expected to be. And it was torn away from you in the worst possible way. It's okay to be angry. It's good, even. Better than stifling those feelings to the point of not being able to function."

"I've *been* functioning," Andy said defensively.

He just looked at her.

"Have you found a job yet?"

"Cash register and waitress at a coffee shop. Just two days a week, but it helps pay for my part of an apartment."

"What about nursing?"

She shrugged. "Who wants to hire someone who

hears a noise and drops to the ground screaming? Wouldn't instill much confidence in patients. Not to mention a bum hand. I can operate the cash machine and take orders, but I can't carry heavy trays."

"There's a lot of fields in nursing where you *can* work."

She looked at him with hostile eyes. "Doc, I really don't think I can do that." Dammit, he *knew* why. He knew all the reasons. He knew everything about her. Well, *practically* everything, after two visits a week for the past six months, including two months while having surgeries and later as an out-patient for PTSD.

"We're getting pressured to let you go now that your medical discharge has gone through. You'll transfer to the Veterans Administration."

"I'm losing you?"

"I thought you didn't like me."

"I didn't like where you made me go."

"Today is important, Andy. I'm not saying to-morrow is going to be easier. What happened today will happen again. You'll see someone who re-minds you of Jared. The anger will come flood-ing back. But it's the beginning of taking your life back."

She looked doubtful.

"Have you cried yet?" The question came out of nowhere. Or maybe not. He'd asked it a month ago.

She thought about lying, but what the hell. "No,"

she said. It was unnatural. She knew it, but she hurt too much for tears.

"You can only keep them inside so long," he said.

She only nodded.

He sat there studying her. "I have a proposal for you," he finally said.

"What?" she said suspiciously.

"I wouldn't have suggested it yesterday. You weren't ready. You still might not be, but given the circumstances I think it's worth a try."

She waited.

"There's a cabin in a small town in Colorado that's available," he said slowly, and she knew he was carefully choosing his words. "It belongs to a veteran who recently married. It was passed to another vet who no longer needs it. The town has a large number of veterans, and they look after each other."

She hated his calm, reasoning tone. She didn't want reason. She wanted to turn back the clock to a time before her world had fallen apart. And she didn't want to go to someone else's cabin.

Andy knew she didn't have many choices. She had worn out her welcome at the military hospital. She couldn't go home. She didn't want to take her grief and anger there or be a burden on her family back home. Jobs were rare, if not nonexistent, in a dying coal town, especially for a surgical nurse who would start trembling uncontrollably at loud noises and who had a hand that didn't work. Never mind the nightmares that made a night's sleep rare.

She should be married now, making a home with the man she loved with all her heart, maybe even beginning a baby they both wanted. That dream was gone, and there was precious little left.

But charity…

A Stuart didn't take charity. Never had, no matter how bad the times, and they had been bad most of her life. She never wanted to live in a small town again. She'd felt trapped as a child and later as a teenager. She'd been different. A nerd in a town where half the kids didn't finish high school and most went into the mines, and, if they didn't, they left as fast as they could hitch a ride out of town.

Her out had been the ROTC and a ROTC scholarship for a nursing degree. She was the first and only member of her family to go to college, much less obtain a four-year degree. The price had been ten years in the army, much of it in Iraq and Afghanistan field hospitals.

And now…now there was nothing. She'd sent most of her salary home to her mother and youngest sister in West Virginia. It would be a while, apparently a long while, before she received back pay and disability from the army. The backlog was as much as two years long. She was, in effect, the next thing to being dead broke.

"I don't want charity," she said again.

"It's not charity," he said, leaning across the

desk. "You might say it's meant as a way station for returning vets while they find their legs. It sits alongside a lake fed by the mountain streams, and there's a large number of supportive vets, some of whom have gone through much the same thing you're going through now."

He paused, then added, "As for charity, you'll probably be asked, but not required, to do something connected to the town. The last vet taught computer classes for senior citizens."

"Where is he now?"

"He joined the police department there. He's being groomed for chief."

"What was he?" she asked, curious despite herself.

"A chopper pilot. Suffered a head injury that kept him from flying again. I have to say that he had the same reaction as you have but decided to try it. He's very happy that he did. He said you could call him if you want."

"You told him about me?" she said.

"Not you specifically. Not without talking to you first. I just said there was someone who could be interested in the cabin."

"And no one wants to know more?"

"Nope."

"I think it's weird," she said.

Dr. Payne smiled. "It's a good kind of weird. But the vets are a close-knit group. They have a weekly poker game," he said with a grin. Somewhere in all their discussions, she'd let it slip that she had become a good poker player during the slow times at the field hospital.

"All guys?"

"Don't know. Didn't ask. Doesn't matter. They take care of each other."

"I don't need to be taken care of." She feared she sounded like a child. She wasn't going to admit that maybe, just maybe, she did.

"If Covenant Falls doesn't work out for you, you can always get into a PTSD program in Denver. There's a good one there."

She looked at him warily. He knew her financial situation. In fact, he knew a great deal about her. She had been in a stupor for months after Jared's death. He had tried to make her want to live again, to believe that was what Jared would want.

"Give it a try," Dr. Payne said, obviously sensing victory. "You don't have to stay. It's not a jail sentence. If you're uncomfortable or just don't like it, I'll find something else."

"I'll think about it," Andy said. She really didn't care where she was. And he was right. She wouldn't have to stay.

"Do you like dogs?" Dr. Payne asked unexpectedly.

"Sure. Who doesn't?" Andy replied, relieved to be off the subject. "Never had one. Money was too tight when I was a kid, then a dog doesn't really fit into army life unless it's military."

"There's several programs, including one near here that matches shelter dogs with vets who have PTSD. They're trained to sense when a PTSD attack is coming and alert their vet."

She hesitated. A dog? How could she take care of a dog when she couldn't take care of herself right now? Dr. Payne waited, then said gently, "You would be saving a life." He paused. "And I can probably win you a few more days here."

He was trying to force her to make a decision, but the idea suddenly appealed to Andy. Loneliness was like a shroud around her. And a dog wouldn't ask questions or give sympathy or question her choices. "Would the cabin owner approve?"

The psychologist grinned.

"He adopted a retired military dog with PTSD. The woman he married has four rescue dogs and, from what I hear, two horses, a cat and a son. He was a dedicated loner before he went to Covenant Falls."

She couldn't hide her skepticism. The loner probably hadn't seen his fiancé shot down in a hail of bullets by one of people he was trying to help. "How much is a dog? I don't have much money."

"It's free. The dog has all its shots, is well trained and there's equipment provided, as well. A dog bed, dishes. Food. Toys."

She felt like a fish being reeled in. She didn't like being manipulated, but she had to make a decision. And fast.

Dr. Payne waited, as he always did. He rarely appeared to push, but in his own devious way, that was exactly what happened.

"Maybe I'll give the cabin a try," she said reluctantly.

"What about the dog?" Dr. Payne said.

She hesitated, just as she hesitated at any move forward these days. Inertia had taken over her life. Decisions were difficult if not impossible. That was entirely new for her. She had been making decisions since she was little older than a toddler. When set on a course she could be rarely be deterred. But that was before. Now…nothing was important.

"Andy," Dr. Payne said, changing from his usual formal "Lieutenant." "Give it a try. At least talk to the trainer. See the dog. You don't have to make a decision this minute."

There was that reason again. Sometimes she hated it.

She nodded her head.

THREE DAYS LATER, she drove with Dr. Payne to meet the dog. She braced herself for meeting someone new and having to make a decision.

Dr. Payne had warned her that the trainer wouldn't let the dog go with just anyone. There had to be "a fit." She swallowed as Dr. Payne turned the car onto a well-rutted dirt road. What if the dog rejected her? She didn't know whether that was what she wanted or not. She had decided that if it did work she was going to keep an emotional distance from the animal.

Why had she let Dr. Payne talk her into this?

"You're second-guessing yourself again," Dr. Payne said.

"You didn't trust me to get here on my own," she accused him.

She'd been surprised when he'd offered to drive her down on his day off. Probably because he feared she would back out, or not make it in the Bucket, her ancient Volkswagen.

If the introduction went well, she would be expected to stay at the trainer's ranch for several days for intense training and to ensure the match would be successful.

Maybe it wouldn't be. In the past few days, she'd read enough about the program to know there had to be trust on the part of both the veteran and the dog. She didn't know if she could give that.

Dr. Payne turned onto a dirt road that led to a small ranch house. There were also stables, an oblong building with a chimney, kennels and a fenced-in area. Several dogs came to the fence and barked as Dr. Payne parked the car.

A wiry woman came to the car as Andy stepped out. "Lieutenant," she said. "I'm Karen Conway. Call me Karen. Everyone does." She held out a weathered hand, and Andy took it.

"We won't waste time," Karen said. "I know Richard…Dr. Payne…hasn't much of that."

The way she said *Richard* startled Andy. There was a warmth in it, as if they were more than simply acquaintances. Dr. Payne never talked about his private life.

Before any more thoughts flickered through her mind, she was herded into the ranch house. A dog was at the window, watching. He didn't move until they were all inside and Karen said, "Joseph, say hello."

The dog approached obediently. He was medium size where she had expected a larger animal. Maybe a German shepherd. But this dog more resembled a small Lassie; his coat appeared woven of shades of tan and black and gray. He had blue eyes that regarded her as cautiously as she expected hers were.

"Joseph?" Karen said again.

The dog held up his paw.

Andy took it gingerly. The fur was soft, and the dog's gaze seemed to reach inside her and ask questions she couldn't answer. Then his tongue flicked out and licked her hand.

"He likes you," Karen said. "It took much longer for Adam to win a kiss."

Andy found herself petting the dog.

"Try behind his ears," Karen said. "That and his stomach are his favorite places."

Andy followed the advice and with her good hand rubbed behind the dog's ears. Joseph turned on his back and bared his stomach. She rubbed it, stopped when she heard a rumbling noise.

"That's a groan of pleasure," Karen said with a smile.

"You sure about that?"

"I'm sure."

Andy went back to rubbing his stomach before straightening up.

"You think he will do?" Karen asked.

Andy stood and Joseph sat in front of her. She hesitated. Joseph lifted the same paw that he had before and looked expectant.

"He's accepted you. Now it's up to you," Karen said. "He's a smart dog, one of the smartest I've trained, and that says a lot. He had to be to survive. If you feel through the fur, you'll find scars. He's had some rough times. Some hikers found him badly hurt in the mountains. They assumed he'd been dumped by someone and had a run-in with wild animals. One of the hikers, a donor to this program, took him home, but he already had several dogs.

"He called me," Karen continued. "Said Joseph had a natural empathy that makes him ideal for our purposes. If you have a nightmare, he knows to wake you up. He will remind you when it's time to go to bed. Panic attack? He will physically interrupt you and redirect the panic."

Andy was stunned. She had read about dogs and

vets but hadn't realized exactly what they did. "All of that?" she asked dubiously.

"And more. He can find and locate objects, like your shoes, or your phone or keys. In other words, he can pretty much do anything you want to teach him to do."

Andy found it hard to believe he could do all that. But if he just interrupted the nightmares, she would be grateful.

"I know it's hard to believe," Karen said, "but it's really remarkable what these dogs can do."

"Dr. Payne said they are free. How can you do that?"

"I have sponsors. Dr. Payne is one of them. But there's others, including area veterinarians who donate their services. I do it because my son had PTSD, only it wasn't recognized like it is now." She paused, then added, "He committed suicide."

"I'm sorry," Andy said.

Karen simply nodded. "If you decide you want to come into the program, you'll stay in the bunkhouse with the dog until I think the two of you are ready. But I want to know for sure that you're committed, that you will stick with it. I don't want Joseph disappointed again."

"What happened?"

"Adam took Joseph home and then discovered his wife was extremely allergic to dog hair. It was either her or Joseph." She looked sternly into Andy's eyes. "You don't have anyone allergic, do you?"

"No."

Andy looked down at the dog. He looked up at her. "Are you ready for me?" she asked.

She would have sworn the dog smiled. "Why the name Joseph?" she asked.

"Of the coat-of-many-colors fame," Karen said. "You will be expected to stay here a short time. Maybe a week, maybe less, maybe more. You'll live in the bunkhouse with the dog while you get to know each other. He's trained, but you're not. You'll learn what he can do for you, and learn to accept what he has to offer."

Karen paused, then added, "You up for the challenge?"

Andy looked down at Joseph. The brightest blue eyes she'd ever seen looked back as if to say, "What are you waiting for?"

She nodded. She had to be. It was what Jared would want. He used to say that what first attracted him to her was her strength. Instead, she had been a zombie these past months. She hadn't even been able to cry since she'd woken up from surgery. She hadn't remembered everything then; she'd just had a head full of dread. Then it came back slowly. The first gunshot...

"Good," Karen said, breaking into that memory. "Joseph has had all his shots, and when you're ready to leave, we'll give you supplies. After that, it's up to you, but we ask that you keep in touch and if for some reason you feel you can't keep Joseph, return him to us."

Joseph made a low sound, like a rumble, and moved closer to her. She felt his warm body through the jeans that were much too large for her. She reached down and stroked his head. He licked her hand and looked up at her as if she were a goddess.

"When can you get started?" Karen asked.

Andy looked at Dr. Payne.

"Three days?" he asked. "It will take a few days to do the paperwork, discharge you from my care. And it will probably take you that long to buy a few things."

She bit her lip. Everything was going so fast. "Trying to get rid of me?" she asked.

"Now that you mention it…" He smiled.

"I have to give notice at the coffee shop, but I don't think that will a problem. I broke more than a few cups."

"Good. Now that's settled," Karen said. "Can you stay for dinner?"

"Wish we could, but I have a meeting tonight," Dr. Payne said. "And I imagine Andy has some planning to do."

He ushered Andy out the door and into his car. Once settled, he asked, "Should I accept the use of the cabin in Covenant Falls on your behalf?"

"You're pushing it, Doc."

He shrugged. "You can always cancel it."

She still wasn't sure taking on a dog was a good

thing. Since the violent afternoon that had taken everything away from her, she'd changed from a hard-charging, ambitious army officer to someone who couldn't make a decision on what to eat. Mainly because she hadn't cared. Didn't want to care.

Neither was she sure she wanted to form a close bond with the dog. In fact, she was quite sure she didn't. But maybe the dog *would* help. Anything to keep from falling to pieces whenever she heard a loud noise. She would just have to maintain an emotional distance, that was all.

She looked at Dr. Payne. "I'll give it a try."

She had made her first decision in months.

CHAPTER TWO

NATE ROWLAND WIPED the sweat from his forehead and looked at his watch. Time to leave and meet the incoming vet.

He took one last glance at the interior of the reception area of the inn he and Josh were transforming from an old by-the-hour motel, then locked the door and headed for his pickup truck.

He was the designated welcoming committee. Josh, who owned the cabin, was in Denver, and Clint, the second vet who had been in residence at the cabin, was completing a law enforcement training program in Colorado Springs.

Nate had volunteered before he learned the new occupant was a woman, and an officer at that. Officers didn't bother him much. The woman part did. He'd made an art of avoiding them for the past four years. Burned once, her fault. Burned twice, his fault.

Josh's cabin seemed to have come under a spell. First Josh. Then Clint. After moving in, Josh had gotten married, and now Clint, the second occupant, was more or less engaged. Hopefully. Nate had never been superstitious, but damn, there was something about that cabin that brought even the most marriage-averse people to the altar.

He looked around the freshly painted lobby—warm sand tones with a huge oak beam reaching across the arched ceiling and a stack-stone fireplace. He was more proud of the inn than anything he'd previously built. Josh had provided his own money and a bank loan and turned Nate loose on design. They'd stretched every penny a yard long. The furniture was coming from a firm going out of business, and it was quality at a low price.

All they needed was guests.

The preview opening was scheduled in seven weeks, which was why Josh was in Denver. He was making the rounds of the state tourist association, tourist publications and newspapers. They were offering complimentary three-night stays to anyone who could help them promote Covenant Falls.

He glanced at his watch again. He wanted to be at the cabin at 8:00 a.m. The newest vet was expected between nine and ten. He'd stacked wood for the fireplace yesterday, and he knew that Josh's wife had stocked the kitchen.

He locked the front door of the Covenant Falls Inn and drove to the cabin. The mayor, Josh's wife, called it the Rainbow Cabin. She'd fallen in love with Josh there, almost, she said, from the moment she had seen him. The same thing had happened to Clint when he'd met the town veterinarian.

Josh had said the new resident was a military

nurse, a lieutenant. All he knew was that she had been injured and had PTSD. She would be the first female veteran in town, and he wondered how she would fit in, particularly at the Monday-night poker games. But he would do his part in making her welcome. He fervently hoped she was plain and obnoxious.

The cabin was spotless. Someone, probably Eve, had placed flowers in vases on the dining table and on the table next to the sofa. There was a platter of Maude's sweet rolls in the kitchen.

He made a pot of coffee and walked outside to the porch swing. It was a fine April day with a cool breeze and bright sun. He thought about the day he'd met Josh, when he'd hired him to replace the floor on the cabin. His life had changed dramatically. Even the town had a new vitality since Josh's arrival. Clint added his own impact.

Nate wondered if this military nurse would also rock the Covenant Falls boat.

He was looking at the lake when an old Volkswagen turned into the driveway. Yellow. And not old, but ancient. A relic, really. His gaze followed its path until it stopped. He stood, opened the porch door and went out to meet the new resident.

She didn't move. She just sat in the car looking at the cabin. A dog sat protectively next to her. Then, as he reached the car, the driver opened the door and got out. Reluctantly, it appeared.

His worst fears were realized. She wasn't drop-dead gorgeous. Not in the accepted sense. But she had a quality even more dangerous. She was slender, even gaunt, but her face was something out of a painting. Strong lines and jaw, with striking, haunted light gray eyes that dominated all the other features.

Nate realized he had been staring. "Lieutenant Stuart," he said, holding out his hand. He tried to steady his voice even as he was affected by the ethereal sadness in her. He noticed her left hand was in a leather brace.

"I'm Nate Rowland, your welcoming committee," he said. "If it's okay with you, I'll show you around, give you the keys and answer any questions."

She nodded and took his hand, but there was no heart in it. "Thank you. And it's not lieutenant. Not any longer. I'm just Andy Stuart." She turned, and the dog, outfitted with a service animal's coat, jumped out and stood close to her. "This is Joseph. We're just getting to know each other. I was told he would be welcome."

"More than welcome. This is a very dog-friendly community," Nate said. "Can I get your luggage?"

She hesitated, and he sensed that she was reluctant to take any help. "I don't have much," she said, "but perhaps you can help with Joseph's belongings. He has more than I do."

She waited while he opened the trunk that was filled with dog food, a dog bed and a cardboard box full of dog dishes, toys and a leash. She was right about her luggage. He saw only a medium-size duffel.

Only too aware of her presence, he picked up the dog bed and the big sack of dog food while she reached for the duffel with her good hand and used the wounded fist to slam the trunk closed. Then she followed him inside. He watched surprise spread across her face as she took in the comfortable interior. "It's very nice," she said after a moment. "Are you the owner?"

"No. Just a friend of the owner." Nate placed the dog bed in front of the living room window and, still holding the dog food, led the way into the kitchen. "I made some fresh coffee, and the owner of the town's diner sent over some sweet rolls. They're great. The owner's wife also filled the fridge. You'll find a couple of casseroles and cold cuts along with bread, eggs, milk and sodas."

"Thank you," she said. It was politely said with little emotion.

"There's a bathroom next to the master bedroom down the hall. There's also a second bedroom that's mostly a library now. Help yourself to any of the books. There's a desk in there, as well." He paused, then added, "As for town, you probably drove through it. There's a general store, grocery, hardware store and pharmacy there, along with Maude's Diner. The food is very good, especially the steaks, and they're easy on the wallet."

She nodded. "I'll remember that."

She was scarce with conversation, but that was all right. So was he. Usually. "How long have you been driving?" he asked, strangely reluctant to leave.

"Since midnight. I like driving at night and dawn when there's little or no traffic."

He suspected it was more than that. Depending on the severity of PTSD, late-night and early-morning driving had fewer distractions.

"That car looks like a real collector's dream," he said, probing for more information, even as he knew he should be leaving. And quickly. She was distant.

"The Bucket," she said with the first hint of a smile. "She's been with me fifteen years, and she was pretty ancient before that. I've nursed her back to health more times than I can remember, but she's a tough old lady. I couldn't leave her behind."

He mentally filed that information. Nursed back to health? The car? Was she a mechanic, too?

He was lingering. He had intended to say, "Hello, here's the keys and goodbye." He gave himself a mental kick. That was exactly what he should do.

"I'll leave you to get some rest," he said. He took out a sheet of paper he'd prepared. "My number is there, along with several others you might want to know. The veterinarian. The town doctor. Josh Manning, who owns the cabin."

She nodded.

He handed her the keys to the cabin, then leaned down and scratched the dog's ears. "Joseph? Of the many-colored coat?"

"It seems to have been the inspiration. I had nothing to do with it," she said defensively.

"He'll have a lot of company around here," Nate said. Damn, he was rambling on, but he didn't want to leave her alone. There was something broken inside her. Her voice was soft, Southern, but it carried no strength, no conviction that would be expected of an army officer.

He was nearly undone by those haunted gray eyes. They were framed by brown hair that fell to her shoulders, a simple style that he thought was probably for utilitarian reasons rather than vanity, although it suited her. She wore jeans and a simple white T-shirt and looked to be in her early thirties.

He suddenly realized he was staring. "I had better go," he said. "The television is satellite and has a lot of stations available. There's a path just to the left of the cabin that goes up the side of the mountain. There's some great views there." He cocked his head. "Anything else you would like to know?"

She shook her head. "It's far more than I expected." She hesitated, then added, "Dr. Payne said there might be something I can do to pay for the use of the cabin." It was a question more than a statement.

"Is there anything you like to do?"

"I'm a surgical nurse. Or was one before my hand was damaged. I don't really know anything else."

"I'm sure Josh and Eve will find something if you're interested. Eve's uncanny in ferreting out talents."

"Dr. Payne said she's the mayor?"

He grinned. "And a damn good one."

She nodded, obviously absorbing the information, then went to the door. "Thank you for the welcome," she said.

It was an obvious dismissal. "Don't hesitate to call if you need anything or have questions," he said again as he walked toward the door. "Covenant Falls is very safe, and the sunsets are great. Oh, and every Monday night we have a meeting of vets. Seven p.m. at the community center. It's right at the end of this road."

"And play poker?" Her lips eased slightly into an almost smile.

"You heard about that?" Nate said with a grin. "It's just penny ante. But we enjoy it. And we're happy to have new faces." Particularly a pretty one, he suspected. He kept that thought to himself and hurried on. "You can bring Joseph. Josh always brings his dog, and everyone has gotten accustomed to having him there." He headed for the door. He had already stayed longer than necessary. He forced himself down the path to his pickup.

As he opened the truck door, he glanced back.

Andy Stuart was watching as he left. Slim and straight and still, she looked like a statue.

He started his pickup and headed toward Lake Road. He swore to himself. Dammit. Why couldn't she have been gruff and rough and thoroughly disagreeable? Instead, she was soft-spoken and appealing. More than appealing. He suspected the haunted gray eyes would stay with him. It was something he did not need at the moment. Or ever.

Hell, he had always been a sucker for a damsel in distress. That particular weakness had nearly destroyed his life. He'd sworn it wasn't going to happen again. He had a chance now to rebuild his career, and he damn well wasn't going to let anything, especially a woman, risk it.

He was going to stay away. A long, long way away.

Andy watched him drive away, then turned back to explore the cabin.

Her first impression of the cabin was warmth. Someone had loved this cabin. And that made her ache inside. It was just like the home she and Jared had planned to buy. A large living area with expansive windows, hardwood floors and a huge fireplace.

She went into the kitchen and poured a cup of coffee from the electric pot. Mr. Rowland had put out a cup and bowls of sugar and creamer. She liked her coffee black, and the stronger the better. She had become addicted to it in college and later during long hours in operating rooms.

She took a plate with two rolls outside and returned for the coffee. She didn't want to risk spilling either one with her bad hand. She sat in one of several chairs on the screened porch and ignored the swing. Joseph followed her and sat at her side and regarded the roll enviously.

Andy couldn't help but smile as the dog's tongue lolled out the side of his mouth. She steeled herself against getting too attached to the dog, but she had to admit he was growing on her. She couldn't resist giving him a piece of roll.

She looked out through the pines to the lake. The sky was impossibly blue against the mountains, and a cool breeze was refreshing. The scent of pines perfumed the air.

For the first time since she set off on this journey, she relaxed. Maybe this *had* been a good move, temporarily anyway. She liked Nate Rowland. He hadn't pushed but made her feel comfortable in a strange place under strange circumstances. He was lanky, like Jared, and had a warm smile.

Grief filled her as she saw Jared's smile again, slow to come but then widening until it filled her heart. It was as real today as it had been seven months ago.

She felt the darkness descending again. The despair. Joseph nudged her, and she stood, remembering what Nate Rowland said about the mountain. A walk. Fresh air. That was what she needed. She looked up and saw the path he had mentioned.

"What do you think, Joseph? Should we try it?"

Joseph wagged his tail eagerly.

She silently admitted to doubts. Her hand would be no use if she needed to grab something. But the path was there. Taunting her. Inviting her to leave her safety zone.

She could hear Jared now. *Go for it.*

A breeze brushed her face, as if he were there next to her.

She started up the path. Joseph went ahead of her but kept looking back to make sure she was keeping pace with him. She didn't realize how out of shape she was. She hadn't run since Afghanistan.

She was breathing hard when she reached what was obviously a lookout. She paused and looked out over the town of Covenant Falls. It looked like a toy town from here. The lake appeared an even richer blue. On its border was a large park with a beach, gazebo, swings and a large rambling building. Four church steeples were also visible. The main street was the only one that looked busy.

A peaceful town where everyone probably knew everyone. It wasn't what she and Jared had planned. He'd been a top surgeon specializing in traumatic injuries. He had already been offered positions in several practices in Chicago and Richmond, Virginia, at the end of his service commitment. Richmond had been her hope, but she'd suspected Chicago had been his.

Nor was Covenant Falls anything like the mining town where she had been raised. That town had the scent of poverty hovering over it. Hardscrabble houses and bare yards. There was always the smell of coal and dust and the sound of heavy machinery.

Joseph made curious little noises in his throat and licked her hand. "Sensing something, huh?" she said. "But I'm okay. Really, I am."

He looked at her with those clear blue eyes. He seemed to be saying, "I'm here now. You're not alone."

Not alone. Then, why did she feel she was? Nate Rowland seemed nice enough. But he was a stranger, and she intended to keep him that way.

He'd looked Western inside and out with his hard, lean build, plaid flannel shirt with the sleeves rolled up, worn jeans and boots. His hair was a little long and looked as if it had been combed with his fingers, and his eyes were a cool hazel. His hand had been hard with calluses.

Jared's hands had been so different. His fingers had been long and smooth and supple, as if designed to perform the most delicate and precise surgery. His dark eyes were always intense…

Don't! Don't do this! She filled her lungs with

fresh air and the rich smell of pine. She swallowed hard. Joseph nudged her again, and she reached out and scratched behind his ears. He was a dog. A smart one, but could he really read her mind?

She hadn't had a nightmare or panic attack since the third night at Karen's ranch, but then that had been only a few days ago. Her problem was she never knew when they would strike. That uncertainty kept her from searching out a nonsurgical nursing position.

Rested, she looked at the towering mountains in the other direction. Snow-covered peaks glistened in the noon sun. How she wished Jared could see it, too.

She could almost hear his voice. *Live, sweetheart. Live for me.*

He wouldn't be happy with the way she had closed herself off from life.

And yet pain was a living thing inside her. It had been for months. She couldn't let go of it. She didn't want to let it go. It would be a betrayal of those who died that day. But maybe here—away from the military and everything that reminded her of her former life—maybe she could manage it. Maybe she *could* take pleasure in a deep blue sky and a fresh breeze without feeling guilty.

She started down the mountain. The path was well trod but steep. She had to concentrate on every step—a good thing, in her mind. She was winded when she reached the bottom. She remembered when she could run ten miles without breathing hard.

But that was a lifetime ago. Now she had to face new challenges. She only hoped she could.

CHAPTER THREE

ONCE BACK IN the cabin, Andy decided to explore. She'd had very little sleep last night, but she hated the very thought of sleep these days. Too many nightmares.

She was curious about Covenant Falls now. Curious about the cabin and its owner and past occupants. She'd been stationed in Texas and had visited Colorado during leaves, but she'd never heard of Covenant Falls. She wanted to know more about her mysterious benefactor who would offer a very comfortable cabin to a stranger.

She checked out the kitchen fridge and cupboard. As Mr. Rowland said, both were filled. There was a small room in back with a washer and dryer.

Then she went through the living room to a large bedroom. The bed was a double and looked comfortable. The headboard faced a window that framed large pine trees. The bathroom was medium size with a large walk-in shower.

Then she inspected the desk in the second bedroom, which apparently served as an office and library. She found pens and notebooks, along with reams of paper as well as stacks of books. She carried a notebook and a couple of pens into the living room and settled in a big comfortable chair.

She started writing, making notes about Dr. Payne, Karen Conway and Nate Rowland and what she knew about them. Impressions, really. It had been a habit of hers since she left home for college.

There had been so many new people, and notes helped her to remember them all. She turned the notes into journals when she went on active duty. There had been so much to see and remember.

She hadn't written anything since the attack, nor had she ever asked about the journals or her other property left in Afghanistan. She hadn't wanted anything. They had been stored with other items in a storage unit near the base. There had been so much about Jared in the last one, and she couldn't bear to read it.

When she finished, she turned on the television and ran through the stations, stopping only at a news channel when she heard a commentator mention Afghanistan. More troops were pulling out. Her team had been among the last medical teams remaining. The rest of the unit had probably been dismantled after the attack.

Just the thought of Afghanistan sent familiar images swirling through her head: the day she had arrived at the forward base, the first time she'd met Jared, the last time she had seen him. Blood had been everywhere then...

Joseph moved closer to her, nudged her and made

guttural sounds in his throat. She assumed that was his way of reassuring her. "It's okay," she said and rubbed his ears. The guttural sounds turned into something more like a purr.

Andy turned the television off and looked at the clock. Just after noon.

She should fix lunch. She wasn't hungry, but she needed to eat. She was foraging in the fridge when the phone rang.

"Hi" came the cheerful voice on the phone when she picked it up. "I'm Eve Manning. I hope I'm not intruding, but I wanted to make sure you had everything you need. I would have been there to meet you, but I had a meeting in town."

"Mr. Rowland was very helpful," Andy replied.

"Are you up to a visit? And don't be polite."

Andy hesitated. It was the last thing she wanted. She was tired and tense from the drive. She had met one stranger, had imagined his unsaid questions. She didn't want more. But the caller was the mayor, and Andy had accepted use of her husband's cabin. She sighed. Maybe coming here hadn't been the best idea.

But then she probably couldn't sleep, either. "That would be fine," Andy said, hoping the delay in her reply didn't say more than her actual words.

"Would one be okay? I can take you to Maude's or we can stay at the cabin. You decide."

She needed to get out. She knew that. She couldn't retreat into a safe place again, as she had done with the hospital. She had taken one step forward in coming here. It was time to take another. "Mr. Rowland mentioned Maude's."

"Good. I can show you around town. I have to warn you, though, that everyone will want to meet you. They mean well, but they sort of take vets under their collective wing whether or not you want to be there."

"I'm warned," Andy replied.

"Nate also said you have a dog," Eve said.

"Yes, Joseph. He's a service dog, although not the kind that can go in restaurants." Apparently the law only permitted dogs for physically handicapped vets.

"Here he can," the mayor said. "Maude has a soft spot for dogs, and the mayor's just fine with it. Your predecessors both take their dogs inside."

"Then, I will," Andy said. "We're new to each other and this is a strange place for him." *For both of us.*

"You'll have to introduce him to my crew," Eve said.

"Crew?"

"Five dogs," she said. "And a cat." She hesitated, then added, "Well, one is strictly my husband's. Amos was a military dog and highly disciplined. The rest of my group are rather unruly."

"Sounds…interesting."

"Terrifying sometimes. I'll be there at one."

The phone clicked off.

Andy took a deep breath. Had she done the right thing in agreeing to go to a public place? What if she had a panic attack? She knew, though, she *had* to get busy doing *something* or she could sink back in inertia.

"What do you think, Joseph?" Despite her vow to the contrary, she found herself talking to Joseph often.

Joseph stared at her with those penetrating blue eyes. He barked.

"I'll take that as a yes," she said. She filled Joseph's water dish, then went into the bedroom. She opened the duffel and took out a sweater and a clean pair of jeans and headed for the shower.

THE MAYOR ARRIVED just as Andy's watch hit 1:00 p.m.

She didn't know what she'd expected, but when she opened the door, she saw a tall, attractive woman with shoulder-length dark hair, a pug nose and a wide smile.

"I'm Eve," the mayor said simply.

"And I'm Andy," Andy said.

"Andy it is. Welcome back to the civilian world." Eve leaned down and rubbed Joseph's ears. "And who is this?" she asked as Joseph frantically wagged his tail.

"Joseph," Andy replied. "He's only been with me a short time."

"Ever had a dog before?"

"No. Dogs and the army don't go together, and my family never had one when I was young."

"Watch out. They steal your heart in no time."

Joseph's tail wagged happily as they walked to the pickup parked next to the Bucket. Eve opened the passenger door and invited Joseph inside and showed him a spot behind the front passenger seat. Andy climbed in after him.

"Thank you for including him," Andy said. "And thanks for the use of the cabin."

"That's my husband's doing."

"Why?" The question was abrupt and probably rude, but it had been pricking at her.

"His best friend owned the cabin and was killed saving Josh's life. Josh had a lot of grief and anger when he left the army. He directed it toward rehabbing the cabin he inherited from his buddy. Rehabbing it was therapeutic for Josh, but when we married he moved in with me. The cabin needed a new resident, and Josh wanted something good to come out of a tragedy."

Andy felt an instant kinship with the owner. No wonder she'd felt more at home here than she'd expected.

They left the cabin, and Eve drove out of the driveway. "That's a great car," she said of the yellow Volkswagen. "My husband will go crazy when he sees it. So will Stephanie, our veterinarian. How old is it?"

"Nearly forty," Andy said.

She didn't add that she'd feared she wouldn't be able to drive it again after the injury to her hand, but she had practiced for hours until she felt confident she could steady the wheel while working the clutch.

"I'll give you a quick tour," Eve said, interrupting that thought. "The second cottage down from you belongs to Mrs. Byars," Eve explained. "Her son was killed in the service, and she loves veterans. She'll probably be by in the next few days with something wonderful to eat."

They reached the end of the road. A park was on the right. "That building is our community center. If you don't have a computer, you can use one there. It's free. That's also where the veterans in town meet every Monday night. I'm barred, but you'll be invited."

Eve turned right toward the center, then a left. "This is Main Street," Eve said. Andy looked at the modest houses lining the street for six blocks before hitting businesses on the left side of the road. "That's the city hall, along with the police and fire departments. The police are paid, but the firefighters are all volunteers except for the chief. He's a retired firefighter from Pueblo and receives a small salary for keeping the equipment and conducting training.

"On the left is the veterinarian practice. Stephanie Phillips is one of the best and most caring vets you'll find. A few doors down is Doc Bradley.

He's nearing seventy, and a bit grouchy, but he's a very good general practitioner and can usually be reached day or night. In between the vet and doctor is the real estate and insurance office. A small bank branch is located inside the building.

"There's also a small grocery, a general store and a hardware store. The pharmacy around the corner has office supplies, books and small tech supplies."

She parked in a space with a reserved sign in front of the city hall. "One of the few benefits of being mayor," Eve said. "Maude's is across the street," she added.

Andy felt comfortable the moment she stepped inside the diner. It looked much like the one back home where all the kids went after school.

The diner was busy, but a middle-aged woman who looked as if she was fond of her own food met them. "I'm Maude. You must be Josh's new veteran," she said, then looked down at the dog. "Looks like a fine service dog," she added with a wink. She didn't wait for an answer but led them to the back booth.

After they were seated, Andy asked what was good.

"Josh would say steaks, but I like patty melts."

"Patty melts?"

"Hamburger with onion and melted cheese on rye bread. They are sinful, and I try to limit myself to one a week. I don't always succeed, but I do try."

"You sold me," Andy said, and they ordered.

She wasn't sure how she felt about Maude already knowing who she was. She'd always been a private person except for the close-knit surgical teams with which she'd served...

The memories came flooding back. Her hand crushed the napkin in her lap. Joseph moved closer to her, put his head on her thigh.

She looked up and saw Eve's concerned gaze. "My first husband died six years ago," she said in a low voice that wouldn't carry beyond the booth. "We were childhood sweethearts. I loved him very much. He was a coach, ran in marathons, and I thought he would live forever. He died one afternoon while on the field with the football team he coached. He was running with them when he suddenly dropped to the ground. A heart defect no one had detected. If it hadn't been for Nick, my son... I don't know what I would have done."

Andy suddenly felt betrayed by Dr. Payne. "You know...what happened to me?"

Eve shook her head. "I only know that pain in your eyes. I saw it in my mirror for a long time. If there's ever anything I can do..."

"There is," Andy said. "I need something to do. I don't have much money, but Dr. Payne said it was possible to help in the community. I've always paid my own way."

"What did you do in the army?" Eve asked.

"You don't know?"

"No. Dr. Payne says very little about his recommendations to my husband. Josh probably says even less to me. He figures if you want anyone to know your business, you'll tell them. He's a sphinx where other vets are concerned."

"I think I'll like him."

"You will. He would tear off his arm to help someone, particularly a vet."

"I've known someone like that." Andy bit her lip as the image of Jared popped up again.

Eve looked at her. "They are rare," she said. "Are you interested in history?"

An odd question and quick change of subject. But she nodded.

"Do you like writing?"

"I've kept a journal, that's all."

Eve's eyes suddenly lit. "We're trying to grow the town, create more jobs. We think tourism is the first step. My husband and Nate are finishing rehabbing—rebuilding, really—a very nice inn, but we're a fair distance from populated areas. We need attractions, and I think that attraction could be our history."

"Why?"

"The town was founded by a Scot who came here in the 1840s, saw the lake and established a trading post. There were Native raids, but he saved the life of a Ute chief and they rewarded him with protection and the chief's sister as a wife. He basically built the town and became instrumental in the campaign for statehood. Then there's our falls, where much of this happened."

"I'm not a writer," Andy said. "And shouldn't someone from the community write about the town?"

"We don't need a book," Eve explained. "Just a short, coherent narrative we can use in a brochure and advertising program."

"Wouldn't someone who lives here be more qualified...?"

Eve sighed. "There's a few rivalries around here. And different versions of what happened and where we should go in the future. I think an outsider will be objective and produce a narrative appealing to people outside the community. I want fresh, un-biased eyes." She paused. "We've been thinking about hiring someone, but why don't you take a stab at it? We don't need *Gone with the Wind*."

"Where would I begin?" Andy asked, a kernel of interest building inside. She had always liked his-tory, even thought about being a history teacher, but there had been no scholarships for that.

"Probably the best place is the small museum we've started in the community center. There's old newspapers and photos and some mining equip-ment. You can start there, and then contact Al Mon-roe. He's a descendant of the founder of Covenant Falls, Angus Monroe. There's rumors that Angus kept journals. Al might have them if, indeed, they do exist."

Eve's proposal was the last thing Andy had expected. The more Eve talked, the more intrigued she became. It was far more interesting than the pounding nails or filing papers that she'd expected. And she'd always liked research.

Plus, it would absorb her. She needed something like that. "I'll try it," she finally said. "I can't promise anything remotely coherent."

Eve grinned. "I'll try to tone down my expectations."

Their lunch arrived then, and Andy took a bite. "Mmm," she said. "I like this."

"Good," Eve said, and they both concentrated on the sandwiches and fries. Andy couldn't remember when anything had tasted so good. After they finished, Eve looked at her watch. "I have a meeting in twenty minutes. I'll drop you over at the community center where the museum is."

"Should we drop Joseph off at the cabin first?" Andy asked.

"I think Joseph can go almost any place you want to take him in Covenant Falls. Amos, my husband's dog, has pretty well shattered people's opinions as to where a dog should or should not go. He's the town celebrity."

"Why?" Andy asked.

"He saved my son's life twice," she said, "but that's a long story and takes time in the telling. Why don't you come over for supper tomorrow night? Clint and my husband both want to meet you. It will be really relaxed. You can leave any time you want, no explanations needed. Joseph is invited, as well."

Andy wasn't sure she was ready for a social event yet.

"I don't want to pressure you," Eve said, obviously sensing her hesitation. "So say no if you're not ready. God knows my husband and I both understand. He was the loner of all time when he first moved into the cabin."

"And now?" Andy asked.

"He still has a tendency to run off to the woods on occasion, but he's adapting," she said with a grin. "Not easy in my household."

Andy surrendered. It was impossible to say no to Eve Manning. "Okay," she said. What was that saying? In for a penny, in for a pound.

CHAPTER FOUR

IT WAS MIDAFTERNOON when Eve drove into a parking area in back of the two-story brick building she'd pointed out earlier. A sign outside identified it as the Covenant Falls Community Center.

Andy was quickly having second thoughts. Why had she agreed to Eve's suggestion of writing a history of the town? But she *had* agreed to try, and she did need a job, a goal, a diversion. She needed to start living again, even if it was so damn hard.

Andy reluctantly followed Eve up the step, through the unlocked door and into a vestibule. A gray-haired, wiry man rose from a desk in a corner. She noted a Western novel on his desk.

"This is Bill Evans," Eve said. "He manages the center. Bill, this is Andy Stuart. She moved into the cabin today. And this is Joseph."

At the sound of his name, Joseph barked and wagged his tail.

Mr. Evans leaned down and scratched the dog's ears. "He's a handsome fellow." Joseph wriggled with pleasure at the attention.

Then the man straightened and held out his hand and she took it. "Real pleased to meet you," he said. It was a firm shake, and she warmed to his friendly grin.

"Thank you," she said.

"Bill, I wondered if you could show Andy around the center and particularly the museum," Eve said. She turned to Andy. "It's on our wish list to do more with it, but money is tight. I'm leaving you in good hands. I have a meeting. It seems I always have a meeting. But Bill will take good care of you. He can drive you and Joseph back to the cabin."

"Not necessary," Andy said. "Joseph and I can make it alone. We walked up the mountain earlier."

"Okay, but if you have any questions, don't hesitate to call me," Eve said, "and we'll see you tomorrow night." And then she was gone.

"Is she always so...busy?" she asked.

Bill Evans grinned. With his thin hair and neatly trimmed mustache, he looked to be in his late sixties. "Yes, and as a fellow vet, I feel it necessary to warn you about our mayor. She's really good at keeping others in the same state."

"She suggested that I try to write a short history of Covenant Falls for a brochure."

"That's what she *suggested*, huh?" he said with a twinkle in his eyes.

Andy wasn't sure she liked the way he said it. "Is there a problem?"

"No, no problem at all," he said. "Sounds like a good idea. You a writer?"

"Nope. A nurse by training," she admitted.

"Ah, one of the angels. I served in Vietnam and that's the way we thought about the nurses. And the doctors. They saved my life, for sure."

She didn't reply. She was still pondering his previous—enigmatic—words.

He didn't seem to notice. "I'll show you around." He walked to the left and stood in an open door while she looked inside. "This is our library and computer center. Nate Rowland, another one of our vets, built the shelves for the books."

Andy peered inside. Large windows were framed by cheerful drapes. Books filled shelves that lined one wall of the room. Several worn but comfortable-looking chairs were scattered in front of them. Two preschoolers were sprawled on throw rugs in front of the shelves. Several older children were browsing through books on higher shelves.

Two teenagers and an elderly woman sat in front of three of the ten computers lined up on a long table. Not wanting to disturb them, she joined Bill Evans, who was waiting in the hall.

"Nice," she said.

"The center is all Eve's doing. This building used to be a restaurant, and it stood here empty for nearly twenty years until Eve decided we needed a community center. She badgered the city council into making repairs with volunteer help."

He led the way across the hall to a door and opened it. "This is our meeting room. We vets meet here every Monday night. You're invited, of course."

"Nate Rowland mentioned it," Andy replied.

"You've met Nate? He's a good guy. He's the one who really started the Monday-night get-togethers. It's helped a bunch of us, just talking about things we can't talk to anyone else about. I hope you come. You'll like everyone, and we need new blood. You play poker, by any chance?"

"I've been known to," she replied modestly.

He eyed her suspiciously for a moment, then grinned. He rambled on, "We're not the only ones who meet here. We just claim Monday night."

Andy admired the room. Like the other one, it had an eccentric charm. Three elderly overstuffed sofas of varying colors and design were scattered throughout the room. An equally aged television sat in a corner. A battered bar ran along the back of the room with mismatched bar chairs. Card tables and folding chairs lined one of the walls.

"I like it," she said. "It looks...comfortable."

"Ah, a diplomat," he said. "It's all donated except for the folding chairs."

"In an odd way, everything fits," she said. Then she remembered why she was there. "And the museum, Mr. Evans?" she prompted.

"It's Bill. I hope I can call you Andy."

"I would like that," she said.

"I should warn you about the museum. We're just beginning to put it together. We've been spending the past several months asking for contributions. Not money, but letters, photos, old newspapers, vintage clothing. Right now it's just scattered pieces of our history. I've been going through it, but I'm no curator. In fact, I'm just a volunteer who kinda hangs around here."

"Are you doing the sorting?" Andy asked. She was getting a suspicious feeling about this museum.

"When I have time. The library and computers came first."

"Okay," she said, trying to determine his role. "You take care of the library and computers, the meeting room and now the...museum, and you're a volunteer?"

Evans looked embarrassed. "I like keeping active. I sold the general store to my nephew last year. It was a huge mistake. I was used to being busy." He shrugged. "Retirement isn't all it's made out to be. Within a month, I was driving my wife and myself crazy. So this is not exactly slave labor for me," he said with a grin. "It's just that one thing kinda leads to another, and before you know it you're hooked like a fish. Eve does have a way about her. Watch yourself." He led the way up a flight of stairs to a door at the top.

"I'm only going to be here for a short time," she said.

"I've heard that from your predecessors at the cabin. They're still here."

Despite herself, Andy was curious. And also wary. "What did *they* get hooked on?" she asked carefully.

"Well…quite a few things, actually."

Andy sighed. "Eve just wants a short brochure. Shouldn't take long."

"Right," he said, but there was doubt in his voice as he unlocked the door and stood aside as she entered.

Newspaper-size bound volumes sat in a pile on a table. Other tables held scrapbooks and photo albums. Unopened boxes filled another table, with even more boxes tucked underneath. She glanced through several of them: menus from the '20s, a bill promoting a traveling circus in 1888 and several wanted posters from around the same time. Another box was filled with school pictures that looked as if they went back as far as the late nineteenth century. A stack of high school yearbooks was in the corner.

Bill Evans looked embarrassed. "We…I…really haven't had time to look at all of it." He brightened. "We also have a fool's-gold nugget, along with a real one and some mining equipment. A few diaries."

"Any of it cataloged?"

"Afraid not."

She looked around helplessly. This wasn't a museum. It was a disaster. An earnest disaster, maybe, but a disaster nonetheless. It would take months to find anything and more months to get the museum in shape.

"You can spend as much time as you need here," he said.

"Maybe I could talk to…a descendant of the founder of the town…Mr. Monroe?"

"You *could* do that," he allowed.

She eyed him. "What's wrong with that?"

"He's a bit…difficult."

"Eve didn't mention that," Andy said. She tried a different possibility. "Is there a newspaper in town?"

"Yep. There's only one now, of course, but there's been a number throughout the years. We have bound copies of some of the editions."

"What about talking to the editor?"

"Well, the newspaper's been around, but the editor hasn't. He's only been here two years. Inherited it, and doesn't give a damn about it or the town. He would sell it in a New York second if he could find a buyer. It's not a very good paper."

That wasn't encouraging. Andy liked newspapers. In fact, she'd been addicted to them. She'd had a really strong curiosity about almost everything, although it had been dormant for the past months. She hadn't wanted to read or hear about the Middle East or any kind of violence. It came to her too often at night.

Then she remembered what Eve had said. A Scot and a Ute princess. Gold. She'd been intrigued by the story. It was obvious now, though, that writing it would probably be more difficult than the mayor implied. Now she understood what Bill meant by a hook...

It didn't make any difference, though. Now that she had committed to at least taking a stab at putting something together for a brochure, she wanted to get started. It was time to stop hiding from the rest of the world. And to do that, she had to join it.

Prying into the town's history seemed a safe way of doing it. Having no goal was like looking into an abyss. She owed Jared more than that. She owed the others more than that.

She had to live for them.

But it was so damned hard.

EVE GREETED HER husband with a huge hug. "I've missed you," she said. Josh Manning bent his head to her upraised face, and their lips met. She wondered if the heat would ever cool between them, prayed that it wouldn't.

"Hey, Josh." Nick bounded out of his room, Amos beside him and the other dogs following him. "Amos was so excited to hear your Jeep."

"Hi, champ, thanks for taking care of him," Josh replied as Amos pressed between them and leaned against Josh's legs, making little crying noises.

Josh knelt down and rubbed his fur. "Sorry, guy, but you were better off here for three days."

"How did it go?" Eve asked.

He grinned. "I have acceptances from eight in

the travel industry, including two newspapers, a business magazine, the tourism bureau, several travel agencies and a freelance writer who specializes in writing about Colorado for major travel publications. I have a couple more maybes."

"What date?

"Eight weeks from today. Clint will be back then and can give us a hand."

Josh was talking more, and faster, than since she'd had met him nearly a year ago.

"Clint's with the police department now," Eve reminded him.

"I know, Mayor. But it's the weekend, and hopefully his boss will let him off for a day then."

"It depends on whether we have a massive crime wave."

He grinned and kissed her again. "Anything happen while I was gone?"

"The new resident of the cabin arrived."

"Have you met her?"

"Today," Eve said. "I like her."

"You like everyone."

"There's a few exceptions."

"Not very damn many. What is she like?"

"Quiet. Grieving. Do you know what happened…?"

"I didn't ask and the shrink didn't tell me. I got the impression, though, that whatever happened was pretty bad."

She had to smile at his use of the word *shrink*. She knew who he meant, knew how much Josh respected Dr. Payne, but he would always be *the shrink*.

"She's coming over for dinner tomorrow night," Eve said. "I volunteered you to grill steaks. Clint will bring Stephanie. I'm debating about asking Nate."

His face suddenly went serious. "He met her at the cabin, right?"

She nodded.

"Then, he'll be a familiar face. Let's ask him. Maybe he can drive her over."

Eve stared at him. "You're not thinking...?"

"Me? Hell, no," he said. "You know the way I feel about interfering."

She raised an eyebrow. "I seem to recall you nudging Clint and Steph together."

"Your imagination. Now tell me more about Lieutenant Stuart."

"She's getting a fast indoctrination. She volunteered to write our history for the brochure. She's going through the museum now."

"Volunteered?"

Eve shrugged innocently. "She wanted to do something to pay for the cabin. We need a history written for your opening. It seemed...fortuitous, don't you think?"

"Can she write?"

"I don't know, but she said she keeps a journal

and likes history. She really needed something to do. She's lost, Josh. Really lost."

Josh took her in his arms. "I love you, Eve Manning, you and that huge heart of yours."

"Me, too," Nick piped in.

Amos barked, and a chorus of sounds came from Nick's four dogs.

CHAPTER FIVE

ANDY SPENT THE rest of the afternoon looking through boxes at the community center.

Bill Evans had brought a chair inside the "museum" after she started glancing through some of scrapbooks, then he disappeared, apparently in pursuit of other volunteer duties.

Joseph lay beside her, his head resting on his paws, his tail wagging occasionally, apparently to remind her that he was there. She didn't have to be reminded. In a few short weeks he'd become her lifeline. She had someone to feed and water and take for walks. She hadn't realized how much she'd needed that.

She found twelve different newspapers that had apparently come and gone in the more than 150 years they documented. Some were little more than a single page. They were in chronological order but some years were missing. Still, it was like filing through snapshots of history.

The faded pages presented a glimpse of the town: the marriages, the births and the deaths. The marriage of a Nathan Rowland to Edna Redding caught her eye. The date on the newspaper was May 16,

1930. She counted back. He was probably Nate Rowland's great-grandfather. The story was accompanied by a photo.

The Nate who had greeted her earlier in the day resembled the groom, except the latter sported a handsome mustache and looked uncomfortable in a black suit and white shirt with a stiff collar. The dark-haired bride was very pretty. Andy turned to another article. The country was deep in the Great Depression. There were rumors, denied, that the bank in the town would close. She suspected she would find out if it had.

Fascinated, she'd turned to the next issue when she heard footsteps behind her. She looked at her watch. Nearly six. She was amazed at how much time had passed.

"Hi, again" came a voice from behind her, and she whirled around. Nate Rowland stood in the doorway. "I hope I didn't startle you," he said. "You looked completely absorbed."

"I was," she said, feeling oddly as if she knew him better after reading the marriage announcement. "These…are fascinating."

"You really think so?"

"Don't you?"

He shrugged. "I grew up on this area's history." He knelt next to Joseph, who promptly turned on his back, baring his belly. Nate rubbed it as Joseph hummed with pleasure.

"He's shameless," Andy said. "And easy."

Nate smiled, a slow twist of his lips that was surprisingly attractive. She found herself smiling back. She hadn't really managed a real one for months, not until several days after she was introduced to Joseph. It was impossible not to respond to an animal that lived every day just to please you and intuit your every mood. It was also...difficult not to respond to Nate Rowland's smile.

"You must be exhausted," he said.

She shrugged. "I don't sleep much."

"I get that. I didn't, either, when I returned from Iraq."

She turned back to the newspaper and closed the bound volume. "It's probably time for me to go back to the cabin and feed Joseph."

"Bill had to leave. Something for his wife," Nate said. "He asked me to close up for him and drive you home. He said you were so engrossed in the files, he didn't want to interrupt you."

"That was considerate of him," Andy said, "and you, but I can walk home. Joseph and I need the exercise."

"He thought you might want to take some of the material with you."

Surprised, she blurted out her first thought. "I would think he, or the town, would want keep it under lock and key."

"I don't think he's worried about you taking off with anything in here," Nate said with that wry smile again. She was prepared for it this time.

She stood, stretched. She considered the newspapers she had been reading. It was either that or a book tonight, and she was becoming intrigued with Covenant Falls. It was the first time in months that she'd felt even a smidgen of interest in anything around her.

She was grateful for it, for anything that kept her mind from going back to Afghanistan. But if she took the bound newspapers home, she couldn't hold Joseph's leash. She would need a ride.

"Thank you," she said. "I'll take that ride."

"Good. Can I carry that down for you?"

She hesitated, then nodded. The last thing she needed now was to fall down a flight of stairs.

He picked up the heavy, awkward book with ease. He waited for her and Joseph to lead the way down the stairs and he followed.

The building was empty. She waited as Nate locked up the building, then walked with her to his blue pickup.

"What time does it usually close?" she asked.

"Five on Friday. Seven the other weekdays so kids can do homework. Then it's open Saturday from nine to five."

"And it's after six," she said. "I didn't realize..."

"Not to worry," he said. "Bill saved me from doing some paperwork that's on my desk. Now I can foist it on Josh." He paused, then asked, "Have you had dinner?"

"No, but I had a late lunch with Eve Manning

and there's enough food in the fridge to feed an army."

A light seemed to go on in his eyes. "Ah, now I understand," he said.

"Understand what?"

"Why you're here. Eve is behind this."

"I like to pay my own way."

"I get that, too," he said as they went down the few steps to the ground. They reached his pickup and she wondered whether everyone in Covenant Falls drove a truck. The Bucket was definitely going to be out of place.

She opened the passenger door before he could reach it and climbed inside. Joseph hopped in and squeezed next to her, then she took the bound newspapers in her lap.

It was warm outside and it seemed to get warmer when Nate stepped inside. The sleeves of his blue shirt were rolled up, displaying bronze muscles. She hadn't noticed that much this morning. She'd been tired and anxious to get inside and settled, at least as much as she could in a cabin that didn't belong to her. She had worried every mile of her drive that some loud noise or headlight would send her back to Afghanistan and off the road.

But now she was running on adrenaline. The lunch with Eve Manning had given her something she very much needed: an immediate goal. She liked Bill Evans and thought he could be a friend.

Maybe Nate, too, although she wanted absolutely nothing outside a casual friendship.

She leaned against the seat.

"What exactly does Eve want you to do?" Nate asked.

"A brochure about the town's history," she said.

Nate didn't say anything, but then silences seemed to be a part of him.

A minute later they were in front of the cabin. He turned off the engine. "If you want to know the history, you should talk to Al Monroe."

"Eve mentioned something about him, but Bill indicated he might be difficult."

"He might. He might not," Nate said. "But it's worth a try."

"Could you ask him?"

"I think you should do it yourself," he said. "He respects strength and directness. And even if not, I'm the last person to ask him."

"Why?"

"As far as he's concerned, I've been wrong on every side of an issue in Covenant Falls."

"That's intriguing." She waited for him to continue, but he didn't. Instead, he stepped down and went around to her side of the pickup and opened the door. He reached for the book, but she shook her head.

"I can take it from here," she said.

His gaze met hers in the internal light of the pickup. His eyes were predominantly a golden brown but with shades of gray and green mixing with it. What was striking, though, was not the color. It was something she couldn't define. It wasn't kindness, but more of an empathy. She resented the hell out of sympathy, or pity or its like, but this was neither. *I've been there. I know what you're going through. I respect it.*

She suddenly realized she was still sitting in the seat, holding the book as if it were a lifeline. Joseph barked as if to jar her into moving. She handed the bulky volume down to Nate. He took it, and she stepped out and followed him to the cabin. "I can take it now," she said, but as she took it from him once they were inside, her bad hand failed her and the heavy volume started to fall. He caught it.

"Where would you like it?" he asked as if nothing at all had happened.

"The table, I think," she said, biting her tongue in mortification.

He placed it down on the table, then he turned to her. "Think about contacting Al Monroe," he said. "I think he would like you."

"Why?"

"Because I think you have a hell of a lot of grit, and he respects that." She was too stunned to reply. *Grit?* Not recently.

"Listen," he said. "I don't know what the hell happened to you out there, but here you are, in a strange town, standing up tall and ready to take on a challenge because you're not giving up."

"But I *was* giving up," she admitted honestly.

"*Was* doesn't matter. *Now* is what matters. Just know we all have your back. Okay?"

He was willing her to believe it. She took a deep breath. "Okay," she said.

He just nodded. "Call if you need anything, or just want to talk. You'll be coming to the vet meeting Monday night?"

"You said they play poker?"

"Yeah. We've been known to do that."

"You betcha, then." False bravado, but it just popped out. She was as surprised as he looked.

He simply nodded, his eyes hooded. "Welcome to Covenant Falls," he said as he headed for the door.

NATE'S THOUGHTS WERE in turmoil as he drove away from the cabin. He had not meant to say what he had said, nor do more than leave her at the door. The look on Andy's face when she'd nearly dropped the heavy, bulky book had changed his mind.

She looked so fragile and yet she had the strength to plunge through whatever pain she had. She'd traveled to a strange place with a determination to reclaim her life. She had apparently grabbed at whatever Eve had offered.

Be careful! Women, particularly pretty ones with wide eyes and sad stories, were poison for him. It had taken him five years to claw back from the hell Maggie had put him through. The last thing he needed was any kind of involvement with a woman.

He would keep his distance. He had given her a challenge by mentioning Al Monroe. He suspected she couldn't ignore it if she was the fighter he thought lurked within her. He'd done his part. He turned on the highway. He had other stops today.

CHAPTER SIX

ANDY WOKE TO sunlight streaming through the bedroom window. She felt a furry body next to her. It was the first full night's sleep she'd had in months. No demons. No blood. Just a soft snoring.

Joseph opened one eye and peered at her, as if asking whether he could stay. She remembered her resolve three weeks ago. She wasn't going to get too emotionally invested in the dog. It was a sound decision. It had lasted until the first nightmare, when he'd woken her, crawled up on the bed and let her cling to him.

Bright blue eyes regarded her solemnly now, and she couldn't help but rub his ears. So much for not getting invested.

She looked at the clock on the stand next to her bed. Nearly seven. She rarely, if ever, slept that late, but then yesterday had been a very long day. She had gone nearly twenty-four hours without more than a nap yesterday morning.

Even after arriving back at the cabin, she'd looked through more of the papers.

One item had jumped out at her. The mention of a camel ordinance being defeated…

For a few hours she hadn't thought of Jared, of her friends, of the hand that didn't work very well.

She stretched out in the bed and thought about the day ahead of her.

Saturday. She was committed to dinner tonight. She wasn't sure whether she was ready for it, but Eve Manning was a force of nature.

She rubbed Joseph's fur, and he rewarded her with a sneak-attack kiss. As a nurse who had never had a dog before, she was appalled. But then, she reasoned, a lot of people apparently had canine companions and stayed healthy.

Joseph hadn't attempted such an overt show of affection before. She apparently had passed the Joseph test.

"Time to get up," she said. She was hungry. Appetite was something else that had been missing. She was actually hungry now. Dr. Payne would be proud. She might send him a text.

She went into the bathroom. The shower was great. She stayed there for a long time, washing her hair, then just reveling in the hot water. It was almost symbolic. Washing away some of the anger and hopelessness that had smothered her.

She stepped out. Joseph stood and wagged his tail. "Want to go out?" she asked.

The tail moved faster.

Andy went back in the bedroom and slipped into jeans and a T-shirt, then went to the back door and opened it. Joseph dashed out.

She stood there and watched as the dog explored the area in back, then did his business and returned. She had been afraid at first that he would run away, but in the two weeks she'd been with him, she'd learned how well he was trained. The word *come* would bring him immediately.

She prepared coffee. It was slow because she had to do nearly everything with one hand. Then she fried three eggs. One went into Joseph's bowl along with dog food. Her two went on a plate with one of the sweet rolls Maude had provided with the cabin.

Andy carried her plate outside. She left the front door open for Joseph to join her.

The lake was visible through the trees. The scent of pines perfumed the air. A few wildflowers peeked up out of the ground.

Her thoughts turned to Nate Rowland. *Grit.* Just his saying the word helped her battered self-image. Grit was something she needed, something she respected, something she'd once relished and in the past months had lost.

Or maybe she hadn't.

She hadn't been a victim in his eyes. She was a person with grit, and that was a gift.

So was a purpose. There were interesting tidbits in the newspapers but very little about the beginnings of the town, and that had been the carrot Eve had offered. Traders. American Indians. Gold. That was the core, the mother lode.

She picked up the plate and coffee cup and went

inside, placed them in the sink and looked at her watch. It was a little after eight. She washed the dishes, put them away, then called Eve.

After the preliminaries, she got to the point. "You and Nate mentioned Al Monroe, that he might have original journals from 1850. I would very much like to read them. Question is, how do I approach Mr. Monroe?"

"Quite honestly, I think if you called, he would say no," Eve said. "He's had a couple of tragedies these past few years, and he's retreated from nearly everyone. But he's very proud of his family roots. We'll talk about it tonight."

"You think he would approve of me writing a short history of the town?"

"I never know with Al. I'm not one of his favorite people, but he surprises me at times. He was a curmudgeon on the town council, but under a gruff exterior he really cares about Covenant Falls."

Andy digested that answer. It raised several questions. And suspicions. She didn't like being manipulated, either for her own good or for someone else's.

But despite any misgivings, she was hooked. One of her character flaws was an obsession to finish whatever she started. "What time tonight?" she asked.

"Around six," Eve said. "Oh, I asked Nate to come as well, since you've already met him. If it's okay, he'll pick you up. Josh will be working his magic with steaks, and we're a bit hard to find."

"It's fine," Andy said and with a goodbye hung up. She stood there for a moment. It wasn't fine at all. Nate was being thrown at her, and she resented it. He probably did, too. He had been helpful last night, but the last thing she wanted, or needed, was a matchmaker hovering around. *Damn.*

NATE AND JOSH spent Saturday-morning meeting with the newly hired manager for the Covenant Falls Inn. The daughter of one of his mother's friends, Susan Hall, had been a hotel manager in Las Vegas—not for one of the huge luxury hotels, but a small boutique hotel.

She was recently divorced and had been looking for a job far away from the ex-husband when her mother had heard about the opening for a manager. Susan was hired after the first interview.

"It may not be permanent," Nate had warned. "We're all out on a limb here."

"It doesn't matter. Right now, it's a godsend."

"You can hire the rest of the staff," Nate said. "Let us know what you need and recommended salaries."

"We'll start off slow until we know about the market," she said. "I can fill several positions. We'll need a night manager. I'll take care of the day desk."

"We'll need a cook," Nate said.

"A *chef*," Josh said with a wry smile.

"A *cook*," Nate insisted.

Susan laughed. "Maybe we could get Maude."

"Hell, no," Nate said. "The town would drive us out on a rail. But we have other great cooks in town. We start out using home talent. Mrs. Byars, for instance, could provide brownies for each room, and Ethel Jones is a great cook. She's widowed and could use money. We could hire a young person to help her while getting training."

"I like it," Josh said. "The whole idea is to bring jobs to the town."

"I'll talk to Mrs. Jones," Nate said. "I have better diplomatic skills than Josh."

"I resent that," Josh said. "Eve says I'm one hundred percent improved."

Nate rolled his eyes. "One hundred percent of zero is still zero."

Susan laughed. "I think I'm going to like this job." She looked down at the dog sitting next to Josh. "I take it the inn will be animal friendly."

"Yep," Josh said.

"Take a hard look throughout the property, Susan," Nate said. "See if there's anything we missed or that we need. We used every wholesale and going-out-of-business company in the country. Call me or Josh anytime with a problem. I'll take the easy ones, and he, as president of this budding firm, will take the hard ones."

"When do we open?"

"We have an informal opening in seven weeks. We've invited a number of travel agents and tourist information people. We have about eight couples who have accepted. I would like to open to the public shortly after that. As soon as you think we're ready, we'll put out news releases saying we're open."

"I have contacts with travel magazines and websites," Susan said. "I'll get in touch." She hesitated, then said, "You don't have the sign yet."

"No."

"You might want to think about the name. Something chic and catchy."

"The Covenant Falls Inn isn't chic and catchy?" Nate asked.

"Truthfully?" Susan answered.

"We'll think about it," Josh said. "We haven't confirmed the design yet with the sign company." Josh stood, ending the meeting. "We're really happy to have you," Josh said to Susan.

"Not nearly as happy as I am to be here. We'll make it work," she replied.

Nate and Josh walked out together. "She might just do that," Josh said.

"I like your enthusiasm," Nate replied drily.

"I hear you're coming to dinner tonight."

"All Eve has to say is 'steaks.'"

"I also hear Eve conned you into meeting our new arrival."

"Yep."

"That tells me a lot," Josh said.

"She's like most of us when we got back. There's a lot of pain there."

"You liked her."

"She's nice enough. Obviously hurting. But don't you or Eve even think of matchmaking. She's certainly not ready, and neither am I."

"I would never harbor the thought," Josh said. "A confirmed bachelor is a confirmed bachelor." He smirked.

"I mean it," Nate said.

"I know you've been avoiding every woman in town and something bad went down. You don't talk much about personal things, my friend."

"Not just bad. I was an idiot. I fell for a pair of blue eyes and a sad story. I thought I could fix things. I discovered I'm not worth a damn in fixing broken things. I married for the wrong reason and to do the right thing, and it exploded on me. My ex-wife had totally different motives, including another guy. I ended up losing my career as well as everything I had saved."

Josh knew the results. Nate had returned to Covenant Falls two years ago. He'd worked at every construction job he could find. It was how they'd met—Josh had needed help installing a new floor and hired Nate. He found a talented craftsman with three years toward an architecture degree in addition to eight years in the army.

Nate had shared stories about his time in Iraq but

not the years afterward. Josh had never asked and never would, but he knew Nate carried a load of hurt. He'd just had a glimpse of how heavy it was.

Josh gave him a searching look, then nodded. "Eve is going to ask you to pick her up tonight. She and I will be cooking, and Andy doesn't know Clint or Stephanie. Do that, and I'll tell—ah, ask—her to refrain from asking anything else. Okay?"

Nate nodded. "Deal."

They separated, Nate going to his truck and Josh, Amos at his side, to his Jeep.

ANDY WAS RESTLESS. She'd finished the last few issues of the bound newspapers. She had scrawled a couple of notes of dates and events she thought might be important.

She wanted to know more about the Monroe family. If she was going to talk to the man, or even try to, she needed as much information as she could find. She decided to drive to the community center, return the volume she had and look at more recent newspapers.

She drove the Bucket, since she had the newspapers with her. Bill Evans wasn't there, but a Mrs. Wilson was.

"Bill told me you might be showing up. I'm real glad to meet you. My husband is Calvin Wilson. He and my son run the hardware store. You need anything—a replacement lightbulb, anything at all—you call them. They would be real proud to help."

The *real proud* reminded Andy of home. It sounded like her mother. It also reminded her she needed to call her mother, make sure everything was all right and let her know where she was. She had made duty calls once a week, but she knew they had been more worrying than comforting. She had repeatedly refused to go home to heal. She didn't want to add another burden to a family that already had more than they should have to handle.

"You need anything, you just call me," Mrs. Wilson said. "There's usually coffee in the club room."

"Thank you. I might try that." After Mrs. Wilson left, Andy looked through the stacks of bound newspapers and picked up one that covered the years 2005 through this year. Someone, probably Bill Evans, had conscientiously added each newspaper.

After flipping through them, she understood exactly what Bill Evans had meant when he'd dismissed *The Covenant Falls Herald* as a serious newspaper. The editions were little more than a collection of gossip, dry recounts of city council meetings and legal ads. She flipped through them until she came to a headline—Councilman Monroe Resigns After Arrest of Nephew.

She read the article. Al Monroe, chairman of the city council, had resigned when his nephew was arrested for kidnapping. Her interest boiled over when she read that the victim had been the mayor's son, who was rescued by the mayor's current husband and her husband's dog, Amos.

Maybe Covenant Falls wasn't quite as tranquil as she'd thought, and now she understood, at least in part, why the mayor indicated she wasn't exactly the councilman's favorite person. And maybe, just maybe, why she wanted an outsider to write—attempt to write—the history of the town.

Strangely enough, it deepened her interest. She had been intrigued before, but now her thoughts were going at warp speed.

She turned to the next week's news. Nothing much of interest.

The nephew was being held for trial. Al Monroe disappeared from the papers.

She kept turning the pages. The wedding, four months later, of Josh and Eve Manning. Then the arrival of chopper pilot Clint Morgan last fall was duly reported.

Andy closed the paper. This was getting her nowhere. She wanted to go farther back. She wanted to know Covenant Falls when it was little more than a trading post.

She checked the other bound volumes of papers, but none went back farther than 1919, unless there were scattered editions in the pile of boxes lining the room.

Then she found what she was searching for: a box marked "Early Years."

She wished she had a computer. She hadn't bothered with one in the hospital or the months of recuperation. The purchase of a cell phone after her release from the hospital had been a big deal.

Note to self—laptop computer. It would take a bite out of what little money she had, but it was necessary. Not only for this task but for day-to-day living now that she'd decided to be a functioning person again. She opened a box and started prowling through it.

CHAPTER SEVEN

WHAT *DO* YOU wear when meeting your landlord and a bunch of strangers while dining at the house of the mayor?

Eve had said it was casual. But there was casual, and then there was more casual. Unfortunately, she didn't have much of a choice. Her wardrobe was limited, and that was an understatement. Her pre-deployment clothes had been much too large by the time she left the hospital, and she hadn't had the heart, desire or reason to buy more than basic necessities.

That translated into three pairs of jeans, one pair of black pants, two sweaters, three T-shirts and several shirts, including two pullovers. Her choice of footwear was a pair of lace-up walking shoes, a pair of sandals and one pair of well-worn loafers.

She chose the best pair of jeans and a blue-gray shirt with long sleeves. After running a brush through her hair, she added a touch of lipstick, then stared at herself in the mirror. Really looked for the first time in months. Her hair needed a cut. Badly. She was thin, too thin. Her cheeks were hollow.

Joseph watched every movement, following her

from room to room as if afraid someone would snatch her.

"It's okay," she said. "You can come with me."

The doorbell rang. Joseph barked. "It's a bit late for that," she told Joseph. "You're supposed to bark before the bell rings." She hurried to the door and opened it. Nate stood there, a rueful smile on his lips.

"Hi," he said. "I'm really not stalking you."

"Are you sure?" she asked with a slight smile.

"Nope, I swear. Eve will vouch for me."

He wore jeans and a casual blue pullover cotton shirt with short sleeves that showed off muscled arms and a fit body. A shock of unruly chestnut hair fell over his forehead.

"Tell me about the other people at the dinner."

"Josh is a former loner who finds himself surrounded by people and animals and can't quite figure out how it happened. Clint is the opposite. He's never met a stranger and could charm a rattler. Clint likes to tease Josh about his current zoo and a wife with a finger in a hundred pies."

"And you enjoy standing back and enjoying it."

"Guilty. But then Stephanie and Clint are interesting, too. Clint's the outgoing one, and Stephanie is all practicality."

"Should make for an interesting evening." Andy turned to Joseph. "Let's go." Then she glanced back at Nate. "Eve said it was okay to bring him."

"I would be shocked if he wasn't invited," Nate

replied as Joseph picked up his leash and brought it to her.

"Eve will be impressed," Nate said as he opened the door for her, then the screen porch. "Her dogs never do that."

She'd expected the pickup but instead he led her to a middle-aged Buick sedan. "My mom's car," he said. "I thought it would be more comfortable."

"She lives here?"

"It's one reason I came back. She's getting older." A shadow crossed his face and she realized there was probably more to the story. But she knew better than to probe. She didn't want anyone to probe into *her* life.

Once they were on the road, he turned to her. "Everyone who'll be there tonight is good people. Really good people. They'll understand if you need to walk away. Just nod at me, and we'll leave. Okay?"

She swallowed hard. *He understands.* She hadn't been around more than a few people since...waking up. She'd refused group therapy. No way could she talk about what happened.

"Thank you," she finally said.

He turned on some jazz in the car and they rode in silence.

Nate drove to a parking area in front of a one-story ranch house. A screened-in porch, much like her own, stretched across the front. A boy—maybe ten or so—opened the door and approached the car. He waited as Andy stepped out of the car.

"Hello," he said.

"Hello to you," she said with a smile.

"I'm Nick. Mom told me to bring you inside. She said you might have a dog. I have four. They're inside because Mom says they can be too much for a visitor." He hadn't taken a breath between all the sentences.

"I think I can handle a few dogs," she said. "And I do have one in the car. Would you like to meet him?"

Nick nodded eagerly.

Nate had walked around the car, and he opened the back door.

Joseph jumped down and stood protectively next to Andy.

"Can I pet him?" Nick asked.

"I think he would like that."

"What's his name?"

"Joseph."

Nick knelt and rubbed Joseph's ears. "He's a fine dog," he said.

"Every dog is a fine dog to Nick," Eve said as she walked up. "Welcome. The guys are around at the grill in back. Would you like to come in and have a glass of wine before joining them?"

Andy nodded. "Sounds good." She followed Eve inside while Nate strode behind the house. Joseph was at her heels, and Nick at his.

She stepped inside the porch. "Looks familiar," she said.

"Josh built the one at the cabin and liked it so much he added this one after we were married. He's great with his hands."

They went inside to the kitchen. Eve poured two glasses of red wine and handed one to her. "Bill Evans said you stayed at the museum until late."

"You piqued my interest," Andy replied.

"Good."

"But there was nothing about American Indians and gold mines and Scottish traders."

"I have to admit we have a lot of work to do on the museum, but you'll find bits and pieces of the history. Some exaggerated, some not. Gold was found in the mountains around us, but no one found the amounts discovered farther north. As for the natives, the Utes lived in this area until they were moved west and were mortal enemies of the Apaches, who wandered this way occasionally."

"And the trader? Angus. I didn't see much about him."

"You'll find it as you delve into it."

"The journals you mentioned? Am I going into a minefield?" Andy asked.

Eve looked startled, then she smiled. "You're direct. I like that." She took a sip from her glass. "A little history will probably help," she said. "I was city clerk before running for mayor. The former mayor did very little to nothing, which made Al Monroe happy.

"After my husband died," she continued, "I was at a loss. The mayor decided not to run again, but I'd really been doing his job. My father-in-law urged me to run and, on a dare, I did. No one was more surprised than me when I defeated Al's chosen candidate. We were at loggerheads for the next three years. He made it nearly impossible for any businesses to move here while I watched all the young people leave town."

Interest stirred in Andy. "I saw in the local newspaper he'd resigned from the council?"

"His nephew, Sam, was on the police force. He wanted to be chief, and I was opposed to it. So Sam decided to make a name for himself. He committed some petty burglaries and tried to frame Josh, the newcomer to Covenant Falls."

Andy was feeling more at ease as Eve talked. She didn't seem to be holding anything back.

"When Josh first arrived, he was in pretty bad shape. He was rude to everyone and stayed to himself. He was the perfect foil."

"Obviously not," Andy said wryly, "since you married him, you're still mayor and the ex-commissioner is nursing his wounds."

Eve grinned at her. "Obviously not," she agreed. "But that wasn't the worst of it. Sam kidnapped my son. Josh and his dog, Amos, found him."

"Where is the nephew now?"

"In jail. He pleaded guilty and received a short sentence, but Al felt he had to resign from the commission. He apologized, which I think was very difficult for him to do, and retreated from everything but his business. He owns the real estate and insurance companies, along with an interest in the bank, which has a branch in his offices."

"And he harbors bad feelings toward you?"

"Against the whole town, I think. It elected me mayor twice, and he feels it was a repudiation of him. It wasn't. They're just scared the town is dying."

"And you're sending me into the lion's den?"

"Nothing as dramatic as that. Thing is, I like him. He's had a lot of tragedies. His wife couldn't have children and she's been ill. She pretty much dropped out of everything. His only other family was a sister, but she and her husband died in a car crash. Al raised their boy, Sam. Spoiled him. The whole kidnapping thing destroyed him."

Sympathy surged through Andy. She knew loss all too well.

And she suddenly realized why Eve had asked her to write the history. "Were you going to ask me to do this before you met me?"

"No."

"You think Al Monroe and I would be good for each other?"

Eve sighed. "You're too perceptive. I won't lie to

you. I had that thought. Not romantically, of course. He's happily married. But he needs something…"

"You baited me neatly." Andy couldn't keep the disappointment from her voice. She'd liked Eve, but she didn't like being used.

"No. The town really does need a history. Al does have his supporters. The town is divided, and neither side trusts the other. That's why I thought an outsider would be a good idea. After I met you, I sensed that you might get through to Al. I don't know why."

It was an apology of sorts, and even an implied compliment. Her resentment faded away. "Has anyone seen the journals?" she asked.

Eve shook her head. "His nephew bragged about having seen journals, but when I asked Al about them, he was very non-committal."

"Maybe there's something in them that he doesn't want someone to see," Andy surmised.

"After a hundred and fifty years?" Eve said.

"Or," Andy said, "maybe they don't even exist."

"That could be true, too," Eve said, "but he's never denied their existence. I think he's just proud and stubborn."

Another voice broke in. "Are you ever going to bring Lieutenant Stuart out to meet the crew?"

Andy turned. Josh Manning—it must be Josh Manning—filled the doorway into the kitchen. He was tall, solidly built with tawny hair and emerald green eyes.

"Hello," he said to her. "Welcome to Covenant Falls. I'm Josh, and I've come to save you from my wife."

"Hi. I understand you're my landlord. Thank you."

"Thank my buddy. He left the cabin to me. It's what he would have wanted." His green eyes clouded over for a split second, then cleared. "I hope you're comfortable."

"It's very nice. I took a walk up your mountain yesterday."

"I did that on a regular basis. It usually cleared my head." He peered down at Joseph. "Who is this?"

"Joseph."

Her host leaned down. "He's a handsome fellow. Okay to pet him?"

"Sure. He loves attention," she said, suddenly at ease with Josh as he leaned down and rubbed Joseph's ears.

"Come and meet my particular savior," he said. "Or one of them." He led the way outside, where a dog resembling a German shepherd stood at the step. "This is Amos, a Belgian Malinois," he said. "He was a military dog before he became my best buddy."

The two dogs, Amos and Joseph, looked at each other, sniffed each other thoroughly, then wagged their tails before retreating to their humans.

Andy took several steps down to a large patio,

and Josh guided her over to a man and woman who were drinking long-necked beers. "The lady is Stephanie, veterinarian superb," Josh said, "and the loafer is Clint Morgan, chopper pilot, police-chief-to-be and your predecessor at the cabin."

Stephanie smiled. "Welcome," she said. A striking redhead, she was nearly as tall as Clint. She eyed Joseph. "Shelties are great dogs. Where did you find him?"

Andy hesitated. She really hated to admit she'd needed help.

But then she shrugged. "A group specializing in matching dogs with veterans. A psychologist at the hospital arranged it."

"How long have you had him?" Stephanie asked.

"About three weeks."

"He's obviously well trained. He doesn't take his eyes off you."

"We're getting used to each other. I thought there would be other dogs here."

"We tried to restrain ourselves tonight," Stephanie said with a big grin. "I have two at home. Clint has one. Josh has Amos, and Eve has four rescues. We thought to keep your first visit relatively peaceful. We didn't want you to run back to Texas on your second day."

"Sit," Josh said. "I'm putting steaks on the grill. How do you like yours?"

"Medium." She put her drink on a table and sank

down into one of the lounge chairs. She looked at Stephanie. "Are you a native of Covenant Falls?"

"I've been here a little more than five years," she said. "I'm one of the newcomers. If I had been here twenty years, I would still be a newcomer, but that's okay. We're not too discriminated against."

Andy decided she needed a longer conversation with Eve about Covenant Falls politics and, more specifically, about Al Monroe, but this was not the time or place.

Andy sipped her glass of wine. She drank very little since her return to the States. Her medications had narrowed to two, one for panic attacks and the other for insomnia. She hadn't used those in several days, but she was still cautious about alcohol.

The sun was going down, and vivid scarlet, pink and coral ribbons crossed the sky and blessed the mountain.

Nate returned and Andy looked at the three men—Nate, Clint and Josh—around her. They had served, probably survived horrors as she had. But she still felt apart from them. They seemed at ease, living in the moment. Talking about events that had nothing to do with her. The shadows inside were still too strong, the memories too recent.

She saw the affectionate banter and touches between Josh and Eve, and Clint and Stephanie, and she resented them. She shouldn't. They were going out of the way to make her feel at home, but... dammit, she did. That anger and resentment she'd felt the morning she saw the couple in the hospital returned.

"Andy?" Nate walked over to her chair. "Why don't we walk to the corral? The horses are out."

Gratitude filled her. He had sensed her discomfort. She nodded and stood, the brace on her left hand hitting the table beside her and knocking the glass over. It exploded like a shot, and the wine splashed up on Nate's clothes and began to spread. A red stain spreading...spreading...

White lights. Shots. Screams. Her screams. More shots. Pain. The mountains faded into the field operating room. Blood was everywhere. "No," she heard herself screaming. Jared stepped in front of her and... *God, no... Jared! Jared! Don't...*

She was only vaguely aware of someone touching her, talking to her, but she couldn't understand the words. A loud bark, a warm furry body pressing against her...

She felt herself being lowered to a sitting position. Images still darted in and out of her brain. *The man with the gun... Her friend...*

She couldn't breathe. Then she felt arms going around her and carrying her. Strong. Like Jared. *He isn't dead!*

"Andy. Breathe. Take a deep breath. Breathe," the voice commanded. *It isn't Jared.* Despair flooded her.

"Breathe, dammit." The voice was louder, too strong to resist.

Air rushed in, then out.

"Andy?" The voice was gentle now, even tender. "You're safe now." Something wet licked her face. A furry body tried to crawl up on her. She grabbed him, held him close as the images started to fade away in a fog.

She was aware, barely, that fingers were taking her pulse, then her blood pressure. She knew her pulse was racing, and her blood pressure was probably sky-high. Her eyes were wet. Sore.

She was inside a room. Not a tent. Joseph was madly licking her hands. She saw Nate's face then. Worried. His hands were busy taking her blood pressure.

Stephanie was by her side, holding a glass of water. "Hey. Glad to have you back with us," she said in a matter-of-fact voice. "Take a sip of water."

Andy did as she was told. "I'm so sorry," she said after a swallow. "I don't know..." But she did know, and she felt humiliated beyond words.

"No apologies necessary," Stephanie said.

"Damn right," Nate said. "I've been there. So has Josh."

"I shouldn't have come..." She remembered the steaks then. Probably burned by now. She didn't care for herself. She wasn't hungry. She felt sick. And incredibly tired.

"Anything I can get you?" Stephanie asked.

She shook her head. All she wanted to do was flee, but she didn't want to ruin everyone's evening, and that was what would happen if she left now. She had to stop running, no matter how much she wanted to at this minute.

"I'll be all right," she said, starting to rise.

"No," Nate said. "Your pulse is too fast. Your blood pressure isn't that great, either. Just relax for a few minutes. Okay?"

Her eyes asked the question.

"Just some medic stuff I picked up along the way," he said. "It's not that hard to feel a pulse or take blood pressure when you have a hostess who keeps a monitor around."

She was grateful he wasn't asking any questions. "I'm feeling much better now, thank you," she said formally. "I just haven't had much sleep lately."

"I certainly understand that," he said.

Andy tried to emerge from the dark mist that still lingered. "Where am I?"

"In Eve's bedroom," Stephanie replied. "Feeling better?"

"How did I get here?"

"Nate carried you," Stephanie said. "He went through medic training in the army. I only treat animal patients."

"I'm sorry," Andy said. "I'm really sorry. I must have ruined your dinner."

"We're just glad we were here," Stephanie replied. "Don't you worry about anything. Every guy here has gone through the same thing. God knows it's nothing to be ashamed of."

"I should…control them…"

"I still have flashbacks," Nate said. "Rare now, but they pop up. It's why we vets meet."

"But dinner…"

"Not to worry," Stephanie said. "The steaks are in the warmer. Everything else is fine." She paused, then asked, "Or would you like to go home?"

She wanted nothing as much. She felt lousy and weak and tired but she didn't want to ruin everyone's evening, not any more than she already had. And to leave now would be cowardly. She wouldn't feel any better at home, and maybe, just maybe, she needed company right now. "I want to stay."

She looked for Nate, who stood up.

"You should be fine now," he said.

She thought she saw a glimmer of admiration in Nate's eyes, but how could that be? She had unraveled at the sight of spilled wine. She had made a spectacle of herself. She had, she noticed now, stained his shirt with red wine.

"I'm sorry about your shirt. I'll pay—"

"No, you won't," he said. "I have several just like them, and this is the oldest. No big loss. In fact, the wine gives it more character."

"It looked new to me," she said.

"Looks can be deceptive."

She suspected that he was just trying to make her feel better. "You do know there are ways of removing wine stains?"

"I've had some experience. I'll leave you with Stephanie and let everyone know you're okay."

She didn't want him to leave, but his tactic worked. She *was* slowly relaxing. Her head ached. Her eyes were probably red, but to her surprise his light banter made her feel human again. She tried a smile. "Thank you. I'm ready…"

Nate leaned over and whispered so softly she knew he meant only her to hear, "Good for you."

Andy took a deep breath and stood. She could do this.

CHAPTER EIGHT

ANDY TRIED A smile as she entered the kitchen.

Eve was checking something in the oven. She straightened as Andy and Nate entered, followed by Stephanie and Joseph. "Okay?" she asked, worry in her voice.

Andy nodded.

Nick looked up at her anxiously. "When I feel bad, I want to be with my dogs. Would you like to meet them?"

"Nick, I don't think…" Eve started.

"Yes," Andy said. "I think I would like that." Anything to delay meeting the gazes and sympathy of the others. She was still shaken, still trembling slightly within if not outside. "I think Joseph would, too."

Nick's face lit up like a sudden burst of fireworks. He reached for her hand and led her through a hall to a closed door. There was trust in that hand, trust she didn't have for herself. Joseph stayed at her side as the boy led her to a bedroom and opened the door. Four dogs looked up, two from dog beds on the floor and two on the bed. Two raced over to her, and the other two regarded her warily.

"This is Lulu," Nick said of the young dog who jumped on her. "She's pretty new. But she's learning. And the beagle is Miss Marple. She's a thief. The two shyer ones are Captain Hook, the Chihuahua, and Fancy."

She was enchanted by the names as well as the obviously odd collection of dogs. Fancy was…the homeliest dog she'd ever seen. Yet her happiness at meeting someone was endearing. Joseph sniffed each dog, then returned to her side, apparently convinced she was in no danger. She stooped and petted each of the dogs and was rewarded with licks.

"Mom calls them her motley crew, but I don't think they're motley at all. When I asked what it meant, she told me to look it up in the dictionary," Nick said.

"And what did it say?" she asked, completely enchanted.

"Composed of diverse, often incongruous elements," he recited like a small scholar.

"And what does *incongruous* mean?"

"I looked that up, too."

"And?"

"I didn't understand completely. *Different*, kinda."

"Well, your dogs *are* different, and in a good way," she said. "They're different in the way they look, but they're alike in that they love you."

He beamed. "I like your dog, too."

"He's my first one. You might have to give me some advice."

"Is he a military dog like Josh's?"

"No, but he's been trained to help me." It was the first time she'd admitted to anyone other than Dr. Payne that she needed help.

"Josh has nightmares," Nick confided. "I've heard him. Amos helps him, too."

That didn't seem right. Josh had appeared so confident, so in control. He was starting a new business, had taken a wife and gained a child…a rather precocious one, at that.

They were interrupted by a knock. "Dinner's ready," Stephanie said.

Andy nodded. She concentrated on controlling the tremors that sometimes continued after a PTSD incident. That was what she called it: an incident.

She was self-conscious, embarrassed, unsteady, even nauseous, but she darn well wasn't going to show it. She stood. "I think I should wash first. I have dog all over me."

"That happens around here," Stephanie said.

Andy went into the bathroom, washed her face and looked at herself.

She looked washed-out. She walked unsteadily into the dining room. Joseph stuck so close to her she almost tripped against him.

Then she was at a table loaded with food. The steaks had been cut into individual pieces and looked a bit charred. But no one said anything. Instead, they dug into a huge salad and baked potatoes.

She listened as Nate and Josh talked about the new inn. "Susan, our manager, is not that excited about the name. She's great at marketing and thinks we should look at something more...descriptive than Covenant Falls Inn."

"I like Covenant Falls Inn," Eve said.

"We haven't finalized the sign yet," Josh said. "Any suggestions are welcome."

He turned to Andy. "I heard you've been delving into some of our newspapers. Find anything interesting?"

She tried to think of something. "A lot," she said. "I followed several generations. But there was one thing I didn't understand. A notice about the city council failing to pass something to do with a camel."

"The camel!" Nate said. "I almost forgot about it."

"It definitely caught my attention," Andy said.

Josh and Clint looked just as mystified as she felt.

Eve glanced at both as if she were sharing a delicious secret. "Angus Monroe," she said, "bought two camels that were brought to the United States from Egypt. They were the brainchild of Jefferson Davis, who was secretary of war for the United States before he became president of the Confederacy.

"There's a lot of conjecture," she continued, "but apparently Davis was concerned about transportation in the southwest. A general had read a book about travels in China and Turkey. It included a passage that camels could travel long distances on difficult terrain and with little water. Money was appropriated and a ship was sent to Egypt and Turkey to buy camels and hire camel drivers.

"The Camel Corps, as it was named, was sent to Camp Verde in Texas and used successfully to take supplies to California. At the beginning of the Civil War, though, the Camel Corps was dismantled. There apparently were difficulties with camels spooking mules and horses. The animals were sold to private individuals or escaped into the desert.

"Angus bought two of the camels from a roaming circus, which bought them from the army. The idea was to take supplies up to the gold mines. He was always thinking of ways to increase his business. It apparently worked for several years. Then one died. The other reportedly was a lonely old lady who followed Angus wherever he went. He kept the animal in back of his house, but it often escaped, mangled yards, bit people and spit on them."

Nate took up the story. "Finally, it was too much. The town council passed a no-spitting-in-town ordinance. It sounded fine to Angus until he discovered it was meant to banish his camel. Then it was too late. And, if Angus was anything, he was a law-abiding man. He had also become very at-

tached to the camel. He built a ranch outside town
for his family and the camel. After that camel died,
the owner of a saloon tried to repeal the no-spitting
law, but the ladies of the town bullied their men-
folk into defeating it.

"There've been other attempts to repeal it, but
the original families liked to tell the story, so it
stayed on the books," Eve finished. "It's one of our
eccentricities."

"That's a great story," Andy said, the earlier em-
barrassment forgotten.

"I haven't heard it before," Clint said.

"I haven't, either," Josh added.

"It was a long time ago," Nate said.

"But the inn…" The words were out of Andy's
mouth before she could stop them. "The gold
mines, using the camels to get to them…what about
the Camel Trail Inn?"

Five pairs of eyes riveted on her. "I mean…it's
none of my business, but…Eve said you wanted
history to promote the town. That's really neat history."

"Damn," Josh said after a short silence. "That's
perfect. There's a Camelback Hotel in Arizona, but
Camel Trail? That's unique and implies adventure."

"The sign could include a camel," Nate added,
his eyes lighting. "The restaurant's napkins and
stationery, as well."

"And the website," Eve added.

Andy looked on as all five of her dinner companions bounced ideas off each other. Josh threw her a grateful look. "That was a stroke of genius."

She didn't think so. It just seemed to fit. But a sense of accomplishment glowed inside, the first she had felt in a long time. She wanted to add ideas, suggestions, but then she stepped back.

"What do you think?" Josh asked her directly. "It was your idea."

"I don't know enough about the hospitality business to answer that," Andy replied.

"Okay, then as an individual, would all things camel attract you?"

Andy's lips twitched. "Maybe not *all* things. Beef would be better than camel."

"We couldn't very well serve our symbol," Nate said, the area around his eyes crinkling with amusement.

"Maybe we can find a real camel?" Nick inserted happily. "It would be so cool to have one."

Josh looked horrified. "No," he roared.

Stephanie had been quiet during the discussion, but now she grinned. "Might be interesting. I've never treated a camel."

"Tsk-tsk," Clint said. "Remember the no-spitting ordinance."

"Joy killer," Stephanie shot back.

"It's just that you're a pillar of the community now and…"

Stephanie turned to Eve. "Do you ever feel like doing bodily harm to your husband?"

"Often," Eve agreed.

The lighthearted comments triggered Andy's loss again. Had Jared and she been so at ease with each other, so full of joy? They'd never really had the chance.

Nate stood. "I think I should take Andy home. I have work to do tomorrow, especially after this discussion. I have a tough boss."

Josh raised an eyebrow.

Eve pushed back her chair and stood. "I'm so glad you came over, for more reasons than one. That was a terrific idea. And I'm so pleased you're interested in the history project."

"I'm glad I could be of some help," Andy said. "It was a good dinner, certainly the best I've had in months." She looked down at Nick. "And thank you for introducing me to your friends. They made me happy."

Nick grinned. "You and Joseph can visit them any time."

"We would like that."

She finished saying goodbye and joined Nate at the door.

Once in the car, she sat back in the seat.

She still felt shaky.

"I HOPE THAT wasn't too much too soon." Nate said.

She hesitated before answering. "I thought it might be," she said frankly. "And I was sorry to spoil dinner, but I think it was good for me to get out."

"That really was an inspired idea about the inn. I'm sure we'll use it. Thank you. And don't worry about the flashback. There's tremendous respect for the way you stayed and hung in there. You made a friend for life with Eve at the way you talked to Nick."

"He's a nice kid."

"Yeah, and smart as hell, just like his mom."

She was silent the rest of the way. Conflicting emotions bombarded her. There had been some very good moments and some very bad ones on her first social adventure outside the hospital. The good had been the comradery, the conversation that included her. It had been Nick and his dogs.

The bad...

Best not to think about that.

When they arrived at the cabin, she swung the door open the second he stopped. "You don't need to walk me inside," she said. "But thank you for everything tonight, especially for looking after me so well."

"Not a chance," he said. "My mama taught me better than that." He left the car and opened the back door for Joseph. She stepped out before he could help her.

When they reached her door, she put the key in the lock and turned back to face him.

"Are you okay?" he asked.

She wasn't sure she wanted to go inside the empty cabin after the attack, but neither did she want to invite him inside. She wasn't ready for that. "Yes," she said. "I think I am, thanks to you and Stephanie. I'm just sorry I interrupted the evening."

"Most of us have been there," he said gently. "Clint, Josh, myself… We've all had flashbacks. I'm just glad you stayed. We never would have thought of Camel Trail Inn."

"I really am sorry I ruined your shirt," she said. "I'll replace it."

"No, you won't. I wasn't fibbing. It really was an old shirt and one I didn't like that much."

Their gazes met and suddenly her heart beat a little faster. Warmth flashed in his expression. She wanted him to touch her. To hold her.

No! How could she?

She turned and fumbled with the doorknob. "I really must go inside. I ate well, but poor Joseph…"

He took the hint. "G'night," he said. "Call if you need anything. The number is on that sheet I gave you."

"Thank you."

After a searching glance, he turned and she watched him stride to the car.

Andy stepped inside and leaned against the door. She didn't look out the window, but she sensed he was still there outside. It was another moment before she heard the car start up.

She flipped on the light, sat in a chair and thought about the extraordinary evening. The wine spill, the flashback with all its terrors, then the convivial dinner. Terror and laughter. But the only time she had really felt at ease was with the boy and his dogs.

And then that brief connection at the door. So brief and yet…real.

She felt disloyal to Jared, to the others. She was living…

She fed and watered Joseph and watched as he went outside and did his business, then joined her inside. He followed her as she changed into the overlarge T-shirt she slept in, then jumped up on the bed and put his head on her chest, looking up at her with his intelligent eyes.

"We did okay today, didn't we?" she said. She had not run after the flashback. She had stayed and taken part in a conversation, an important part. And she had enjoyed most of it. She had laughed. Actually laughed about Nick's camel.

She turned the light off. But she doubted she would get much sleep.

CHAPTER NINE

WHEN NATE REACHED HOME, his mind was in turmoil.

He'd been reluctant to take Andy Stuart to Eve's house that evening. He'd been attracted to her at their first meeting, and warning signals had flickered in his brain since.

It was especially true when she'd had the flashback. He'd been closer to her than the others and had caught her as she fell. Then the medic in him had taken over. He wondered whether the others had noted his slight hesitation before carrying her into Eve's bedroom. He didn't want to be involved, dammit. But she was a vet in need of help.

That her flashback had been terrifying was clear, and he admired how she had tried to shake it off, the gallantry in returning to the others and even participating in a discussion that had little to do with her. Or perhaps that was why she'd participated. Why she had so quickly wrapped herself in Covenant Falls history. She could avoid the present.

He, on the other hand, wanted to remember the past so he could reshape the present.

But, dammit, he'd had that sudden urge to hold

her at the door, to try to erase some of the pain from those very wide gray eyes. He'd wanted to kiss her. Hadn't he learned anything from Margaret?

He'd watched her go through the door, and then the lights go on. He'd done his job. He had seen her home safely. Joseph would take over now.

So why hadn't he driven off? Maybe *he* needed a Joseph.

He wondered whether both he and Eve might have underestimated Ms. Stuart. It had taken courage for her to move to a totally new town, especially having PTSD.

He hesitated, then did something he never thought he would do—he went online and ran a search. He shouldn't have. It was none of his business and she was entitled to her privacy, but her reaction to the wine spill prompted him to learn more. Several articles came up almost immediately when he searched her name, *army* and *Afghanistan*. One article mentioned she was the lone survivor during a terrorist attack on a field hospital in Afghanistan eight months ago. He remembered reading about the attack when it happened, but no names were mentioned at the time. It had been big news, especially in the military community.

Nate continued his search and then found an article that stunned him.

Lieutenant Andrea Stuart had been engaged to one of the two murdered doctors.

Nate took a long, deep breath. He closed his eyes

and he saw the attack in his mind. The intruder, the shots, the blood. Probably everything she had seen again last night.

He had no intention of sharing that information with anyone else, not even Eve and Clint, although they might know, since Josh was instrumental in bringing her here. He had intruded into something extremely painful, more painful than he could have imagined.

No wonder she'd had a panic attack last night. He had lost friends in Iraq. Too many of them, but she had been a healer, not a warrior.

After a sleepless night, he rose early, took a shower, drank a cup of coffee and walked several houses down to his mother's. Her home, which had harbored three generations of Rowlands, was close enough that he could keep an eye on her, but far enough that they were independent of one another. She, and her failing health, was one reason he had returned to Covenant Falls after his divorce.

They usually had Sunday breakfast together, and he rather dreaded it this morning. His mother had been curious about Covenant Falls's newest resident, particularly when she'd learned it was a woman, and she would want a full report.

He would edit it considerably. He would omit Andy's PTSD episode, and the way he'd felt as he'd helped her.

He liked her. He admired her courage. Even worse, he was attracted to her and far more intensely than he'd been to any woman in a very long time.

That disturbing discovery meant he had to keep his distance, although it would be difficult. Eve had evidently taken her under her wing. And he was in business with Eve's husband, which meant they would be thrown together. Often.

Nate sure as hell wasn't ready for any kind of relationship. Neither was she. She had stay-away signs all over. And himself? He doubted he would ever be ready to trust any woman again.

But dammit all, she wouldn't leave his thoughts.

Hell with it. He could avoid her as much as possible. *He would.*

Agnes Rowland greeted him with her usual wide smile. "My turn this week," she said. "Pancakes okay?"

"Sounds great."

His mother wasted no time in getting to the point. "What is she like?"

"Nice."

"Nice? That doesn't tell me much."

"You'll like her," he added.

"I like everyone."

"Well, then, there you go."

"Nate!" she said in a disgusted voice.

"You'll meet her and make your own decision," he said. "Eve has sort of trapped her into writing a short history of our town. I expect her to be talking to a lot of people."

"She's smart, then."

"Very. She came up with a new name for our inn. Susan thought Covenant Falls Inn didn't have much kick to it."

"I thought Covenant Falls Inn was a good name," she said as she poured pancake batter in the frying pan. "Are you going to keep me in suspense or should I ask Josh?"

"The Camel Trail Inn."

His mom burst out laughing. "*That* certainly does have a kick to it. A pun. From you. I'm amazed. Now I'm more curious than ever about her. When do I meet her?"

"She just arrived, Mom. She needs to take things a little slow."

"Should I take her some chili?"

"I would wait a few days," he said. "She's been flooded with food."

Her eyes danced with curiosity but thankfully she dropped the subject. For the moment.

The pancakes were great as usual, and afterward he drove Agnes the four blocks to church, then headed to the inn to discuss the proposed name change with Susan and Josh.

SUSAN LOVED RENAMING the inn. It was different enough from Camelback that there should be no confusion, not to mention that their inn was a speck compared to the mammoth in Arizona.

They had planned a simple, stylish sign, but now

Josh suggested a weathered wood sign with the name and a camel silhouette.

"No ordinary camel," Nate said. "We need one with an attitude."

"I'll pass that on to the artist," Susan said. While they were there, Susan called an artist she knew who said he would send three logo designs by midweek. She thought the sign company could expedite the work.

"It's going to be an expense we didn't expect, but I think it will add a quirky twist that sets it apart," Josh said.

Susan grinned.

"As soon as we get a design," Josh said, "I'll send it to Clint and he can redesign our website. In the meantime, I'll send those who accepted our invitation for the preview a letter explaining the name change."

"It was Andy's idea," Nate said. "Maybe she could write a few paragraphs, an explanation of the name. We can use it on menus and a card for each room."

"Will you ask her?" Josh said.

Nate hesitated. He'd put his foot in it again. Why had he mentioned it?

Maybe because he had seen the flicker of interest in her eyes when she'd suggested renaming the inn, and he wanted to feed it. He'd experienced aimlessness when he'd returned from Iraq.

"Okay," he said. "I'll ask when I see her." That

gave him some time. He might not see her for a while.

The discussion then went to other details. Mel Edwards, a local rancher, had offered the use of several of his horses for trail riding in hopes of building another source of revenue. Then there was the old but lively Herman Mann, who knew the area's mountain trails and mining sites like the back of his hand. Not only did he know mountain lore, but he looked the part, with a full gray beard. He could lead adventure tours to abandoned mines and a ghost town.

"Do you think Herman knows anything about the camels?" he asked.

"If he doesn't, he'll make it up," Josh replied.

"We could always buy a camel," Nate mused in jest.

He choked when Josh said, "Good idea. Find one."

It wasn't until Josh, who almost never joked, grinned that Nate realized he was kidding.

With a straight face, Nate replied, "What's my budget?"

Their inn manager merely shook her head. "I am not feeding and boarding a camel."

"But it would make a great mascot," Nate said slyly. "I bet I could convince Eve if I found a camel in distress." He glanced at Josh.

"One word to Eve," Josh warned, "and we end this partnership. I'm sure she would find an orphaned, moth-eaten camel somewhere, and heaven help us if young Nick even got a hint of it. He would be on the internet in seconds and would have several candidates he couldn't live without."

Nate knew this was only too true. He'd been cruel to mention it. He chuckled. "Love sure does change a man."

"Just wait until you get bitten by the bug."

"Been there, done that. No intention of ever doing it again."

Josh just smiled.

"I think I'm going to love working for you guys," Susan said. "But right now you have decisions to make."

They went through the items one by one.

The inn was just outside the city limits, and he'd had to get permits from the county. It passed the building inspection with flying colors, but there were a dozen last-minute details. The hiring of staff, training, final purchases.

"Oh, I called Mrs. Byars," Susan said. "She would be delighted to provide brownies for our guests. I didn't give her a price yet, but if it meets your approval, I figured twelve dollars for two dozen. It would make it worth her time and wouldn't bankrupt us. We also have to decide whether we want to offer free wine and tea in the afternoon."

"What do you think?"

"Clients really appreciate it. It makes them feel as if we're going the extra mile. I know you haven't settled on final prices, but a glass of wine when guests come back after a busy day more than pays for itself in goodwill and repeat business."

Josh nodded. "I know damn little about the hotel business, but I trust your judgment. Nate?"

"Agreed."

Susan nodded. "I'll have some figures ready for you next week. I know you've been quoting some promotional rates, but they're a bit on the low side."

"We're not trying to make a lot of money," Josh explained. "It's the first step to revive the town, to introduce it to Denver and maybe get another couple of businesses going."

"Understood. But I don't want you to lose money, either."

"I like that," Josh said.

Josh and Nate walked out together. "Thanks for recommending her," Josh said. "I'm not sure how all this would go without her."

"We were lucky. Our moms are good friends and when she wanted to leave Nevada, Mom thought she might be just what we needed."

"She's pretty," Josh noted.

"Yeah, I guess she is."

"Any interest?"

"Nope," Nate said. "She was a couple of years ahead of me in school. Too familiar, I guess. Besides, she just left a bad marriage and I left a bad one in Seattle. I suspect neither of us wants to repeat that experience."

Josh changed the subject. "How was Andy when you drove her home?"

"Embarrassed, I think, though God knows she shouldn't be. She's been through hell."

Josh shot him a look. "Did she say anything?"

"No, but I guessed from last night it was pretty bad."

"Dr. Payne didn't give me any details. He just told me that she needed a safe haven right now." He took a long breath. "I know how that feels."

Nate felt even worse now that he had snooped into Andy's story.

"Dr. Payne never tells me much. That's kind of one of our rules for the cabin. I'm there if he, or she, needs help, but otherwise it's up to the vet to decide what, if anything, they want to reveal."

"I know," Nate said, "but last night…"

"She came out of it, and joined us. She listened and even made a contribution. A darn good one, I might add. I called Dr. Payne and told him about it. He thought it was a huge step forward."

Nate nodded.

"I have to get home while I still have a family," Josh said, hesitated, then added, "It still sounds strange saying that. Family. Getting home."

"You've got a good thing going."

"I know," Josh said somberly. "At times, I can't quite believe it." He hesitated again. "I know I said I wouldn't push you and Andy together, but she needs to see the falls to really understand Covenant Falls, and I just got home from Denver. She's also very alone. Can you take her there? Fill her in on what we talked about today? I swear I won't ask again."

"I seem to remember we had a deal. I would pick her up for supper yesterday and you would desist from calling on my services again."

"I promised for Eve, not myself," Josh replied with a smile, then he lost it and his tone changed. "That was before last night. You saw how devastated she was after the flashback, then how she changed when we talked about the history of this area. I think we should encourage that interest."

"Don't you think we might be pushing too hard? She's only been here three days."

"Maybe, but she doesn't have anyone here. It can get lonely in that cabin."

"I thought *you* liked it that way."

"Don't rub it in," Josh replied with a grin, "but it's up to you." He climbed in his Jeep and drove off.

ANDY HAD A touch of cabin fever on Sunday. She and Joseph headed for the mountain. She was relieved to note it was easier today than it had been before.

The blue in the sky was so pure she ached with the beauty of it. She and Joseph sat there, trying to erase the memory of last night. Well, who knew what Joseph was thinking. He cocked his ears at the chirping of a bird or a rustle of a squirrel or rabbit, but he didn't move from her side.

After their walk, she played with Joseph, or tried to. He was obviously as clueless at play as she was. She would throw one of the dog toys she'd been given by Karen. Joseph just sat there and regarded her with a puzzled expression.

She threw out a ball and said, "Catch," and he looked at her as if she were crazy. She would go get it, stand where it landed and hold it out. Joseph would trot to her, waiting patiently for his person to do another crazy thing.

She dropped to her knees and gave him a big hug. Proper, solemn Joseph. He licked her hand in appreciation, then rested his head on her arm in a gesture of trust. Warmth filled her at the unquestioning affection he offered. "You're such a good boy," she said, "even if you don't know how to have fun."

She shouldn't be critical. She hadn't known how to have fun, either.

She'd been so intent on leaving her hometown that she'd studied every spare minute she had. Every moment, that was, that she wasn't helping her mother raise two younger children. After her father died when she was fourteen, her mother waitressed in the only café left in town. Tips were rare, and they mostly lived on leftovers from the café.

That reminded her. She should call her mother. She had promised to do that when she reached Colorado, but so much had happened so fast she'd barely taken a breath. She punched in her mother's number on the cell phone she carried with her when walking alone. It was answered immediately.

"Hi, Mom." She forced cheerfulness into her voice.

"Hey, baby. How is everything?"

"Good. The cabin Dr. Payne found is great. So far, I've met three other vets, and they're all helpful. To help pay for the cabin I volunteered to write a short history of the town. I may not be able to send you anything for a while."

"That's the last thing I care about," her mother said. "I saved some of that money you sent. We're fine. Joy's husband got a job as a mechanic at the mines. Thank God, he doesn't have to work in them."

"And Barb?"

"Honor student," her mother said. "Says she wants to follow your path. She's thinking about trying for one of those ROTC scholarships, as well. Sure would be fine to have two college graduates in the family."

Andy wasn't so sure she wanted her younger sister to go into the army, but, except for that last week, the army had been good to her. And the war in Afghanistan was winding to a close.

"That's great," she said.

"When are you comin' home?"

"You know there's nothing there for me," Andy said.

"Dr. Odum said he could use a nurse. Can't pay much, but he's a good man and you would be home."

Except for her family, home was the last place she wanted to be. "I can't go back to nursing," she said. "Not yet."

"Okay, baby, take your time. We'll be here for you."

"Thanks, Mom." She hung up, feeling a familiar guilt. She had escaped, and she'd sent money home to assuage that guilt. Now she couldn't do even that. She should be helping…

"Damn," she said to Joseph. The peace of the morning was gone.

Her phone rang. She hesitated before answering. "Hello."

"Hi," Nate said. He didn't have to identify himself. She recognized that deep voice, but it was hesitant. He had never seemed the hesitant type. "I hope I'm not interrupting anything."

"No," she said.

"Josh thought you might like to see the falls, where everything happened back in the 1850s. I'm going out there to look for a location to place signs. I could stop by and pick you up. We won't be gone long. No more than an hour and a half."

She had been thinking about driving to the falls,

but she had no idea how to get there and she hadn't wanted to call anyone, not after the scene last night. Nate made it sound like the most natural thing in the world. Business.

"It sounds good," she said. "Thank you."

"Great. Twelve thirty okay?"

"Sure."

"I'll bring some sandwiches," he said and hung up.

CHAPTER TEN

TELEPHONING ANDY HAD been more difficult than he had expected. He was stepping across a boundary, a protective boundary.

After his talk with Josh, he'd weighed the pros and cons. He thought about her alone in the cabin in a strange place with people she didn't know, then how her face had become animated for the first time when they were discussing Covenant Falls history and those darn camels.

He knew from experience Andy would be feeling the emotional hangover after last night. She'd seemed to snap out of the flashback, but he was personally familiar with them. He suspected she felt very much alone.

There was also a business reason. Andy Stuart should see the falls before she talked to Al Monroe—if, indeed, she did. She should have a good idea of why Angus Monroe had chosen this place in the 1850s and what had kept him here. What kept most of the families here.

He was surprised when she'd agreed to go to the falls. It meant he was right. She needed company today. He would keep it friendly and no more, and then he would have done his duty. She would meet the other vets Monday and have a support group.

He didn't need to change. He'd dressed casually for the meeting at the inn. Jeans and a light V-neck sweater. He ran a comb through his hair and headed to Maude's.

Maude greeted him as he came in. "Your mother and her friends are in back."

"I'm just here for takeout," he said. "Two ham and cheese, two roast-beef sandwiches and some of that great slaw."

"Gotcha. Be ready in a jiffy. Want something to drink?"

He hadn't thought about that. "Make it two lemonades."

"Okay."

He stood to the side. He noticed the Presbyterians apparently heard a shorter sermon than the Baptists, since his mother was already seated and the Baptists were just coming in. He wondered whether the pastors got together on Friday and decided the length of their service so their congregations wouldn't all converge on Maude's at the same time.

He went over to say hi to his mother and her friends, a group of widows who banded together for church and other events. He was grateful to them on his mother's behalf. They played bridge twice a week and had organized a book club and a club where each member hosted a full dinner once a month.

"Have lunch with us," said one.

"And learn all the secrets of this formidable group?"

"More like they want to interrogate you," his mother said with a smile. "I told them you wouldn't tell me about your dinner last night."

"Yes, I did. I told you the steaks were great and it was a companionable evening. The dogs all behaved themselves."

"He's a very exasperating son," Agnes told the others. "He doesn't gossip."

He winked at her. She'd neatly stopped any more questions.

He asked about the ladies' families, then said, "I have to work, and I think my takeout is ready."

It *was* ready when he returned to the counter. "Love ya, Maude."

"Have a good time with whoever you're lunching with," Maude said with a wink.

"Work, Maude. Just work."

"Okay, but I stuck some pieces of pie in there, too."

Nate just shook his head. Maude seemed to know every move anyone made in town. If she didn't know, she guessed. Usually correctly. But not this time. This *was* business. Just business.

He arrived at Josh's cabin exactly on time in his pickup. Andy and her dog sat on the porch, and the funny little lemon bug sat in front. He would love to drive it.

She walked through the porch door and down the few steps just as he opened the door on the passenger side of the pickup. Joseph jumped in first, and then Andy stepped inside. She was back in jeans and this time wore a red-and-white-checkered shirt. She looked like a waif. He tried to picture her in uniform, but he couldn't.

"Hello," he said after they were both in the pickup.

She smiled. And he had a glimpse of the woman she'd been before Afghanistan.

"Hi," she replied.

"I thought you might like to hear about the meeting this morning. We took a vote, Josh and I, and changed the name of the inn to the Camel Trail Inn. Thank you. The reward is a great sandwich from Maude's."

"I was at Maude's Friday with Eve. I take it she's an institution in Covenant Falls."

"She's the heart. She and Eve."

She didn't say anything for a moment, then said, "I've been walking up the trail next to the cabin. It's...beautiful. Peaceful."

"Wait until you see the waterfall," Nate said.

"I don't understand why you don't have more people here. I would think retired folks would be banging on your doors."

"We don't have any industry and minimum services. We're well off the interstates, and we had a city council that didn't want anything to change and passed enough restrictions to discourage newcomers. Eve and the new council are trying to reverse that. She doesn't want to change the character of the town—she grew up here—but she does want to bring in jobs. Tourism will do that faster and with less disruption than anything else.

"How far are the falls from town?"

"As the crow flies and by horseback, about eight miles, by the roads about twenty minutes. Earlier generations of the Monroe family managed to keep it within the city limits. It makes for a strange map—it looks like a giant puzzle piece."

Joseph made a little sound like a moan behind her.

"He doesn't want to be in back," Nate guessed. "He was worried about you last night." He'd hesitated to bring it up, but he wanted to know she was all right.

"He's a worrywart," she said. "He wouldn't let me out of his sight when I got home." She paused, and he saw that her hands were knotted together in her lap. "He curled up next to me as if he knew…" Her voice trailed off.

After a moment, she asked, "Do you have a dog?"

"I did as a boy, and then Mom had a little beagle until he died about six months ago. I guess I considered him partly mine. She hasn't been ready to get a new one, and my schedule doesn't exactly work for a dog. Eve's been hounding me about taking one of her rescues, though, and I'll probably do that once the inn is squared away. She has several in foster homes."

A few miles later they stopped at a narrow asphalt road that turned left up into a forest of pine trees. He pulled onto it, then stopped. He stepped out and looked around. The road needed a sign and he thought he found the right place for it. He staked it out in his mind.

"This road takes us up to the falls," Nate said when he returned to his seat. "A sign will go up next Wednesday. It's never been marked because the former city councils didn't want it marked. They wanted the falls for Covenant Falls people only."

He started the car again and drove up the twisting road. He glanced at Andy. She looked far more relaxed than she had when he picked her up. Her hands had stopped twisting together. The windows were open, and a breeze ruffled her hair. He wondered whether she had any idea how pretty she was.

He immediately banished that idea. Everything in his life was coming together. He was building again. Designing. And even better, he felt he was helping to bring life back into the town and people he loved. Andy would be going back to her roots just as he had come home to his.

The road needed some repair, but Andy didn't

seem to notice as she stared out at the forest around them. It was slow going because of the winding turns, but then he turned onto another road and, in a very short time, stopped at a large grassy area, which served as a parking lot.

"We have just a short walk," he said as he stepped out of the pickup and hurried around to her side before she could get out on her own. He opened the door and held out his hand. "The ground is uneven," he said as she took it and stepped out. He let go of it almost immediately. The last thing he wanted was to frighten her off...

ANDY HEARD THE roar up ahead and stopped.

"Come with me," Nate said. She walked with him to a wood railing and looked down about 150 feet. A creek meandered below, the water so clear she could see rocks beneath it.

"The falls are just around that stand of trees," he said.

They continued toward the sound of thunder, and once they passed the trees Andy stopped and stared with awe at the torrent of foaming water tumbling over rocks into the river below. Spray spun into the sky to create a perfect rainbow. Her breath caught in her throat and without thinking, she reached out and touched Nate's hand. He clasped it and grinned.

"Your town has been selfish," she said. "It's... grand."

"*Grand.* I like that word," Nate said. "It's our

gem, and we've been protecting it, but it's time to share if we want Covenant Falls to survive."

"Everyone seems happy."

"But you don't see many people our age," he said. "Josh and Eve want to change that, although it's damn strange, because all Josh wanted when he arrived here was to be left alone."

"The falls changed him?"

"Well, I think Eve had more to do with it, but the truth is the falls seems to have some magic, and this observation comes from a very pragmatic person," Nate said with amusement in his eyes. "Me."

"I don't see you as pragmatic," she said.

"Why not?"

"Your eyes lit up when I suggested Camel Trail Inn, and I think it's more inspirational than pragmatic to reframe an entire town."

"We're just building an inn."

"I don't think so," she said slowly, thoughtfully. "I think you and Eve and Josh are trying to kick this town in the ass and get it moving, and it's going to change far more than you suspect."

He raised an eyebrow, apparently at the words she used. She was appalled at the vehemence with which she'd said it. Where in the heck had it come from? Why did she care? She had been here all of three days and already she felt invested.

He chuckled. "I guess you're right. I hadn't exactly thought of the inn as doing that."

"I think Eve has," she said. "I suspect the community center was only the beginning."

"I can see she's already drawn you into it."

"I've always liked stories," Andy said, "and Eve fed that instinct. When I was a kid, I would make them up about people I knew. They would be horrified at some of them."

"What did you do to them?"

"You really don't want to know."

"I think I do."

"I murdered some of them."

"Kids or adults?"

"I was an equal-opportunity slayer," she admitted wryly.

"And then you became a nurse to save them," he said with a twinkle in his eyes.

Andy wondered why she had told him about her childhood fantasies about bullies. But then she knew. She didn't have to pretend. He had seen her at her worst last night. She looked up at him, at the warm hazel eyes and the hank of chestnut hair that fell over his forehead.

She sought frantically for something to say, to divert her thoughts from his face. It was much too attractive, too rugged. "Thanks for bringing me here. Is this what brought and kept Angus Monroe here?"

He shrugged. "I don't know what was in his mind. Probably it was the lake. The land east of here is—or was—all dry. The lake was a draw to every wagon train and wanderer that came this way.

It was a perfect place for a trading post. He made a treaty with the Utes after saving a chief's life. He married a Ute woman and had three children. Everyone pretty much agrees on that."

"And after that?"

"He became very powerful in the state and amassed a lot of land, some of it, according to various stories, by not very savory means. Original settlers filed claims for land, then he bought them out cheap. But that's just rumor. The fact is, no one really knows a lot about his early years here, which is why the journals are important."

He was intellectually seducing her, and he realized she was enjoying it.

"There's no more?"

"That's why we're curious about the journals. When his nephew mentioned the journals, Eve and Al were at loggerheads. Al headed the city council and pretty much controlled the town for years. Nothing happened without his approval. When Eve was elected, his influence was substantially reduced. They disagreed on nearly every issue. He didn't want anything to change. Eve did."

"Why would he let me read them, or even talk to me, if he won't talk to anyone here in town?"

"He probably won't. But there's a chance. He's proud of his heritage and you're an objective stranger."

"Am I? I'm indebted to Eve's husband. He's probably aware of that."

"I'm sure he is, but you're writing a brochure about his town. He certainly would want his family portrayed well."

"A short history," she corrected. "A few pages for a pamphlet, and it might be terrible. I'm not a writer. I told Eve that. I'm telling everyone that." She bit her lip. "I'm beginning to feel manipulated."

He shook his head. "Then, don't do it. That's the last thing anyone wants. There's absolutely no obligation, and I sure as hell don't want you to think there is. Neither would Eve or Josh. Eve just thought you might be interested."

She believed him and relaxed. But he was right, and so was Eve. She *was* intrigued. As someone who loved history, the thought of reading a journal written 170 years earlier was more than beguiling to her.

"If I don't get his cooperation, will you tell me the rest of the story, or at least a version of it?" She couldn't stop a smile.

"I swear," he said. "On my honor." Then he added, "I left the sandwiches in the pickup. Why don't you stay here while I get them?"

To her surprise, she was hungry. She nodded.

While he was gone, she gazed at the falls, thinking about what he had said. She pictured Angus Monroe. He would have been tall, with dark hair, and he would be honorable.

She felt a growing excitement.

Joseph barked. She glanced up, startled, to see

Nate approaching with a box. "You looked a thousand miles away," he said. "Should I ask what you're thinking about?"

"Angus Monroe," she said, a half truth.

He put the box on the table and opened it. It was loaded with food. He took out two paper plates and plastic spoons.

"The pie was Maude's idea," he said. "I didn't know what kind of sandwich you like, so I got two ham and cheese and two roast beef. There's lemonade in the cups."

"I'll take a roast beef," she said, "and lemonade sounds perfect."

The falls and fresh breeze were intoxicating, and she enjoyed every bite of her sandwich. She kept her eyes on it rather than the attractive man across from her.

When she turned her gaze back to him, he was studying her, and she felt a sudden warmth. Then guilt struck her like a sword. How could she even think of another man? The food suddenly felt like cotton in her mouth and her throat closed.

No. No. No. Not now.

Joseph whined next to her and put a paw on her knee. She fought the panic. She willed herself to breathe until it came naturally again. She looked up and met Nate's concerned expression. She took another deep breath. "It's okay," she said.

"Do you want to go?" he said softly.

"No," she said. She leaned down and put two

hands on Joseph's head, just touching him. She struggled for normalcy, for something to say. Then she remembered what Nate said last night.

"You said you were a medic," she reminded him, hoping her voice wasn't strained.

"No, I said I had medic training, but I was just a soldier. I was with the Strykers in Iraq."

"You were in the middle of combat," she said.

"You know it?" he said in surprise.

"I was in the ROTC in high school and college. It paid for my degree. You learn military history. The Strykers are well named."

She was quiet for a moment. He reached out and touched her hand. She was surprised at how comforting it felt. Human contact. She bit her lip. The guilt struck again.

Nate must have seen it in her eyes because he dropped his hand.

"Ready to go back?" he asked.

She nodded. "But you're right. It is beautiful here. It's a shame not to share it."

"I agree."

"Thank you for bringing me here," she said properly, the formality maintaining a distance.

"You're very welcome." He gathered up the remainders from lunch and packed them in the box.

They walked back toward his truck. She paused just as they approached the stand of trees that framed the falls.

The rainbow was gone.

NATE NEEDED A very cold shower when he returned home.

The house was lonely. He hadn't really noticed that before. After the bitter end of his marriage four years ago, peace had been a much-appreciated balm.

Covenant Falls had been safe as far as any romantic risks were concerned. Nearly everyone he knew was married, engaged or in some other town. He hadn't been tempted.

Until now. Andy might look fragile, but she sure as hell wasn't. Field medical personnel couldn't be. They had to be tough physically, mentally and emotionally.

Right now, she was in a battle for herself. He tried to convince himself that he was only concerned as one vet would be about another. But he knew that wasn't true.

She stirred something in him he'd thought he'd conquered. He cared. He cared much more than he'd ever thought he could again. And it could only lead to disaster. She would leave Covenant Falls, probably sooner than later.

He headed for the cold shower to inject some reason into himself. It did nothing to relax him. He couldn't stop thinking about her. The attraction had been immediate. It had grown even stronger today although he knew it boded no good for either of them. He was still seared by his ex-wife, and she obviously still mourned the man she'd loved and lost in front of her.

After the shower, he buried himself in work. While the inn was the major focus of his partnership with Josh, they also did renovations for both homes and businesses. The inn was in good shape with Susan now in place.

He studied plans for an addition to a ranch house outside town. He had purchased the materials and they should be at the ranch next week. He'd hired two other men to join him and Josh at the site. They wanted to be finished in three weeks, sooner if possible, and Josh wouldn't be there all the time. The framing shouldn't take long, but the electrical and interior work would. That meant twelve-hour days.

In the meantime he was doing a pro bono job for June Byars, who lived just two houses away from Josh's cabin. It was a good thing. No time to think of Andy, much less see her, even if they were just a few hundred yards away from each other.

He needed another cold shower.

CHAPTER ELEVEN

ANDY TOOK A deep breath before invading the lair of the dragon.

After Nate left Sunday afternoon, she'd spent an hour sitting on the porch, then walked out to the lake and sat on the dock. She thought about the Scottish trader and a vision that founded a town.

The various descriptions of Al Monroe also challenged her. She had always been good with people. She'd learned how to persist while being so polite no one took offense. She'd used that tactic to get into high school ROTC. It was all guys, and they'd done their best to get her out as they had other girls. But she knew it was her best chance to get into college, and she'd taken their hazing and bullying and even disdain from them and the instructor...

She reassured herself as she took a long hot shower and dressed in the best she had: the black pants that were a little big and a blue shirt. She added a touch of lipstick and ran a brush through her hair. Then she stooped down next to Joseph. "You have to stay here now," she said. "I'll be back soon."

She turned back to the problem at hand. How to approach Al Monroe.

Directness had always worked for her.

She reluctantly left Joseph inside and drove the Bucket to the center of town and parked in front of the Monroe Real Estate and Insurance Company. If she got in to see him, she would not mention the journals, only that she was trying to write a short history and needed his input.

Andy took a deep breath, then walked to the office. Real estate flyers decorated the front window. She walked in. The bank branch was to her right as she entered. It was nothing more than a counter with a young woman smiling hopefully at her.

Andy went up to her. "Hello. Is Mr. Monroe in?"

"Sure is," the young woman said. "Mrs. Stanley over there will help you. I'm Mary Reynolds," she said. "You must be the new veteran in Josh's cabin."

"Guilty," Andy said. "I'm Andy—Andrea—Stuart."

"Welcome to Covenant Falls. I hope you stay awhile. We need new blood."

"Thank you," she said, although she had no intentions of staying. Covenant Falls was just a way station.

She left the counter and walked across the room to the woman staring at the computer. "Hello," she said.

No smile this time from the middle-aged woman.

A gatekeeper, Andy thought. She'd had experience with that certain breed.

"Would it be possible to see Mr. Monroe?" she asked.

"Do you have an appointment?"

"No, but I would really like to meet him."

"Insurance? Or real estate? Mr. Adams is responsible for insurance."

Maybe a small deception wasn't out of order. "More like real estate."

"Who should I say is here?"

"Andy Stuart. I just moved into Mr. Manning's cabin."

The woman gave her a long stare, then picked up her phone. "An Andy Stuart would like to see you about real estate."

After a pause, she nodded at Andy. "You can go in."

Andy's stomach churned. She had managed this far. She hadn't allowed herself to think beyond each step. The first step was to drive here, the second to get into his office…

I can do it. She stood and went to the door, opening it.

She peered inside. A tall, heavily built man stood as she entered. He looked startled when he saw her. "I thought Irene said Andy Stuart."

"That's me, I'm afraid," she said. "Andrea, but everyone calls me Andy."

"You're the new person in Manning's cabin?" He didn't sound very happy about it.

"Yes, sir," she said, reverting to military protocol.

He nodded toward her hand in its brace. "What happened to your hand?"

"A bullet."

"You were in combat?" He sounded surprised.

"I was an army nurse in a combat zone."

"Was?"

To her surprise, she didn't mind the question from him. It was better than the averted glances.

"My hand was injured. I received a medical discharge."

"Why did you come to Covenant Falls?"

It was direct and even a bit rude, but she'd expected that. She sensed that frankness was the best course with him. "I needed a place to...decide what to do next. My doctor recommended Covenant Falls."

"No family?" he asked.

"That wouldn't work right now."

"Sit down," he ordered.

She sat.

"Irene said you were here about real estate."

She thought about lying, then decided that would be a bad move. "Not really."

"Then, what?"

"History. I want to write a short history of Covenant Falls."

"Why?"

"For the community center and to tell people about the town. I want to do something to justify my use of the cabin. No one told me to. But I like history, and this town has so much of it."

"It's really to promote the town," he said with a frown. "Eve wants to bring more people here. I don't. I like it as it is."

"It can't stay as it is if everyone grows old and dies," she said. "You'll just have another ghost town here. I know what it's like when a town's young people feel it's necessary to leave to get a job."

"How do you know?"

"I come from a small coal-mining town in West Virginia. About the only choices were waiting tables in the diner or...leaving."

"We're not *that* bad," he said with what she thought must be a rare smile.

"I would have liked to stay," she said, sensing an opening. "My only family—a mother and two sisters—are there, but I couldn't support myself. It's why I joined the army. It helped me get a degree I might otherwise not have."

He stared at her. "Why are you really here?"

"I've visited the community center and looked through some of the newspapers dating back to 1875. I've heard some stories about the founding of this town. I would really like to learn more about how it started. And about Angus Monroe." She paused. "I could probably sit down now and write some paragraphs about the town that would satisfy Mayor Manning, but I want to do something more. I want to know your ancestor. He deserves more than a few paragraphs."

He lifted an eyebrow. "You know the mayor and I don't exactly agree on the future of Covenant Falls."

"I heard."

"You have nerve coming here," he said.

She didn't answer.

"Give me the real reason," he said, and she realized there was much more to Al Monroe than she'd been led to believe. She decided to answer honestly.

"Because it's the first thing that's interested me in more than seven months," she said.

"And that should matter to me?"

"Maybe not. But I understand Angus became a powerful man. He was one of the first settlers in the state. He has a great story and he deserves to be remembered."

"Why would the history of a small town like Covenant Falls have any interest for anyone? What do you want from me?" Al Monroe asked.

She sat straight up in the chair. "Just what you want to tell me about Angus Monroe. What made him come here, settle here, establish a town that exists today? It had to take courage and vision."

"I don't think Angus thought anything that grand," Al said wryly.

"That's why he's so interesting. He's like so

many other pioneers. They didn't know what they were creating. They just wanted something better for their families."

"I'm not sure that's true of Angus," his descendant said. "He was an unwilling pioneer. He came to America to save his irresponsible brother, only to watch him die. He'd already severed all his ties in Scotland and sold everything there. He had nothing left in Scotland. It was either settle here or go home penniless."

That was already more than she'd known before. Maybe more than anyone knew. Excitement coursed through her. "Will you tell me more about him?" she asked. "I swear I won't use anything you don't like."

He looked at her for a very long moment, then he nodded.

His phone rang. He glanced at what must be the caller identification.

He turned to her. "Come to my house this afternoon. Five p.m.," he said. "It's the large brick house two blocks down Main Street." Then he waved his hand in an obvious dismissal.

She left, a sense of accomplishment lifting her steps. She waved at Mary on the way out.

ANDY DROVE HOME to be joyously greeted by Joseph. She had to admit it was much nicer than entering an empty cabin that belonged to someone else. "I missed you, too," she told him. "But I have to support the two of us in some way." He wagged his tail and licked her hand.

"Come on," she said. "Let's for a walk, then have lunch."

They walked outside and up what she now thought of as her mountain. She talked to Joseph all the way up to the viewing point. "You should be proud of me," she said. "I actually did something useful today."

Joseph barked.

"Thank you," she said. "I think it's progress, too. And I'm seeing the town's bear again this afternoon."

When they reached the lookout, she glanced down at the town below. She wondered whether Angus had viewed the valley below from this point. He must have explored much of the area. Now that she'd embraced the idea, he almost came alive to her.

She was still surprised at the ease of her conversation with Al. After what had been hinted and said about him, she'd expected an ogre, but she'd enjoyed her time with him, with his direct questions. She'd suspected he was testing her and she had passed. In any event she was looking forward to talking to him again.

Maybe she should call and ask whether she could bring Joseph. Or would that be a step too far?

"What do you think?" she asked Joseph.

He nudged her and moved closer in what she took as approval.

"We should go back," she said. She refused to call the cabin home.

It just had to be *back*. It wasn't her home and never would be. She hadn't had a home in years. She'd always stayed in officer quarters to save money when in the States and usually shared rooms or tents overseas. The cabin was the nicest place she'd stayed.

Which led to the future. She hadn't wanted to think about it for months after that last day in Afghanistan. It just seemed so empty without Jared, without her team, without nursing.

She looked down at her hand. Without the brace, the scars were only too evident, which was why she usually wore it. She hated answering questions. Somehow she hadn't minded with Al Monroe. Maybe because, according to Eve, he'd had so many losses himself. She returned to the cabin and turned on the news beamed in from Denver.

She quickly turned it off and searched for something happier. She had three hours before she had to meet Al again. She thought about writing out some questions but then decided against it. She would have to wing it. Maybe she would return the bound newspapers she had and pick up some more.

"Come on, Joseph," she said as she awkwardly picked up the large volume. In minutes, she was parked on the side of the community center. There were other cars there, as well.

She walked up to Bill Evans. "Hi. I'm returning this. I would like to pick up another."

"Good. Are you coming tonight?"

Tonight? Then she remembered the veterans' meeting. Poker. Refreshments. Maybe sharing. She wasn't ready to share. "I'm not sure I can attend," she said. "I have an appointment at five."

She saw curiosity in his eyes but he didn't ask any questions. "Drop in any time. You don't have to be there exactly at seven."

"Thank you," she said and changed the subject. "Do you have a picture or painting or sketch of Angus Monroe?"

"There's a sketch that an artist did for the Denver newspaper in 1877. Legend is they wanted a photograph but Angus refused. An artist did a quick sketch when Angus met with the governor. He'd been a strong supporter of the statehood movement and I suspect he planned to collect on it. Not money but protection of his town and the falls."

Another tidbit Andy filed in her head. As soon as she returned to the cabin she intended to look up the conflict over statehood.

He led the way upstairs and unlocked the museum door. He opened the door and stood aside as Andy entered, then went to one of the cabinets. He unlocked it and took out a faded newspaper page carefully encased in plastic. A sketch was in the lower left-hand corner.

Andy studied it. The artist was good. He'd captured the directness of eyes that seemed to stare at her. Monroe was clean shaven, and a scar ran down his right cheek. Even with the scar, or maybe because of it, the face was arresting. Not handsome but strong.

"Interesting," she said. "Can we get copies made?"

"Don't know why not. The newspaper belongs to us."

"Good."

"There's more bound volumes. Take your pick. I have to go downstairs."

She nodded. "Thanks."

Bill left the door open when he went downstairs. She leafed through the volumes, looking for the oldest ones. Then she found a smaller volume. *The Miner*. They were little more than one-page sheets published in 1878.

She read about a possible gold strike over the next mountain. Several later editions reported the shooting of a miner who had salted his claim with fool's gold and sold the claim. The miner survived the shooting but not the hanging that followed.

Andy glanced at her watch. Nearly four thirty. Where had the afternoon gone?

She hurriedly replaced the volume and met Bill Evans downstairs. "I have to go," she said.

"Not taking anything with you?" he asked.

"Not tonight. I'll be back in the morning if I can't get to the meeting tonight."

She hurried out the door, Joseph at her side. She was back at the cabin in five minutes. She quickly washed her face and applied lipstick. After filling Joseph's food and water dishes, she glanced at her watch again. Ten to five.

Joseph looked at her anxiously as she grabbed the keys to the car. "Stay," she said. He moaned. "I won't be long."

With that promise, she was out the door.

CHAPTER TWELVE

ANDY DROVE UP to the large period brick home precisely at 5:00 p.m.

As she approached the porch, she wished she had brought a notebook or a recorder or something. She would have to depend on her memory if he said anything important.

She felt a little trepidation and then realized how foolish that was.

She'd certainly managed worse situations. She reached the door, rang the bell and was surprised how quickly it was opened.

A young Hispanic woman opened the door and smiled. "Miss Stuart, Mr. Monroe is waiting for you in his study. I'm Elena. Can I bring you coffee or tea?"

That was positive. It meant that Al Monroe expected her to stay longer than hello, goodbye.

"Coffee, please," she said. "Just black."

"That's the way Mr. Monroe likes it, too," she said approvingly.

Elena led the way through the living room, where a slight older woman sat with a book in her hands. She looked wan and thin, but there was an elegant beauty about her. She put the book down. "Hello," she said.

"Hello," Andy said, "I'm Andy Stuart."

"I'm Sara Monroe." She started to rise but Andy noticed she did so with difficulty.

"Please don't get up," Andy said.

Mrs. Monroe sank back into her chair. "My knees aren't that good any longer, but I'm delighted Al asked you over."

"Thank you," Andy said, noting that her knees weren't the only thing wrong with Mrs. Monroe. Her face had an unhealthy pallor. Andy stood there, not knowing what else to say.

Elena saved her. "This way," she said, and Andy nodded at Mrs. Monroe and hurried along beside Elena as she led her down a hall to a large room lined with books. A large mahogany desk piled with papers dominated the room. There was a side extension that held a computer.

This time, Al Monroe rose. "Miss Stuart," he acknowledged. "Are you settled in the cabin?"

"Yes," she said. "It's really very comfortable."

"Manning did a good job with it."

She nodded. That surprised her. She hadn't expected a compliment directed at the Mannings.

"You said you wanted to write about our town," he said. "What do you think you know about it now?"

She noticed the emphasis he put on *think*. "Not a lot," she confessed. "I like history, and the West has always fascinated me. I have a general knowledge about its history. I found a newspaper in the library with a sketch of your ancestor. I know Angus founded the town and he helped with the statehood campaign. You must be really proud of him."

He grunted. A sign of displeasure?

"Why do you think you can write a history on the town better than someone here?"

"Because no one has," she shot back.

He studied her for a long moment. "I'm impressed," he said, "and that doesn't happen often." He hesitated, then added, "My wife has always been interested, as well. She's donated some items to the so-called museum, but lately…" He stopped, then added, "I guess you heard about my nephew."

"A little."

"Sara couldn't have children. Sam became the son she couldn't have when my sister and her husband died in an auto accident. It near killed her when he kidnapped Eve's kid. She has a heart problem but it seems to be under control. The bigger problem is she's lost her spirit. She stopped going to meetings she previously liked and she seldom goes out."

"I'm sorry," she said.

"Maybe you could get her interested in your project. She's a good writer. She majored in English and minored in journalism. I think her heart was with journalism, but those jobs were scarce, especially for a woman, and she turned to teaching English until we married." He put a hand on the table and played with a letter opener shaped like a dagger. "I like your brass in barging in on me. I also appreciate the fact you've been in the army. It takes guts, discipline and honor."

So that was the reason she was asked here. He wanted to use her to help his wife. She couldn't argue with that. His motive was more noble than hers. "Why don't you just ask her to do it?"

He sighed. "She would think it's my idea—busy work."

"Eve could ask her," Andy said, not wanting to get involved in something that was becoming complicated.

"I'm afraid it would be the same problem. She would think I put Eve up to it. You're a newcomer asking questions. I hope she will embrace that."

His brow furrowed as he waited for an answer.

Andy hesitated. She knew how abrupt he could be from their first meeting. She could easily see the difference in styles between Al Monroe and Eve, and how they might clash. They both wanted what was best for Covenant Falls; they just had different ideas of what best was.

Darn, she liked him. He was like her father: irascible but underneath that hard crust he obviously cared about his wife a great deal. "It's just meant to be a short history," she said. "And it's to pro-mote the town."

"I know," he said. "As I said, I usually know what goes on here. But maybe it will get Sara interested in moving on with her life."

She nodded. "I can't promise anything, but I'll try."

"Thank you," he said.

Andy hesitated, then plunged in. "Eve said you might have some journals written by Angus Monroe?"

He hesitated. "Is that a deal breaker?"

"No. They would just be very helpful."

"I'll think about it," he said. "In the meantime, there's letters and news articles and other material. Sara can get you started."

"Is your wife a native of Covenant Falls?" she asked.

"No. That's one of the problems. Even after all these years, she feels like an outsider to people who live here. I suspect some of it is my fault. But, like you, she loves history and has always been more interested in Angus than I was. I always think about the present and the future."

He stood then. "I know it's late notice, but could you join us for dinner?"

When she hesitated, he added, "We'll be finished in plenty of time for you to go to one of those meetings at the community center."

She must have looked surprised, because he added, "As I said, I still know everything that goes on in Covenant Falls. You might tell Eve that."

"I think she probably knows," she retorted.

"She probably does," he agreed with a hint of a smile. "What about dinner?"

"I would like that," she said even as she wondered about the strange circumstances in the past four days. She'd needed something to take her mind off Afghanistan. She'd certainly found it here.

What had Dr. Payne dropped her into?

Al—he was Al to her now, although she wouldn't dream of addressing him that way—accompanied her into the living room, and he helped Mrs. Monroe stand. There was obvious affection between them. He might be a bear with others, but it seemed it was of the teddy type with his wife.

Dinner was served immediately. Pork tenderloin with a whiskey sauce, wild rice and grilled vegetables. "It's wonderful," Andy said after several bites.

"Elena is a great cook," Mrs. Monroe said politely. "Al told me you're living in Josh Manning's cabin. I hope you like Covenant Falls."

"It would be hard not to," she said. "I really enjoy the mountain next to the cabin, and I saw the falls yesterday. It's glorious."

He turned to his wife. "Miss Stuart is writing a brochure about the town. You know as much or more about our history as I do, and I'm busy right now with my accountant. Could you meet with her tomorrow, show her some of our photos and documents?"

Mrs. Monroe's eyes lit. A bit of color came into her cheeks. Andy knew she must have been a real beauty.

"I would like that," Sara Monroe replied.

Andy suggested 2:00 p.m. the next day.

Mrs. Monroe nodded. "That will be fine. We can have tea."

Andy hesitated, then asked, "I have a service dog. Would it disturb you if I brought him?"

"No. Of course not. I would enjoy meeting him." She cast a look at Al as if warning him not to argue. There was iron in her.

"I'm afraid I must go now," Andy said. "But thank you for dinner."

"Miss Stuart has a meeting tonight," Al explained.

"Good," Sara Monroe said. "I understand you've come back from the service, and you have no family here. Please consider us your friends."

Al took charge then and walked her to the door. "Thank you," he said. He looked pleased with himself and she turned and left.

NATE CALLED ANDY as he left June Byars's house Monday afternoon. He'd dropped off some lumber he would need to fix her porch the next morning. He'd hoped to take Andy and Joseph to the community center for the vet meeting. When no one answered, he tamped down the disappointment he felt. He told himself that she was probably doing just fine by herself.

He wasn't so sure about himself. He hadn't been able to get her out of his mind.

Where was she? He worried about her. He felt she was his responsibility, or maybe that was just his excuse. *Dammit.*

He reached home at six thirty, took a quick shower and put on clean clothes, then headed for the meeting. He'd made a point of making the meetings a priority both for himself and the others. Especially tonight. Most of the guys would be strangers to Andy, and news that a new vet—a woman—was in town would probably bring them all out.

He reached the community center right at seven. Five vehicles were already there. He didn't see Josh's Jeep. No sign of Andy's yellow Volkswagen, but she could easily walk from the cabin.

The door was unlocked, and he walked through the entrance to the community room. Johnny Kay, owner of the Rusty Nail and a vet himself, had apparently brought the beer tonight. Bottles were stacked in ice in an office wastebasket. Snacks were already on the bar, including a great-looking dip and chips. He dropped five dollars in a jar for the beer and grabbed a bottle.

Bill Evans stood in a corner, and Nate greeted

the others as he made his way over to him. "Seen Andy?" he asked.

"She was here earlier in the day and said she wasn't sure she could come, that she had an appointment," Bill said. "She was seen entering the Monroe house late this afternoon. That's all I know."

Nate digested that. So she had gotten her foot in Monroe's door! Why was he not surprised?

"Good for her," he said. He hoped it was good. He was never sure what Al Monroe would do. He could be a devious bully, but then he would surprise the town and do something generous. He had certainly startled everyone when he apologized and resigned from the council when his nephew went rogue.

He took a long swallow of beer and helped himself to the chips and dip as others filtered in. As he predicted, it was going to be a full house. They were all curious about the newcomer.

"Army, navy or air force?" asked one.

"Army," he replied. "A nurse, but I wouldn't ask any questions."

"Bad stuff?"

"I think so. Haven't asked, though." Nate put a warning in the words.

Josh came in carrying a large pan of chicken wings. Amos, as always, was at his side. Several of the guys competed with each other as to who would shake his paw first. Then they dived into the chicken wings.

"Hey, save a few," Josh chided.

"Eve make these?" Bill Evans asked.

"Hell, no. She doesn't think they're healthy," he said as he grabbed one. "I picked these up at the Rusty Nail on the way in. I didn't have time for supper. Neither, I think, did Nate, so leave a few for him."

Josh looked around, and Nate knew he was searching for Andy. "She's not here," Nate said. "Someone saw her go into Monroe's house around five."

"Maybe we should send a rescue party," Josh replied.

"Not necessary," Nate said as Andy Stuart walked in with Joseph.

Amos went over and sniffed Joseph, although they had met earlier.

The guys introduced themselves one by one, each identifying himself by the branch of service, teasing the one ahead of him. Nate and Josh stood at the bar, watching, ready to step in if necessary. It wasn't. The vets all knew not to push the newbie.

When all the introductions were finished Andy joined Josh and Nate at the bar. "Beer?" Nate asked. "And Josh brought some spectacular chicken wings."

She hesitated, then nodded her head for the beer and refused the wings. "I just had dinner."

"Bill said he saw you go into the Monroe house," Nate said with a question in his eyes.

"Everyone really does know what is going on in town, don't they?" she said. "Dr. Payne warned me about that."

"And?" Nate said.

"And I heard there was a poker game here," she said, a gleam in her eyes. She looked very self-satisfied. He had to grin even as his curiosity was stoked to boiling.

All of a sudden a large round table filled up. It was all Nate and Josh could do to grab a seat. Some of those who didn't make it turned on the baseball game. Others stood around to watch.

"Ladies first," Bill said and handed the deck to her.

She looked at it, then said apologetically, "Can you shuffle for me? My fingers are a bit stiff."

Bill glanced at the hand brace and flushed. "I'm sorry. Of course I can." He shuffled and handed the deck back to her. "We play penny ante with nickels rather than pennies," he said. "We have a jar if you need any."

"I do," she said. "Five dollars' worth."

"She came to play!" Jeff, the youngest vet, commented.

A hundred nickels were counted out, put in a can and handed to her. The others were putting out cans that clinked when moved.

She gave them a five-dollar bill and asked, "Any rules?"

"Nope. Dealer picks the game. Ante up a nickel," Josh said from his seat next to Nate's. "Andy, as our newcomer, is dealer."

"Mexican stud," she said.

"Ah…could we have a ringer here?" Josh said.

She won the first game.

The players saluted her with their beers and the dealer changed.

SHE HAD DONE IT! She had played poker without breaking down. She had stayed in the present; she hadn't had a blackout or flashback. Mexican stud had been Jared's favorite game. She thought he would be proud of her tonight.

"Andy?"

She looked up and met Nate's gaze. He winked at her. Pleasure spread through her, then confusion. She looked down at her cards.

They played for another hour. Andy won more than she lost, and her jar was heavier when they quit. There was good-natured grumbling.

They quit and watched the baseball game from Denver until it was over. It was late, and everyone started to leave. They all stopped to tell her how happy they were to have a new veteran in town, especially "another poker player," and if she needed anything to call one of them. She felt bundled in care as Nate walked her to the car. "Thank you for pushing me to go," she told him. "It was good."

"They're probably wondering why I brought a card shark," he said with that wry smile that was becoming more endearing. "You play a mean game of poker."

"I used to play a lot in Afghanistan," she replied. It didn't hurt as much to say it now.

They reached her Bucket. "So how was your visit with Al Monroe?" he asked.

"I went to see him at his office, and he invited me to dinner."

"I'll be damned," he said.

"I hope not," she said with a smile. "He and his wife are going to help with the history." She couldn't keep a note of triumph from her voice.

He put a hand to her cheek in a gesture of tenderness. "You're one gutsy lady," he said. Then he opened the door. Joseph jumped in and moved to the passenger's seat and then she slid inside.

Nate closed the car door as she settled into the seat. Then he stood back as she started the car and drove off. She looked back as she turned onto Lake Road. He was still standing there.

CHAPTER THIRTEEN

ANDY WOKE UP the next morning after a rare good night's sleep. The sun streamed through the window. Joseph burrowed next to her and raised his head the instant she stirred.

She scratched his ears. Why had she been so reluctant to own a dog?

She stretched out. Yesterday's meeting with Al had been good, and the poker game was fun. Two successes. Two huge successes.

That didn't mean the end of flashbacks or nightmares, she knew, but a brief reprieve was certainly welcome. She had tapered off her meds and stopped using them altogether.

She had another challenge now. Apprehension crept into her about the upcoming meeting with Sara Monroe. She was out of her element. Everyone seemed to have expectations she couldn't possibly meet.

"Okay, Joseph," she said. "We should get moving. We have things to do today. First a shower," she added, as Joseph's ears went up.

The water felt good, sensual even. She hadn't even thought that word for a long time. She shampooed her hair, although it was difficult working mostly with one hand, then she soaped her body, turning the water as hot as she could bear. When she stepped out, she noted that Joseph had not moved from his watchdog position.

"Just a few more minutes," she promised as she glanced through her slim belongings in the closet.

A trip to the general store was in order. They might have clothes. She didn't like the idea of a T-shirt and jeans in the Monroes' elegant house.

She mentally planned the day as she made coffee and toast for herself and prepared dog food for Joseph. At least now she *had* something to plan. Breakfast and a walk, then a visit to the community center before her meeting. A stop at the general store for clothes. She thought about calling Eve to tell her about yesterday's conversation with Al Monroe and his wife, but decided to wait until after today's visit with Sara Monroe.

She liked Eve, was here because of her husband's cabin, but she also liked Al and Sara Monroe. She had no intention of being manipulated by either camp, but it might mean walking a very thin line.

Or she could just walk away. That was probably the route she would have chosen a month ago.

Not today. She'd agreed to write a short history, such as it might be, and to her surprise she really wanted to do it.

Not so much, however, that she was going to use Mrs. Monroe, who looked as fragile as a leaf. She would not write anything she didn't have permission to use.

After breakfast, she decided to scrap the usual hike up the mountain in lieu of a run with Joseph. She really hadn't explored town yet, and everyone assured her she could take Joseph almost anywhere.

NATE CONCENTRATED AS he tore out the rotten boards on Mrs. Byars's porch. He straddled the ladder and handed another rotting board down to Jim Carter, a man who often worked with him.

The porch was a disaster waiting to happen. Mrs. Byars had nearly fallen through the floor several days earlier and had asked him to look at it. The porch was an addition and not a well-constructed one. The flooring would have to be replaced, but the ceiling above was in even worse shape; he wanted to replace the boards before the roof caved in, especially since rain was possible later in the day. That meant stabilizing the roof first.

He was only too aware that Andy Stuart lived two doors down. He had tamped down the impulse to drive over there before starting at Mrs. Byars's house. He was proud he'd managed some restraint. Damn, but he hadn't been able to get her off his mind.

She'd looked irresistible as she won repeatedly at poker. The challenge of competition made those gray eyes sparkle even as she kept a poker face during the game. The victory was transparently sweet to her.

The mere memory of her smile made him ache with wanting. He'd basically been a monk since he'd moved back to Covenant Falls. He loved the mountains and the people here but, dammit, everyone seemed to be getting on with life, with the exception of one Nate Rowland. He hadn't admitted, even to himself, that he was lonely.

The only woman who had interested him since his divorce was just a few houses down, and he was acting like a besotted high school kid, yearning after the girl he couldn't have. She was definitely off-limits. Since her flashback at Josh's house, he'd felt responsible for her, which was probably the dumbest thing he could do.

She was also here temporarily, and she was still mourning the loss of her fiancé. She was vulnerable, and he would be a true bastard to take advantage. Her only spontaneous smile had been last night and even that had disappeared all too quickly.

Nor was he in a position to even ask for a date. His ex-wife had done her best to send him into bankruptcy before announcing she was in love with someone else. She had lied to him about being pregnant, about wanting a family and about nearly everything else. His trust level these days was a little below zero.

He tried to convince himself that his interest in Andy was concern over another veteran. And his wanting to see her was only because he was curious about what happened at the Monroe home yesterday.

He pulled another board from the ceiling framework and started to hand it to Jim. Through the corner of his eyes, he saw Mrs. Byars approach with a tray. Jim backed up to let her by and bumped into the ladder, which started to tumble. Nate grabbed an overhead brace. The rotted wood gave under his weight and he fell, crashing into the ladder and down through the porch flooring...

ANDY AND JOSEPH had started to jog from her cottage when she heard a crash and a shout. Something about it raised the hackles on her neck.

Instinct took over. She ran in the direction of the sound just as a woman rushed out of the house toward her.

"Miss Stuart," the woman called as she approached Andy. "I heard you were a nurse. Please help. Nathan Rowland just fell while working on my porch. I think he might be hurt bad."

Andy didn't stop to think. "Where is he? Have you called the doctor or medical service?"

"There's just Dr. Bradley. Jim, Nate's helper, called his office while I hoped to find you. Nathan is in the back. He's unconscious and bleeding."

Andy ran alongside the house until she saw the porch and entered through the open door. Nate was lying there, one foot sticking down into a hole on the floor. She knelt next to him. His breathing wasn't labored, but he was unconscious. Blood dribbled from an injury on the back of his head. Then she saw blood pouring from a jagged wound on his leg where it went through the floor.

She stared at it. Saw it spreading. The world turned red, started spinning... She felt herself trembling.

"Miss Stuart!"

The sound of her name dragged her back. *Nate. It's Nate. Don't lose it now. Stop the bleeding first!*

She looked at the young man standing next to her. "What's your name?" she asked.

"Carter, Jim Carter. It was my fault."

"No time for that. We need to stabilize his neck first. Mrs. Byars, hold his head as still as possible while Jim and I get him out of the hole."

She waited while Mrs. Byars slowly, awkwardly, sat on the floor and held Nate's head, then Andy turned to Jim Carter. "Give me your belt and then pull out the boards around that foot so we can get his leg out without more damage."

Before she finished the sentence, the young man took off his belt and handed it to her, then grabbed a crowbar from a large tool chest and carefully inserted it into the hole. A board came up, then another.

Andy put both arms under Nate's shoulders and used her upper-body strength rather than her hands to nudge him inch by inch away from the hole as

Jim carefully eased Nate's foot out. His pant leg was drenched in blood.

"A knife?" she asked Jim.

He pulled out a pocketknife and handed it to her. She took it and cut the leg of his jeans away, revealing a large gash just above his ankle.

She examined it. "A vein," she said. "Not an artery, thank God, or there would be even more blood. Now help me get the belt around his leg. My left hand..."

Her helper lifted the leg slightly and her right hand worked his belt under it. She managed to slip the end into the buckle and pull it tight. Dammit, she needed more help.

She looked at Mrs. Byars, who was still holding Nate's head. "Let Jim take over from you. I need bandages, towels and water," she said. "And any antiseptic you have. As fast as you can..."

She watched as Jim helped Mrs. Byars up and then sat down next to Nate, carefully following directions.

Then the older woman returned, her hands full of towels and bandages, including a large roll of adhesive bandaging. With her help, Andy made a pressure bandage for Nate's leg. Then she looked at his head. There was a wicked-looking cut but it didn't seem deep. The fact that he was unconscious, though, meant he probably had a concussion. She wanted a CT scan.

"We need to get him to a hospital or clinic,"

she said as she checked the rest of him. Plenty of bruises but nothing that seemed life threatening. But the fact he was still unconscious worried her.

Mrs. Byars spoke up then. "I think our best bet is Stephanie Phillips. She has a van and she's a veterinarian. I called Dr. Bradley's office and talked to his nurse. He's at the hospital in Pueblo now with a patient."

"Can you call Stephanie?" Andy asked.

"Of course. I'm so glad you're here," Mrs. Byars said. She punched numbers into her phone and made a hurried explanation when Stephanie apparently answered. "She's on her way," Mrs. Byars said when she clicked off.

Andy turned to Jim. "While we wait, can you make a stretcher out of those boards?"

"I can do that," Jim said, "and I'll call some friends to help carry him." He stood, made several calls on his phone, then lined up three fresh boards next to one another. He sawed a fourth one into three parts. He quickly nailed each of the three smaller sections crosswise to the full boards. He then made four handles from another piece of wood and nailed them to the bottom of the stretcher.

"Miss Stuart?" Mrs. Byars's concerned voice broke through the sudden panic. "What can I do now?"

"Try to reach your doctor in Pueblo again. Tell whoever answers that it's an emergency. A head wound is involved, and he's unconscious." She paused, then added, "I want to talk to him."

Mrs. Byars nodded, tears in her eyes. "I'll do that."

While Mrs. Byars called the hospital, Andy loosened the pressure bandage.

What worried her most was that Nate hadn't uttered a sound or made a move. When he did wake, there would be a lot of pain.

"Dr. Bradley's nurse reached him," Mrs. Byars said. "He should be calling now." The phone rang. Mrs. Byars answered it and then passed it to her.

Andy quickly told the doctor about the injuries, emphasizing the fact he hadn't regained consciousness.

Nate moved, then groaned. His eyes flickered open. He tried to lift his head, but she leaned down, putting her fingers over his mouth. "Don't move, Nate. You've had a bad fall." Then she was back with the doctor. "He's awake."

"Andy..." Nate said hoarsely.

His head fell back. The doctor was still on the line. "He fell back into unconsciousness," she told him.

"Any other injuries?" the doctor asked.

"A jagged tear on his leg. He was bleeding heavily. I put a pressure bandage on it. I loosened it when the bleeding slowed, but he's lost a lot of blood. His ankle could be injured. He fell through some flooring and it looked as if it might have turned. I didn't want to take off his boot to check it. But it's the head injury that worries me."

"Back and spine?" Dr. Bradley said.

"I can't tell," she said. "We're keeping him flat just in case."

"Can someone transport him? I could check to see if a chopper is available, but that might take some time."

"I understand Stephanie is on the way with her van."

"Good. She keeps that van spotless."

"He might have a seizure," she said, expressing her worst fear.

"You're a nurse, right?" he said abruptly. "You'll know what to do."

She wanted to say she was no longer sure of that. She was terrified she might have another flashback.

"You *are* coming with him?" Dr. Bradley asked.

"Yes."

"Well, he's lucky to have you there," the doctor said. "I'll be waiting for you. I'll have the right people here." He hung up.

The phone rang. Mrs. Byars answered it. "Stephanie, I'm so glad you called. Here's Miss Stuart."

Andy took the phone again.

"Stephanie here," said the voice. "I'll be there in five minutes. We'll need a board for him. All mine are dog size."

"Jim Carter made a temporary one."

"Good. We'll need a couple of strong hands to help," Stephanie said.

"Jim Carter has also taken care of that," Andy said, amazed at how everything was coming together.

Stephanie heard her. "Okay," she said and hung up.

Just then two sturdy men, one older, one younger, appeared at the door of the porch. Mrs. Byars introduced them. "Father and son. Craig and Blake Stokes. They're both members of the volunteer fire department."

"Hate to meet you under these circumstances," the older one said. "I'm Craig, and this is Blake. "We were at his son's scout meeting last night or we would have been at the vet meeting." He turned and looked at Nate. His face creased with concern. "Sorry to hear about this. Nate's one of the good guys."

They heard a screech of brakes outside. "That's Stephanie," Craig said. "Let's get him in the van."

"We need one more person," Jim said.

"No, you don't," Andy said. "I've carried my share of wounded."

She supervised his transfer from the floor to the board, which Mrs. Byars had softened slightly with a comforter. She had also torn pieces of what looked like a sheet to keep him in place.

"On three," Craig said, "One, two, three." They all lifted. Blake was opposite Andy and she knew he was trying to help her. Her good hand had gripped the handle. They moved fast and she realized they had done this before. But then, of course they had, if they were volunteer firemen.

Stephanie had moved the van close to the porch door and they needed to take only a few steps to load him into the back.

Andy turned to Mrs. Byars. "Can you keep Joseph with you? He's very well behaved."

"Of course," Mrs. Byars said. "I like dogs. He'll be safe with me."

Andy got into the back of the van and sat on the floor next to Nate. The doors closed, and the van moved forward.

CHAPTER FOURTEEN

NATE JERKED AWAKE in a moving vehicle. His head felt as though someone had bashed it in. The rest of him didn't feel so good, either.

"What…?" he started to say.

"You fell."

He turned his head, although movement made the pain sharper. He tried to focus on the speaker. "Andy?"

"I was running near Mrs. Byars's home when I heard you yell," she said.

"I…was on the ladder…"

"Apparently Jim Carter was startled by Mrs. Byars and knocked the ladder down. You fell. Your right leg went through the floor and you hit your head. You came to for a couple of seconds, then relapsed."

"I don't…remember. Where…?"

"We're in Stephanie's van on the way to the hospital in Pueblo."

He started to shake his head no, then clenched his lips against his teeth to keep from moaning as the pain grew fiercer.

"Don't even try to protest," she said. "You obviously have a concussion, and you *are* seeing a doctor and getting a CT scan."

"My leg?"

"You have a bad gash and lost a lot of blood. You might have a foot or ankle injury as well, but I didn't want to take off your boot. When you landed, your foot crashed through the porch floor. I don't think it is broken."

He noticed then that she was pale. Despite the throbbing in his head, he recalled the other night when she'd had a flashback.

He felt like a damn fool. He hadn't fallen from a ladder since he was eight years old. He suspected that not all his attention had been with the task at hand. He had, instead, been puzzling out his confusion regarding Andy Stuart.

He tried to move again. His shirt was unbuttoned and he was aware his chest was bare and the scar from Iraq was obvious. But then he couldn't seem to focus very well.

Andy didn't say anything, though, and maybe she hadn't seen it. He felt every jolt, every small variation of movement. He closed his eyes.

"Stay awake," Andy said urgently. "Try to stay awake."

He forced his eyes open again but it took even more of an effort.

"Any siblings?" she asked.

"One. One brother."

"What's his name?"

"Allen."

"Where does he live?"

He realized she was trying to keep him awake. "Chicago...now." His voice was unsteady. He hated that. He wanted to be strong for her. She had enough on her plate without...

"Want me to call him?" she asked.

He shook his head. "No. This is just a bump on the head..."

"Maybe, maybe not," she said. "You need to stay awake, okay?" She paused, then asked, "The scar on your chest. Iraq?"

He struggled to stay awake. "Not bad...didn't hit anything...vital."

His eyes wanted to close. He felt her touch.

"Stay with me, okay," she insisted. "What after the service?"

He tried to concentrate. "College."

"What did you major in?

"Architecture. Didn't finish, though. Got married. Mistake. Huge mistake. Divorced..." His voice was trailing off.

"Architecture?" She kept prodding him.

"I...like building things." His head seemed to be exploding. "You?" he asked in a barely audible voice.

"Me?"

"Where did you get your...training?"

"West Virginia University, thanks to the ROTC."

"Was...it worth it?" he asked. His curiosity counterbalanced the pain.

She hesitated, then said, "Yes, I think so."

His eyes closed.

"No," she said. "Stay awake. Just for a few minutes more."

He tried. "Thank you...for being here."

"You did the same for me Saturday night."

"Not...quite even," he replied.

"Tell me more about the inn. How big is it?"

"You haven't...seen it?"

"No."

"Then as soon as..."

Nate felt the van slow down. Maybe now he could close his eyes.

A TEAM WAS waiting at the emergency room door. They rushed him inside. Andy trailed behind while Stephanie moved her van.

An older man in a white physician's coat talked to the paramedics as they rushed Nate inside. Then he left them and walked over to where she stood. "Miss Stuart?"

"Andy," she corrected.

"I'm Dr. Bradley. Tell me exactly what happened."

She ran through what she knew in more detail than was in the phone call.

"Glad to have you in Covenant Falls. We'll talk later. I already have the CT scheduled and called a consulting neurologist. Are you going to stay with him?"

She nodded. She wasn't going to leave him alone now. Joseph, at least, would be cared for by Mrs. Byars. Stephanie had to get back to Covenant Falls. She had bumped her scheduled surgeries and one was urgent. Andy had to call Sara Monroe and cancel the appointment. She hated to do it. It might destroy that fragile connection they had. It might also anger Mr. Monroe. But there were priorities, and Nate had become one.

She wasn't surprised at all that he had been helping Mrs. Byars. She'd watched the ease with which he'd moved among the veterans last night, the interest he expressed for each one. He and Jared had a lot in common.

The thought, so sudden and powerful, struck her like lightning. *No one was like Jared.* How could she even think about comparing the two? Another jolt: she had managed the past few hours without a major flashback. There had been the one brief moment when she'd seen the blood, but Mrs. Byars had jerked her out of it. Progress. She needed to talk to Dr. Payne about it. Later.

Now she had other concerns. She used her cell to call Sara Monroe and explain what had happened.

"Al heard about the accident. Of course you must stay with him," Sara Monroe said. "You just call me when it's convenient. And give Nate our best," she added. "I've always liked that young man. Please keep us informed."

"I'll do that, and thank you," Andy replied. *Al already knows?*

Andy had suspected that Sara Monroe would know as soon as she did. She knew now how fast news moved in Covenant Falls. She suspected the waiting room would soon be full.

"Soon" WAS EVEN quicker than she'd thought. An hour and a half after she and Nate arrived, Eve and Josh joined her in the waiting room. Clint arrived thirty minutes later with a tall white-haired woman.

Clint made the introductions. "Andy, this is Agnes Rowland, Nate's mom. Mrs. Rowland, this is Andy, our newest resident."

Mrs. Rowland grasped her hand. "Thank you," she said. "Thank you for taking care of Nate. How is…?"

"We're waiting for the doctor," Andy said gently. "Nate was talking to me on the ride over here. He has some cuts and bruises but—"

The door to the waiting room opened and Dr. Bradley appeared. "Agnes," he said, going straight to Mrs. Rowland. "Nate has a minor skull fracture. We've cleaned the scalp wound and closed and removed some loose bone fragments," he said. "The good news is a CT scan doesn't show any blood clots or lesions. But I don't want to take any chances. We should keep him here for several days under observation. Head wounds can be tricky. He's also on intravenous antibiotics for the very nasty gash in his leg, and he has a sprained ankle that's going to be pretty painful."

"Is he awake?" Mrs. Rowland asked.

"Yes, and already complaining about being here."

Mrs. Rowland's anxious expression eased. "That sounds like him. It's difficult for Nathan to stay still for more than five minutes. Can I see him?"

"Yes, and stress the importance of staying here for at least two days and even better, three. If you were closer to the hospital…I would feel better about Nate going home, but there could be some swelling, and quite frankly I don't have the equipment I would need."

"He'll stay if I have to sit on him," Mrs. Rowland said grimly.

Relieved, Andy smiled. Mrs. Rowland would have a hard time restraining her taller, stronger son. Her hair was short and simply styled and she wore slacks and a shirt with a button undone halfway down. Andy judged her age to be in the late sixties. The idea of her sitting on Nate made Andy smile. Inwardly.

As if sensing Andy's perusal, the woman turned and looked at her. "June Byars told me how fast you reacted. Thank you for talking sense to my stubborn son and getting him here." Her tight lips relaxed into a smile.

Embarrassed because she'd really done very little, Andy simply nodded.

"I hope we can get to know each other better," Mrs. Rowland said. "I hear you're interested in the history here. I don't know if anyone told you that Angus Monroe's Bible is at the Covenant Cove Presbyterian Church."

No, they had not.

"Miss Stuart," Mrs. Rowland started.

"Please call me Andy," Andy interrupted. She still wasn't used to "Miss Stuart." For years it had been "Lieutenant" or "ma'am" or just plain "Stuart."

"Andy, then," Mrs. Rowland continued. "I hope I can repay you with a lunch or dinner when Nathan gets home." She turned back to the doctor. "Can I see him now?"

"He's still getting stitched up," the doctor said. "But you can look in there," he said, talking directly to Mrs. Rowland.

Eve turned to Andy. "Do you have a ride back?"

"No." She hadn't thought about that. "Stephanie had to get back, and I wanted to wait for the doctor's report."

"You can ride with me. Josh can go with Clint."

Andy wanted to stay, but she had no reason to do so. Mrs. Rowland was with him. Clint and Josh, his best friends, were staying. He would have the best of care here. "That would be great. I left Joseph with Mrs. Byars."

"You probably want to get cleaned up," Eve added.

Andy looked down at herself. Blood had splattered over her shirt and jeans. She hadn't noticed in her concern about Nate. *She hadn't noticed blood.*

"You're right. I probably look like something from a horror movie."

"Close," Eve said. "But you did good."

She had. A surge of satisfaction swept through Andy. She'd seen blood and hadn't fallen to pieces. Maybe it would come later. Maybe tonight.

"Let's get you home," Eve said. "You can come back with me later if you want."

"I don't think so," Andy said. "He'll need rest."

The problem was she *did* want to come back. She kept seeing Nate on that board in the van.

She swallowed hard and looked around for a purse before remembering she didn't have one with her. She didn't have anything with her.

"Want to stop by a restroom?" Eve asked.

She did. Badly. She had to wash her hands, look at her face. She nodded.

Eve obviously knew something about the hospital. She led the way directly into a nearby restroom. Once inside, Andy took a look at herself. Her hair was a sticky mess where she had pushed some back. There was blood on her face, as well. She took a deep breath.

That was the way she'd looked to Nate's mom? Why hadn't she cleaned up the moment she'd arrived at the hospital?

She knew why. She'd been worried and hadn't wanted to miss the doctor. She knew the danger of concussions, had seen people die from brain bleeds.

She grabbed paper towels and washed her face, her hands, but she couldn't do anything about her hair. She watched the blood leave the towels and run in a pink stream into the sink. She waited for her hands to shake.

"Andy?" Eve's voice filtered into her consciousness.

She dried her hands. "I'm ready," she said and followed Eve out the door.

CHAPTER FIFTEEN

An ecstatic Joseph greeted Andy when she arrived at Mrs. Byars's house. Eve accompanied her inside.

Andy knelt and hugged Joseph, then stood and thanked Mrs. Byars for keeping him.

"No thanks necessary," Mrs. Byars said. "I owe you so much more, and Joseph was a delight. I had forgotten how much I enjoy having a dog around. How is Nate?"

"The doctor thinks he'll be fine," Andy said. "A mild concussion, several gashes, a sprained ankle. He's already complaining about staying in the hospital. But they want him for a few days. He's a hard guy to keep down. So please don't worry."

Mrs. Byars nodded, but all the same she looked worried.

"I'll keep you posted," Andy promised, just as she had Sara Monroe, but then realized it was probably unnecessary. The way news flew around town, Mrs. Byars would probably know before she did.

Eve left her red pickup in Mrs. Byars's drive and walked with Andy to the cabin.

"Need company?" she asked when they reached the door.

"Thanks, but I'm fine, and I have Joseph. I just need to get these clothes off and take a shower."

"Call if you need anything," Eve said. "You did a great job."

"I did what I was trained to do," Andy said. She knew she sounded testy, but she was tired and wanted to be alone. She suddenly realized she didn't have a key to the cabin, then remembered she hadn't locked it. She'd just tucked her wallet in a pocket.

She opened the door and turned to Eve. "Thank you for the ride," she said. "I'll be fine once I get a shower."

Eve nodded. "If you need anything, call." Andy watched until she disappeared down the road. Then she went inside and, emotionally and physically exhausted, she collapsed on the sofa. Joseph put one paw up on the cushion, asking permission to come up with her.

"It's okay," she said. Joseph climbed up, one foot after another as if still unsure of his welcome. Once all the way up he rested his head on Andy's lap as she tried to relax.

She wasn't aware how long she sat there, comforted by Joseph's presence, until she realized she hadn't changed clothes or taken a shower. Nor had she fed Joseph. She stood and he followed as she went into the kitchen and poured dog food into his bowl. While he was gobbling it down, she headed to the bathroom.

She took off her clothes. Her T-shirt was ruined. Her pants were stiff with blood. She threw them in the corner, then stepped into the shower, not even caring that the first stream of water was cold. It soon turned warm, then hot as she scrubbed her body and washed her hair.

She stayed there until the water started to run cold again, then stepped outside and toweled herself down. When she went into the bedroom, she looked at the clock. A little after six. Sleep was impossible.

She was grateful Eve had been mostly silent on the drive back from Pueblo. She hadn't wanted to talk about what happened that morning. She didn't want to relive it. She didn't want to think about the fact that she had nearly flipped out again.

She pulled on her oldest T-shirt and shorts, then threw the bloodstained clothes into the garbage. She grabbed a soda and went out to the porch, where she could see the lake and mountains and sky, all of which had a soothing effect.

She pondered the question Nate had asked in Stephanie's van. Had the scholarship been worth the years she'd spent in the army? That wasn't exactly the way he'd formed the question but it was what she thought he'd meant.

After the attack, she had asked herself that question over and over again. Without the scholarship, she might never have become a nurse. Never gone overseas. Never saved a life. Never fallen in love.

Everything had been intense during those years. Intense training. Intense satisfaction in saving a life. Intense fear. Intense love. Intense grief.

She sighed. Part of her missed the adrenaline that surged when a copter landed with the wounded. The flush of victory when the team saved a life or limb. But then there were the failures...

Then she remembered she'd promised to call Sara Monroe. She went back inside and punched in the number. The maid answered the phone. Andy identified herself and asked for Mrs. Monroe. She came on immediately.

"Miss Stuart. Thank you for calling. How is Nate?"

"Please call me Andy," she said and repeated what the doctor had said.

"Thank you for calling," Mrs. Monroe said. "I know it's late today, but would you like to reschedule our meeting for 2:00 p.m. tomorrow afternoon? I've been looking through letters and other documents."

"I would like that," Andy replied, trying to infuse enthusiasm in her words. At the moment, she was tapped out of enthusiasm.

"I'll have tea ready," Mrs. Monroe said. "Or would you prefer coffee?"

Andy thought the latter was an afterthought. She was a coffee person through and through, but she was a guest. "Tea will be fine."

"I'll see you then, and I'm so pleased about Nate. I'll tell Al."

Duty done, she went back outside. She sat in the swing and stared out at the mountain. She wondered whether it had a name, had ever had a name or was merely a part of the San Juan mountain range.

Images of the morning flickered through her head even as she tried to block them. She didn't want to think of the blood when she'd reached Nate, the way she had almost lapsed into a flashback or how frantically her heart had beaten when she didn't know how badly he was hurt.

How could that be? She barely knew him. She remembered him as he'd been when she left the community center last night. Tall, strong, competent. She had been drawn to him even as she'd tried her best to draw away. She'd felt disloyal to Jared. She still felt that way. She couldn't get away from the fact that she lived because he'd died. He'd taken the bullet a second before armed guards had rushed in and killed the attacker.

She swallowed hard.

"Come on, Joseph," she said.

He brought his leash to her and they walked out. She didn't bother to lock the door. If there had ever been a safe place, Covenant Falls seemed to be it. Not that she had anything to steal.

It was dark, but a part moon lit the night enough to follow the road. She walked down Lake Road to the beckoning lights in the park and sat on one of the swings. There were others in the park. A woman pushed a boy on a swing. A couple sat on a bench facing the lake. Young. Fresh faced. They were holding hands and leaning against each other.

She'd never had young love. She'd been too different in high school, too busy in college and too careful in the service. Sure, she'd dated, but no one had clanged the bells. And then she'd joined Jared's team. At first she'd been wary. Fraternization was frowned upon, and Jared was all business...

She chewed on her lip as she stood there like a member of an audience staring at a play. An onlooker, not a participant. She'd been kept so busy since arriving here, she hadn't had time to think, to remember. She had gone several days without mourning Jared, but now grief hit her like repeated blows to her midsection.

Joseph bumped her and offered his paw. "You're right, Joseph," she said. "It's time to look ahead." They left the park lights and walked back to the cabin. She would choose a book tonight and read. And hope the blood this morning would not bring on the nightmares.

NATE DRIFTED IN and out during the day. His leg hurt like hell. At least he'd been assured that no permanent damage had been done. The doctor said he might need crutches for a few days. He supposed he'd been lucky.

It was a freakish accident, one he felt he would never live down. Falling off a damn ladder. Years ago, he would not have been caught off balance. He feared it was because his mind had not been on the job.

If he hadn't concentrated so hard on keeping awake in the ambulance and if he hadn't hurt from head to toe, he might even have enjoyed Andy's attention during the drive to the hospital.

"Nathan?"

He looked up at his mother. "You don't need to stay," he said. "The doctor said I'm fine."

"Sorry, but he didn't say that. He said he wanted to observe you for a few days. I'm simply helping him do that."

He knew that look. He gave up. "Could you get me something to read?"

"Magazines? A book?"

"Whatever they have downstairs. And get something to eat. Okay? I'll be fine with all the nurses around here."

"That Miss Stuart sure is pretty. And nice," she said slyly.

"Don't go dreaming up a romance, Mom. You know how I feel about that. And she's not going to be here long."

"Like your friends Josh and Clint?" she replied with a twinkle in her eyes.

"She's hurting, Mom, and two hurts don't heal each other. They just make for a bigger one," he said, not bothering to deny the pain his ex-wife had caused him. "You go home, Mom," he said. "I promise I won't try to escape."

She left then, and he lay back. His mother was right in one respect. It was time to let go. It wasn't that he still loved his ex-wife, although he had, or thought he had, in the beginning. It was all the betrayals...

They had colored all subsequent relationships. He simply was unable to trust again especially when the woman seemed—or was—in need of help. He helped, then usually ran as fast as he could in the other direction. That defense mechanism didn't seem to be working with Andy.

He turned on the television, checking to see whether the world was still spinning. It was. The offerings were sparse, however, and his mind turned back—once more—to Andy. Blood splattered and all, she was one of the most appealing faces he'd seen. He didn't think he would ever forget the intensity in those gray eyes as she demanded he stay awake.

He remembered until the meds kicked in and he drifted off to sleep.

CHAPTER SIXTEEN

THE SOUND OF gunfire erupted outside the operating tent. The team stopped in midmovement as if caught in a movie that had suddenly frozen in place.

Everyone but Jared, who was reconstructing a leg.

Khalid burst into the room, a gun in his hands and an expression she had never seen before on his face. He didn't say anything, just swung the automatic from one of the operating team to another, firing with rapidity, then toward her as if they hadn't just exchanged words about his family thirty minutes earlier.

Jared stepped in front and she felt the splash of blood...

Andy woke screaming. Joseph was whining and pawing at her with his foot. She was trembling and sweating and could barely breathe. She clung to the dog until she could breathe normally again. But when she looked at her hands, they still shook.

Joseph snuggled close, his tongue frantically trying to lick her. She buried her hands in his fur. Comforted by his unconditional love, she didn't move. Her shaking finally stopped as the last of the recurring nightmare faded away.

The result of yesterday's accident? She knew from experience she wouldn't go back to sleep. She padded to the kitchen to make coffee. It was still dark outside.

She wrapped a blanket around her and took the coffee to the porch. Nights were still cool, but she didn't want to stay within four walls where she felt...trapped.

The moon was nearly full and glimmers of light touched the mountains. Grasshoppers chirped but it seemed the rest of the world was silent. No planes arriving or taking off. No alarm declaring incoming wounded. No sandstorms or freezing nights and hell-hot days.

Then her thoughts turned to Jared. She hoped he was playing cards in heaven and keeping the angels busy.

He'd been smart, funny and ambitious. Like her, he'd traded years in the army and—it turned out— his life to become a doctor. He had been due to leave the service at the end of that last deployment.

Until they had fallen in love, she'd planned to stay in the service. She'd liked the challenges of military medicine. She especially liked the comradery of the entire team. They ate together, worked together and played together. Because she liked her job, she'd always been very careful never to get involved with a teammate.

But Jared had courted her from the time they had met. She had resisted until he asked her to go with him to a village to hold a children's clinic. He'd brought toys and supplies that he'd purchased with his own money. When other members of the team had discovered what he was doing, they all pitched in.

Watching him with children had melted every one of her defenses, and they'd started spending even more time together. Four weeks before the shooting he had asked her to marry him when their deployments ended...

She took a sip of coffee. It was cold. She'd been out here longer than she thought. She realized this was the first time she could think of Jared with a smile rather than intense grief.

The rising sun was sending streams of gold across the mountaintops, and her thoughts went back to Nate in the hospital. She wondered how he was faring this morning. Hurting but probably restless. He never seemed to stay still.

She remembered their conversation in Stephanie's van. They'd both probably said things they usually wouldn't say until they knew each other a lot better. She had been doing her best to keep him awake and in doing so had said more than she intended. She suspected he had done the same.

Divorced? The worst mistake he'd ever made? He was good-looking in a rugged way. He was obviously smart and easy to be with. He'd studied architecture but hadn't finished. Was that part of the mistake?

She went inside and helped herself to another cup of coffee. Joseph looked hopefully at the front door. "Shower first," she said, "then walk." His tail wagged eagerly.

She took a long shower, then looked at her laughable wardrobe options. Top of her list today was that shopping trip that had been interrupted yesterday. In the meantime, she resorted to an elderly T-shirt and jeans. When she finished dressing, she toasted two slices of bread and fixed Joseph breakfast. It disappeared in seconds.

What time did the stores open? Nine? Ten? She made a list of things she needed. Clothes. She wanted to see if any of the stores had a tablet or laptop that was affordable. Otherwise she would have to drive to Pueblo.

Nate was in Pueblo.

Better if you stay away, she warned herself.

Joseph nudged her. He had his leash in his mouth. "Okay," she said. "A long walk."

They walked past the community center. Not open yet. No one was in the park, either. There were a few cars driving through town. Cars were parked around Maude's. She noticed that Eve's pickup was parked in front of city hall.

She walked by the real estate office. The lights were on but she didn't see anyone inside. Maybe Al was in the back.

The general store was closed, but she peered in. A tall, full-bodied woman was walking around inside. She looked up, then hurried over to the door and unlocked it.

"You must be Andy Stuart," she said. "Haven't heard of any other new folks in town."

"I am," Andy said. "Are you closed?"

"Putting in new stock, but if you need something, you just come on in. I heard how you took care of Nate yesterday. Is he all right?"

"The doctors are keeping him a few days, but everything looks good. Can I bring Joseph inside?"

"Sure. No one here but me," the woman said. "I'm Heather. My husband owns the store. He'll be in later. What can I do for you?"

"Shirts and pants, mostly."

"Blouses and shirts are on the left rack in back. Pants and skirts in the middle. Dresses on the right, although we don't have many in your size. You'll find T-shirts and jeans on the tables. There's also shorts. I'll just leave you to look while I go do some paperwork."

Andy was startled at the selection. The dresses were obviously aimed at the older citizens in town, but the shirts were both fashionable and reasonably priced. She found three she liked, along with two simple T-shirts and three pairs of pants: blue, black and gray. She'd discovered long ago they were the foundation of any wardrobe.

"Do you have any laptops?" she said.

"We have a few," Heather said. "They're fine, but the internet is still pretty spotty around here. I doubt it's available at the cabin, although we do have it at the community center."

Andy glanced at the selection, then decided to use the ones at the community center. She could always write in longhand at home.

With packages in her arms, she decided to head back to the cabin. She passed the Presbyterian church and stopped to read the historical marker in front: Founded by Angus Monroe, 1865.

She looked at the church. It was a pretty white building with a tall steeple and bell. The architecture was simple with clean lines. It did not look like 1865.

The doors were open and on a whim she decided to go inside.

An older, nice-looking man approached her. He held out his hand. "I'm Reverend Barrett, the pastor here. Welcome. What can I do for you?"

"Hello. I'm Andy Stuart. I'm staying in the Manning cabin, and I wondered if you can help me. I saw the marker outside, and Mrs. Rowland said you have Angus Monroe's Bible."

He smiled. "Obviously this building isn't the one that he had built. That burned down in 1950. But the church family remained and this building was constructed on the same ground as the original, so we still claim him. And yes, we do have his Bible here. Al Monroe's grandmother gave it to us for safekeeping after the fire. We now have it in an airtight, fireproof safe. You are welcome to look at it as long as someone is with you."

"Is someone available now?"

"I am, for the next hour. The safe is in our library, and I can work on my sermon while you look at it."

"Thank you," she said.

"I'm happy someone is interested in the Bible." He led the way out of the sanctuary and down the hall to a room lined with books. There were several tables along with chairs.

He opened up a cabinet and then the safe. Reverently, he took out a weathered-looking Bible. "This came from Scotland. It was the family Bible dating back to the 1700s. It's the one thing he held on to during the trek west."

The minister placed the Bible on a table, opened it and pointed to an entry. "This is Angus's first entry in this country. You might start there."

He left it with her and went to another table, where he worked on a laptop.

She stared down at the handwriting. There was a flourish to every letter, but it was surprisingly readable.

Died: Liam Monroe this 7th day of April, 1849, of drowning. God keep his soul.

The next entry was happier.

*Wedded: Angus Monroe to Chiweta this 20th
day of August, 1852.*
*Born: of Chiweta and Angus Monroe, a daugh-
ter, Lorna, this 15th day of July, 1853.*
*Born: of Chiweta and Angus Monroe, a
daughter, Jenna, this 6th day of May,
1854.*
*Born: of Chiweta and Angus Monroe, a son,
Liam, this 5th day of April, 1856.*
*Died: Chiweta Monroe, this 5th day of April,
1856.*

There was nothing after that.

"I wonder why there's no entries after the last
one," she said.

"I've wondered that myself. You might ask the
family."

She closed the Bible and stood. "Thank you,"
she said.

"Come and see me again," he said. "You're invited to the services."

She just nodded her head. Since Jared died, she'd
not attended a church service.

She and Joseph left. She looked at her watch. It
only eleven. Her appointment at the Monroes' was
at two. She didn't want to go to Maude's. There
would be too many questions about Nate.

She and Joseph headed toward the cabin. They

had gone halfway when Bill Evans pulled up in a car. "You look loaded. Can I give you a lift?"

She nodded. The package of clothes was getting heavier with every step, and not being able to use her left hand made it awkward.

She opened up the back door and Joseph hopped in, then she stepped in the front passenger seat.

"Going home from the looks of it," he said.

Home. She still didn't consider it that.

She nodded.

"I hear you helped Nate yesterday. Whole town is grateful. I checked with the doc this morning. He said reports from the hospital were good."

"They're still keeping him there for a day or two."

"Knowing Nate, I'm surprised they didn't have to tie him down, but I'm not surprised he was helping Mrs. Byars."

She didn't say anything. Nate was in her head. He occupied way too much of it already.

Then they were at the cabin. Bill got out and went around and picked up her package. "Heavy."

"Hey, there's a whole wardrobe in there," she replied.

He took it up the porch. "I'll see you at the community center," he said as he left.

She put the package in her bedroom and transferred the tops to hangers in the closet and the pants to the dresser. She left one of each on a chair. At least she had something decent to wear to the Monroes'. The phone rang.

She picked it up. "Hi," Eve said. "Just wanted to let you know Nate is doing fine. He wanted to come home, but I convinced him that you might leave town if you had to doctor him again. That worked."

"That is Machiavellian," Andy said. She didn't add that she was beginning to expect that of Eve.

"I know," Eve said, sounding very pleased with herself. "I'm a politician, remember."

"Thanks for letting me know he's staying."

"You're welcome. I heard you met with Al."

"It's rather amazing," she said. "I went to his office Monday morning and he invited me for dinner Monday night. I think he believes it will help his wife. I'm going over at two today to look at some letters and other items they have."

"I'm impressed," Eve said.

"I really like them," she said.

"Al does have his good points," Eve replied.

"He really seems to love his wife."

"I don't doubt it," Eve said. "I've always admired him for that. Please don't forget, if you need anything…"

"I was happily surprised by the general store and the clothes they stock."

"Heather has good taste," Eve replied. "If I hear anything more about Nate, I'll call you, unless you want to run up there and see him." She hung up before Andy could say anything.

Andy showered and dressed in a new light blue blouse and blue pants. She then made a sandwich from the cold cuts in the fridge and ate it outside on the porch.

When she glanced at her watch, she was surprised it was nearly two.

"Ready to go?" she asked Joseph. He had, after all, been invited.

The dog wagged his tail and went to the door. She grabbed his lead and followed him.

Elena opened the door before Andy could ring the bell. "Miss Stuart, Mrs. Monroe is expecting you in the garden room."

After greeting Joseph, Elena led the way through the living room toward the back of the house and into a room surrounded on three sides by ceiling-to-floor windows. The sun streamed in, nourishing the many varieties of flowers and plants lining the sides. Mrs. Monroe sat at a glass table piled with folders and bound volumes. The woman started to stand as Andy entered the room.

"Please don't get up, Mrs. Monroe," Andy said. "I need a minute to absorb this. It's really lovely."

Mrs. Monroe slipped back in the chair, and Andy noticed she did so with relief. Her skin was too pale despite the powder obviously intended to cover the fact. "Elena and I planted them. I love flowers, and this is my favorite room." Then her gaze turned to Joseph. "He's a handsome dog."

Joseph offered his paw. Sara took it as a smile spread across her face. "He has very good manners."

"Yes, he does," Andy said, "although I can't take credit for it. He was already trained when I adopted him or, more truthfully, he adopted me."

"Where are you from, Andy? Where's home?"

"I really don't have one," she said. "The army was my home for ten years' active service. Fourteen if you include ROTC at the university. Before that, a small town in West Virginia."

"There's mountains there," Mrs. Monroe said.

"Mostly deserted coal mines, bald tops and few jobs," she said. She didn't say it hadn't been home for a long time. It reminded her that she needed to get her act together and help out her family.

"Then, you will have to consider Covenant Falls home," Sara said.

"I think I already do," she said. "I've never felt so welcome."

"Good. Now, what would you like to know?"

"I went by the Presbyterian church this morning and saw Angus's Bible. I just had time to see the notifications about Angus, his marriage, the births of three children and the death of his wife. I didn't see any successive entries. Did Angus marry again?"

"No, he didn't. A woman from Chiweta's tribe came to stay with him and care for Liam and his sisters."

"What happened to the son? There was nothing more in the Bible."

"Oh, he survived, but he disappeared for years. Rumors were that he was an outlaw. He returned when Angus was dying. Among the papers we have is a pardon from the governor two days before Angus's death, but I don't think Angus forgave him. He became a pillar of the community and is one of Al's ancestors."

"And the daughters? Were they heard from again?"

Sara was silent for a moment, then said, "There was a lot of prejudice then. There had been numerous raids—not so much by the Utes, but most people didn't distinguish between tribes. Angus sent the daughters away to be educated in the east, and that was where they met their husbands."

"Does everyone here know that story?"

Sara shrugged. "They know the rumors. Much of what I said has been passed from one member of Al's family to another. They didn't publicize it. Maybe because they were ashamed of the Ute blood or that one of the relatives had been an outlaw. I thought it rather intriguing," she said. "I always wanted to write the story, but I didn't because I thought it might hurt Al's position in the community."

"He doesn't care now?"

"We talked about it last night. He knows I've always been interested in Covenant Falls history, but he was on the council and was thinking about running for the House of Representatives. After last year, his heart wasn't in it any longer. I think he may even want the story told now."

Excitement roiled inside Andy. A film was rolling though her mind. Angus, his Ute wife, daughters fleeing their heritage and an outlaw son.

"You said 'may,'" Andy said.

"He told me you promised that you wouldn't say or publish anything without approval. Is that right?"

"Yes," Andy said. She wasn't a reporter. It would be fascinating, though, to try to discover what had happened to the sisters. That, though, wasn't her objective. A short, concise history for a brochure was. "I don't want to write a book," she added, "but I think you might."

Sara looked at her with surprise.

"Mr. Monroe told me you were an English major and wanted to write," Andy said slowly. "I'm a nurse. It's what I wanted since I was little girl. I still want it, although I might have to take a different specialty. Maybe I forgot how important it was to me until yesterday when Nate fell."

"How is he?"

"Doing well, I think. He has a concussion and he's staying in Pueblo today and hopefully tomorrow to make sure there isn't any bleeding in the brain."

"What was your specialty?" Sara asked.

"I was a surgical nurse, but a bullet crippled my left hand."

"I'm sorry," Sara said.

Andy just nodded. She wasn't going to say she was the lucky one, that she was the one survivor. And that maybe she wasn't the lucky one at all.

"Would you like to see some excerpts from Angus's journal?" Sara asked.

"Yes." An escape from memories into another world.

Sara reached into an envelope and pulled out three pages.

Andy started reading.

CHAPTER SEVENTEEN

November 5, 1848
Tomorrow I leave my beloved Scotland and
my store in Edinburgh for America. I hear it
is a vast and wild land. It is not my wish to
go. I do so sadly, but I feel it is my duty to my
reckless young brother, Liam, whom I swore
to our parents to protect.

He took funds from our leather tore and,
without my permission or knowledge, took
passage to New York City. Like many here, he
has heard there is gold to be found in America
and he yearned for adventure. He is an irre-
sponsible lad of seventeen and in good con-
science I cannot let him go alone...

ANDY SKIMMED TO the last sentence: *I am beginning*
this journal today to record the journey ahead.

She looked up from the pages Sara Monroe had
given her. "Is the rest of the journal this interesting?"

Sara nodded. "It is to me. There are dry spots
here and there. He recorded every river they crossed
and fauna he found along the way."

"Is there more than one journal?"

"There's five," Sara said.

"What a treasure!"

"I've been telling Al that for years, but the journals have been passed down as private family history. In the beginning I think it went back to a fear that their heritage and Liam's reputation might taint the family, which basically ran this part of Colorado for many decades. Then it became a tradition, one Al didn't want to break. But after our nephew was arrested and convicted, I think Al realized then the myth of Angus Monroe and the influence of the family destroyed his sister and her son."

She looked up with sorrowful eyes. "Al's sister was much younger than he, and when his parents died, he took care of her. Spoiled her completely. She could never do any wrong. She married a con man, a very handsome one. He was an alcoholic abuser, but she couldn't admit she'd made a mistake and dived into alcohol, as well. When they died and we adopted Sam, he was the child I could never have, and we spoiled him just as Al had spoiled his sister."

She had tears in her eyes when she looked at Andy. "He thought he stood above everyone because of the relationship…"

She straightened up. "But I'm wandering. What's done is done, but I think Al feels that some of that aura around the family contributed to his sister's death and his nephew's troubles. I also think he might realize Eve is right about trying to grow the town." She smiled. "Like any man, it's hard for him to admit he's wrong. This is his apology," she added, "although he won't admit it."

"Have you read them all?"

She nodded.

"May I?"

"I think that's why Al brought you here. He doesn't usually take to people right away. His father was that way, too. But he liked your grit, as he put it." She smiled wistfully. "I used to be that way."

"I think you still are," Andy said.

"Thank you for that," she said. "Would you like some tea?"

"Please."

There was more color in Sara's face, even a hint of a sparkle, when she left the room.

Andy turned to the next page and started reading.

New York City, December 15, 1848
I arrived in New York City after a hellish passage on the Mary Ann, *a clipper ship that was said to be seaworthy. We were met with storms and I have rarely been so ill. The food was rotten from sea water and the drinking water scarce.*

Two crewmen were washed overboard during a storm and five passengers in the below deck died of some sickness. The captain had advertised a trip of no longer than three weeks. It took us six weeks, and I fear that Liam will be headed west.

I have found lodgings while I hunt for my brother. The innkeeper told me of several neighborhoods where they say Scots gather. He also reported it was a very dangerous area. I will begin my search tomorrow when I am rested.

From the Journal of Angus Monroe

Feeling increased excitement, Andy turned to the last page.

Yule, 1848
It is a joyful Yule. After ten days of searching, I found my brother. He is with me now. Running low of funds, he had been enticed into a fighting club where he was forced to lose rounds after winning several matches. When he complained about not being paid, he was badly beaten and thrown out on a wintry street in Five Points, an area much feared.

New York is a lawless place. The police are corrupt, asking for money when I sought assistance. I hired men to look for Liam. One stumbled upon him and brought him to my lodgings. A doctor attended him, and he is improving. I asked him to return to Scotland, but he refused.

Despite his injuries, he is determined to go west. The newspapers are full of news about gold finds in California, and there are also rumors of gold in Colorado. I fear if I do not go with him, he will go alone and his reckless-ness will kill him.

I offered to pay our way if he would travel west with me. Liam, now penniless, agreed. I do not seek gold as my brother craves, but I have heard there are opportunities for traders in the West. I have talked to many people, and I am told we should buy goods and wagons in Independence, Missouri, since the journey from New York is long and harrowing with many river crossings. I have also been told we should be in Independence by April to join a wagon train for protection against the sav-ages. I can buy goods then and hire men to drive the wagons.

Since we will be going by horseback, I must leave behind many of my prized possessions. I fear I have seen Scotland for the last time, but there are vast new territories to explore. I cannot deny a hunger for land.

We will have to wait here until the snow melts, but we want to be at the Mississippi by mid-February. They say it is a great river and we will have to find a boat to take us across. I have purchased a book that purports to tell

*me everything we will need on the journey
westward from the Mississippi.
    If only the snow would stop...*

Sara returned then with Elena and a tray with
tea and small pastries.

"I talked to Al," she said. "We would like you to
come to dinner tonight, if you're not too exhausted.
Around seven?"

Andy would have accepted any invitation to have
access to more of the journals. She hesitated. She
had planned to visit Nate, but maybe if she hurried
she would still have time. "I would very much like
to come," she said as she tasted a very good lemon
concoction.

NATE WAS SUPPOSED to rest. However, there had been
a steady stream of visitors on his second day in the
hospital. To placate his mother he agreed to spend
the second night there, but by damn he was leaving in the morning. He had things to do.

Four of the vets showed up together, followed by
Eve and Josh, then Clint.

He really wished everyone would leave him
alone. He was not a good patient, and he felt like
a fraud. He was fine. He had a bloody bad headache, and a small bald patch where his head had
been shaved and the wound closed. The gash on
his leg was still seeping, but he could live with that.

An orthopedist said it was a grade-two ankle

sprain and he recommended crutches for several weeks. Though it was painful, he'd walked to the bathroom without them. He'd walked on worse during army training.

None of the injuries were severe. They just hurt at the moment, and he wanted everyone to leave him to his misery. He hated hospitals; he had spent four very bad weeks in one fourteen years ago. He had to admit, though, this hospital had it all over the military one, not in quality of care but certainly in atmosphere.

Truth was he only wanted to see one person, and that person was Andy Stuart. He wasn't particularly happy about it. But damn, he couldn't stop thinking about her.

By late afternoon, the visitors had left. The nurse came in to put an ice pack on his ankle and made sure it was elevated, then took his temperature and blood pressure. "All good," she said. Then she checked the head wound. "You're going to have a scar there, but you were lucky."

"That's one way of looking at it," he said glumly.

"I don't know who you are in Covenant Falls, but your doctor got you the best specialists."

"What I feel like is the biggest damn fool in the hospital. I've never fallen off a ladder before."

She left and he turned on the television, flipping from one station to another. Nothing caught his attention. He was turning it off when there was another knock at the door. He wanted to say, "Go away," but decided that would be rude. "Come in," he said unenthusiastically.

"Hi," Andy said as she walked in, a book hugged to her chest with her wounded hand. She dropped it on the bed. "I suspected you might try climbing the walls, so I brought a book I thought you might like. He's my favorite suspense writer."

"Where did you get it?"

"In the second bedroom in the cabin. I went through them all."

He took it and glanced at the title. He liked the author, too. "I haven't read this one. Thanks."

"I'll tell you a secret about hospitals. They purposely pick the worst possible television stations so people will leave. Same with the food." Her other hand was behind her back, and she pulled out a box and handed it to him.

"A gift from Mrs. Byars. Brownies, I think. I didn't peek, but I smelled them all the way here."

"Where's Joseph?"

"He's in the car. I left the windows partly open and it's cool outside. I wasn't sure he would be welcome in the hospital and I can't stay long."

He studied her. That triumph he'd seen at Monday-night poker was there again, and her grin was wide. "You look as if someone handed you a sackful of money."

"Even better," she said. "The Monroes are allowing me to read segments from Angus's journals, and what I have seen so far is fascinating."

"I'm impressed," he said, meaning it. "I wasn't sure they existed or, if they did, that anyone could pry them out of Monroe's hands."

"Well, I haven't exactly pried them out of their hands, but I hope the excerpts are only the beginning. I had tea today with Sara Monroe. They've invited me to dinner tonight at 7:00 p.m. I'm hoping they will let me see one of the volumes."

"You've drove all this way for a few minutes?"

"And brownies. Don't forget the brownies. Mrs. Byars saw me drive in, and she came flying over. Well, maybe not flying, but she was moving fast. She had the strangest idea that I might be coming to see you. I couldn't disappoint, could I?"

"Most certainly not," he said, grabbing one. "Tell me about the journals."

"There's five of them. I've just read a few entries at the beginning of the first one, but Sara told me what I might find. I feel like I've found a lode of gold."

Her excitement was contagious. And the fact she'd driven to Pueblo to tell him warmed him all the way through.

"Go on," he encouraged her.

"The first entry is Angus leaving Scotland to follow his younger brother here. He finds him half-dead, then the two go by horseback to Independence."

Nate loved the excitement he heard in her voice, saw in her eyes.

"His brother wanted to look for gold, but Angus figured he had a better chance at growing wealth by trading than by digging for gold. He's a very economical writer, yet the story just flows."

She sat in the chair next to his bed. "I didn't mean to gush," she said and reached for a brownie. "I never gush," she added wonderingly.

"You're welcome," he said drily. "And it's interesting to note you never gush."

"Just this once," she retorted. "And the brownie is my fee for bringing them." She took a bite and asked, "Are you springing this place tomorrow?"

"Hopefully at first light." He was suddenly aware of the new bare spot on his head. His hand went to it before he could catch it.

"It's a unique haircut," she said. "Kind of intriguing."

He knew he was seeing the Andy Stuart before the tragedy in Afghanistan. He didn't know how long it would last, but he liked it. He liked it very much, especially the gushing. Her eyes sparkled with life.

He tried to tamp down that feeling.

"Thanks for coming and bringing the goodies," he said.

"Oh, I was told to tell you not to worry about Mrs. Byars's porch. There's a group of vets over there fixing it. It should be done by tomorrow morning."

He gave her a wry smile. "That's good to hear. I was worried about it."

"It's a pretty neat town you have here," she said. "Yours isn't?"

"I think it was once. It's pretty dismal now. It was a coal town, but the mines played out. It left the old and those too tired to move."

"What about your family?"

"You couldn't move my mother with a ten-ton truck. Her father, mother and grandparents are buried there. So is my father. She practically lives at the cemetery."

"What about friends?"

She shrugged. "I was always the odd one out."

"How?"

"I was the only girl in ROTC, and they gave me a hard time, but I knew it was probably the only way to get a college degree. That and grades. I studied when everyone else was playing."

"I'm surprised a small-town school had a ROTC unit."

"We were bused to a larger school twenty miles away. It was big in athletics and the military. I was able to get an ROTC nursing scholarship."

"Did you like the military?" He knew he should stop asking questions. It was none of his business and it was one of the unspoken rules of the vets. No questions. If someone wanted to talk, then yes, but otherwise…

Her eyes clouded, and he thought she wasn't going to answer. She would probably tell him it was none of his business.

She didn't. "It was important," she said slowly. "I am…was…a surgical nurse. It was always challenging. The…doctor could do magic with some of the traumatic injuries."

"It had to be a challenge coming here, a place where you knew no one."

"I didn't feel I had a choice," Andy said. "I was making minimum wage working in a coffee shop and I was breaking so many cups it was only a matter of time before I was fired."

The comment was light but obviously meant to deflect. Yet he couldn't stop the next words.

"You could always go back to nursing. Doc Bradley needs someone. I certainly can vouch for you after yesterday."

She shook her head. "I can't," she said simply. "I had to force myself to come here today. I never know when I'll have a flashback, and a hospital setting brings…" She shrugged self-consciously. "I just can't."

He suddenly realized why she had seized on the history project. She was running away. He couldn't blame her, and yet he knew from personal experience that you could never run far enough. At one point, you had to turn and face the past. God knew, it took him long enough.

He studied her, wondering whether he should mention what he had read online. Then he knew that it would be dishonest if he didn't. He'd hated dishonesty in Margaret. He wasn't going to follow that path.

"I read about the attack in Afghanistan when it happened. Most of us keep up with news like that," he said.

She stared at him. The warmth in her eyes was seeping away. "I thought I remembered your name," he said slowly. "I checked the internet and confirmed it. It must have been hell."

"Worse than that," she said as she ran fingers through her hair. They were shaking. "I should go," she said. "I shouldn't leave Joseph in the car this long." The sparkle in her eyes was replaced by the curtain he'd seen on the first day.

"I didn't mean to pry," he started to say, then interrupted himself. "Yes, I did. But I like you, and it was obvious something bad happened. I want to help, and sometimes it helps when you talk about it."

"No, it doesn't," she said. "It doesn't help at all." She turned around and started for the door.

Damn. Why had he said anything? He should have kept it to himself, or at least left it alone in the beginning. But he thought it unfair that she didn't know he knew.

She stopped at the door and turned around. "You shouldn't have done that. Dr. Payne swore that no one would know. I don't want pity or understanding or sympathy." She scowled at him. "I discovered everyone knows everything about people in

Covenant Falls, but I thought Afghanistan was off-limits."

"You're right," he admitted. "I should have left it alone, but I recognized…" Nate stopped, then tried again. "I wanted to help."

She gave him a scornful look. "If I wanted help, I would ask for it. And no, you can't help, not unless you can bring the dead back to life."

"I'm sorry," he said. "I should have realized you're a hell of a lot stronger than you think you are. You're a survivor."

"What makes you think I'm a survivor?" she asked.

"The smile on your face when you came in today."

She stared at him for a long moment, then swallowed hard. "I feel guilty every time I do that."

"You should talk to Josh," he said. "It took him a long time to smile, too."

"I'm not Josh."

"You certainly aren't, but you have the same fiber."

"You don't know anything about it."

"Then, tell me," he said.

"No." She opened the door and this time she left.

He sighed. He'd sure messed that up.

But one good thing had happened: she'd had fire in her eyes. He much preferred anger over that old emptiness.

He picked up the book, although he doubted

whether he could read the pages. His thoughts were too full of the woman who had just left.

ANDY'S ANGER SWELLED as she left the room.

It was made stronger by those few moments of intimacy that had warmed her. They had made her forget for a moment, had dulled the sharp slash of memories. She felt betrayed, particularly by someone she liked.

What had been a good day had turned sad, and she resented Nate for doing it. She didn't want to be known as *the* survivor in a massacre.

She drove to Covenant Falls in time to take Joseph home, freshen up and be on time for dinner at the Monroes'. She'd been surprised at being invited twice the same day, but she'd sensed that Sara Monroe was lonely and Mr. Monroe might have second thoughts about sharing the journals.

When she arrived, Al was dressed in a suit. He offered both Sara and Andy a drink. Both requested wine while he had what looked like whiskey.

"Is there anything about the camels in the journals?" Andy asked when they sat down. "I read about the spitting ordinance." She wanted to hear Angus's version. It would make great copy for the inn.

Sara smiled. "Angus bought them from a traveling circus that bought them from the army. They could carry a lot of supplies and go into hard-to-reach camps. But they were fierce-tempered beasts

with a habit of biting anyone or any animal that
came close, and that included Angus and the han-
dlers. No one really liked the camels but Angus.
One bit the wrong man, who promptly shot it. The
shooter was quickly hanged. No one liked the camels, but the camels were citizens of Covenant Falls,
and the shooter was an outsider."

Andy could tell Sara relished the story. "What
finally happened to the other one?" Andy asked.

"Died of old age. An English writer called her
the Dowager, and the name stuck. The town held
a funeral when she died. You'll find references to
the camels in the journals."

"You know that Clint and Nate plan to call their
inn the Camel Trail Inn."

"No, I didn't," Sara said. "But it does have a certain flair about it."

"I'm writing some material for them. Do you
mind if I use what you told me?"

"Not at all. I've always been fascinated by the
Dowager."

Andy looked at Sara. "You've read all of this in
the journals?"

"Some of it. Some came from lore passed from
generation to generation. Whenever I heard any
small scrap, I jotted it down. I love history and
I had a real-life story here," Sara said. "I met Al
at college. I majored in English but I leaned toward journalism until I discovered there weren't

any jobs. Until then, I was bound and determined to be a reporter, but I fell in love."

She looked at Al and smiled. "I never regretted it."

"But she still has that instinct in her," Al said.

Elena announced dinner.

Al stood back while Sara led the way to the dining room and Andy followed. But in Al's last words, she knew exactly why she had been invited.

CHAPTER EIGHTEEN

IT WAS LATE afternoon Thursday before the last physician signed off on Nate and he was finally released. Josh picked him up in his Jeep and started back to Covenant Falls.

"I messed up," Nate confessed as they left the Pueblo city limits.

Josh glanced at him. "In addition to your various injuries?" he asked.

"I told Andy yesterday that I knew what happened in Afghanistan."

Josh looked at him with a question in his eyes.

Nate hesitated, then confessed. "I went online and looked her up. There was an attack on her field surgical team while they were operating. Andy was the only survivor. Apparently, she was engaged to one of the victims, a doctor. You didn't know?" Nate asked.

Josh was silent, then said, "I knew from Dr. Payne that she'd been through a lot, but nothing like this. Being a lone survivor brings a hell of a lot of guilt."

Nate knew that only too well. When he'd served in Iraq he'd been wounded during a search through enemy-occupied buildings. Two of his buddies had been killed on the last mission. He was still haunted by their faces, and that was only a fraction of what she'd suffered.

"She's damned gutsy," Nate said.

"She is that," Josh said. "It explains why she jumped headfirst into our history. She needed something. Just like I did. My salvation was rehabbing the cabin."

"And Eve," Nate said.

"Especially Eve," Josh admitted. He studied Nate. "You like her, don't you?"

"Hell, she's off-limits. If I hadn't known before, I do now. She's still carrying a load full of pain," Nate said.

"You do know, don't you, that every unmarried woman in Covenant Falls has tried to penetrate that shell around you."

"That's about three people," Nate said, "and all over fifty."

"A few more than that, or so my wife tells me."

"She's only here to heal. Then she'll be gone." Nate said.

"Dammit, Nate, sometimes reasons are just excuses. Believe me, I know. If you like her, do something about it."

"She's fragile," Nate protested.

"I think she's discovering she's stronger than she thought," Josh replied. "She faced Al in his den and came up triumphant. Damn if I know how she did it."

"I do," Nate said. "She looks like Al's sister when she was at that age, and he adored her. You wouldn't know that, since you never met Regina."

Josh looked stunned. "For real?" he finally said.

"Eve probably noticed it, as well," Nate said. "Regina was fifteen years younger than Al, and he helped raise her. She and her husband died in a car accident when she was about Eve's age."

Josh pondered that. "I knew about her, of course, because of my problems with Sam. Eve didn't mention the resemblance and maybe she didn't think about it, but then Eve can be devious in pursuing a good cause." He grinned. "Much to my surprise, it's one of the things I love about her. She never gives up on anyone, me included."

Nate didn't answer. He usually distrusted manipulation, even in pursuit of good. He'd had too much experience with the kind that didn't mean well.

Eve and her huge heart was the exception.

"I take it you told her you've checked on her, and she didn't take it well," Josh said.

"Right and right."

"Better you told her than she discovers it later."

"That was my thinking until she pretty much told me to go to hell. She takes privacy seriously."

"So do you, my friend, as a rule. You must have it bad."

Nate shook his head in wonderment. "It's impossible," he said.

"Nothing is impossible. Look at Clint and Stephanie."

Nate just raised an eyebrow. "Andy just lost her fiancé in a hail of bullets. I don't have two cents to my name. Whatever I did have after my marriage is tied up in the inn."

"She's army, and I've seen how easy you two are together, even if you don't."

"Even if I thought it could work, I've blown it."

Josh changed the subject. "Speaking of our last two cents, we need to start working on the program for the preview weekend. The gold mines for sure. I've already talked to Herman Mann about a jeep trip to the gold mine near his cabin, and he knows of several other mines. He and Clint are going to prepare maps. I was thinking we should start with a steak fry up at the falls at sunset," Josh said.

Nate shook his head. "Why not leave the falls for Sunday? End with a Sunday brunch at the waterfalls at noon. If it's good weather, we should have the rainbow. It'll allow everyone time to get back to Denver before nightfall with a great memory. Saturday will be used for activities: the gold-mining tour, horseback riding, hiking, even rafting on the river below the falls."

"I like it," Josh said. "But we have to plan something Saturday and Friday nights."

Nate was stymied. "Damn if I know, but half

of our guests are women. We need something that will appeal to them… Maybe Eve or Stephanie will have an idea."

"Or Andy?" Josh added.

"Or Andy," Nate agreed although he feared she might not talk to him again after his confession. "Maybe we should have a meeting."

"Not today. You, my friend, are going home to bed. You can barely walk on that ankle and you lost blood, not to mention a concussion. An afternoon off is mandatory. Tomorrow will be soon enough."

"But you'll talk to Eve tonight?" Nate bargained.

Josh nodded as they drove up to Nate's house.

Satisfied, Nate left Josh's Jeep and limped up to his house. Ideas were tumbling through his head. An event. They needed an event of some kind. Maybe even one they could develop into a draw for tourists. He knew some towns had really turned around when they held annual events. Covenant Falls needed a turnaround, and quickly.

He limped his way into the kitchen. There was a note on the counter. "Shepherd's pie in the fridge. Just heat at 350 for an hour. If you need anything, call me. Mom."

She knew him well. She knew he disliked being fussed over and she also knew he would probably be hungry. He called her. "Hey, Mom, thanks for the care package."

He hung up after assuring her he was fine, located the shepherd's pie, his favorite, and preheated the oven. He sat at the kitchen table and thought about his conversation with Josh. Disjointed activities just wouldn't make the impact they needed for the preview. He knew enough public relations from his home-building days to understand that a story pulled people in. Right now they just had a hodgepodge of unrelated activities.

He stared at the shepherd's pie. The last thing he wanted now was to eat alone. It hadn't bothered him in a long time, but this afternoon it did. Maybe it was the disappointment in Andy's face when he had mentioned Afghanistan, the fact that he had invaded her privacy. Maybe the shepherd's pie would be a good apology.

He stared at the phone for a long time. Well, hell, what did he have to lose?

His oven pinged, telling him it was ready for the casserole. He summoned his courage and called Andy, hoping that she wasn't over at the Monroes'. She answered on the second ring.

"Hi," he said. "It's Nate."

"You've been sprung?" she asked coolly.

"Finally," he said. He hesitated, then said, "I owe you thanks for the great medical attention, as well as an apology. A very heartfelt apology. I now have in my possession the best shepherd's pie you've ever tasted about to go in the oven. Can I tempt you to come over and let me take care of both matters at the same time?"

He felt like a kid as he held his breath until she

answered. "I love shepherd's pie," she said. "You didn't make it?" she added cautiously.

"Nope. I'm good with steaks and burgers, but a Good Samaritan left it in my fridge."

He felt her hesitation. "I really do want to apologize," he said. "I don't usually pry." He hated the word. "And," he added in desperation, "I also have something to discuss with you. Josh and I were hoping you could help us with something."

"Apology unnecessary. I…overreacted. It's just…"

"Hell, it was none of my business."

There was a silence, then, "Can I bring Joseph?"

"He's always invited." It had never been so hard to ask for a date, nor had he ever been so happy to have it accepted. It scared the hell out of him how happy he was.

"Where?" she asked.

"I'll pick you up," he said.

"No, you won't. I'm through putting pieces of you together. I can follow directions." He thought he heard a smile in her voice.

"Turn right at Maude's, then take the fourth left—Aspen Road. I'm the fourth house on the left. It's a brown bungalow with yellow roses along the walk."

"When?" she asked.

"When can you get here?" To hell with trying to be smooth. He wasn't any good at it.

"An hour?"

"Perfect," he said and hung up before she could change her mind.

Down, boy, he told himself. He didn't believe in romance. Maggie—Margaret—had killed that. He didn't trust his own instincts. And yet Andy had stayed in his head since the moment he'd met her. He had known her only a few days, but it felt much longer. He couldn't remember being so at ease with a woman.

Yet every moment with Andy had strengthened the attraction: the quiet, poignant watchfulness when she'd first arrived, the way she'd come back from the flashback at Eve's house, the mischief in her eyes when she'd won at poker, the competence in treating him and getting him to the hospital, the unique connection she'd apparently made with the Monroes.

There were so many sides to her and he liked every one of them.

Using the crutches, he limped around the living room, piling magazines and books in neat piles and clearing the dining room table. He rarely had company other than the occasional get-together with other vets, and he'd never collected much in terms of dishes and silverware. Still, he rounded up the best he had and put them on the table.

Carefully balancing himself with the crutches, he managed to take the shepherd's pie out of the fridge and put it in the oven, then realized something was missing. Wine. He had beer and bourbon but no wine. He called Josh. "SOS," he said.

"You fell?"

"Nope. I need a bottle of wine. In the next ten minutes."

"Should I ask why?"

"No."

"Ten minutes?"

"Or less."

"What kind?"

"Whatever is good with shepherd's pie."

There was a pause, then Josh said, "Okay, but you owe me," and hung up.

Nate plopped down in a chair. Damn, but it had been a long time since he'd asked a woman to dinner. He knew, though, that Eve and Stephanie both enjoyed wine with dinner and Eve had a ready supply.

Eight minutes later, the door opened, and he knew it was Josh. He slowly stood. His friend had a big smile on his face. "Hot date?" Josh asked.

"Just making amends," he said.

"All we had is white. Want me to put it in the fridge? It's already chilled. I also brought a wine opener. Didn't know if you had one."

"I do," Nate said. "I'm not that hopeless. Thank you, and goodbye."

"Can I have a guess?"

"Nope."

Josh grinned. "Don't think I need one. I'll run

before she discovers you're a clod who doesn't have wine."

"Goodbye," Nate repeated pleasantly.

"I can take a hint," Josh replied. "Don't forget, you owe me." He opened the door and left.

Nate found some cheese that wasn't gray yet and cut it into small pieces. He put two plain glasses in the fridge to chill them. Not elegant, but they would have to do.

Almost exactly an hour had passed when the doorbell rang and he opened the door. Andy looked prettier today than she had yesterday, and more yesterday than the day before. God help him if that trend continued.

Joseph barked at her side.

He looked down and grinned, grateful for the save. "Hello, Joseph," he said.

"Thanks for inviting him," Andy said, then looked around the yard. "I like your roses," she said.

"I'm just their caretaker." He paused. "You look great," he said as he glanced appreciatively at a pair of pants that fit snugly on her slim figure and a dark brown blouse.

"Thank you," she said. "I made a visit to the general store yesterday and discovered there are clothes other than uniforms and blue jeans."

Nate's pulse spiked. His heart thudded faster even as he led her toward the kitchen.

"How are you feeling?" she asked as she eyed his crutches and swollen ankle.

"Probably a lot better than I should, thanks to you. I don't know if I thanked you..."

"You did, and it wasn't necessary. I just happened to be going by." She looked at him with concern. "No headache?"

"The barest shadow of one."

"And the wound?"

"Sore but tolerable. A good meal will help build strong blood cells."

She squinted at him. "Your medical training told you that, yes?"

"My common sense told me that. Along with my appetite."

She grinned. "Shepherd's pie is one of my favorite dishes. I discovered it in Germany, of all places. There was an English pub near the base when I was stationed there."

He limped his way into the kitchen, and she followed. She looked around and through the windows to the garden in back. There were roses everywhere.

"I inherited them," he said with a shrug. "The house belonged to a friend of my mother's. Her son inherited it when she died. But he'd moved away and nothing was selling here. I was just returning to Covenant Falls and we made a bargain. I would rent it, make some improvements and take care of the property until the market turned around. That included the roses."

"How long have you been here now?"

"Three years, going on four. Mom's getting older and I thought I should be near."

"Is your mom the Good Samaritan?"

"Yes. She's convinced I'll starve without her help, or else die early from too many stops at the Rusty Nail."

He opened the fridge with his good hand and took out his newly acquired bottle of wine. "We have a few minutes before the pie is ready. Would you like some wine?"

She looked up at him. "Now, let's see here. You're just home from the hospital with one leg, and I'm driving with one hand." Then she grinned. "I guess Joseph and I can always walk home."

The smile was breathtaking. It lit her face like the North Star.

"I take that as a yes," he said. He took the wine over to the table where he'd put the glasses. Then he made the mistake of discarding the crutch and balancing on the two legs as he turned the corkscrew.

"Nate!" He heard her voice just as his ankle folded under him and he started to fall. She reached out for him with her bad hand, and they both fell against the fridge, her face next to his, her body pressed against his. He held out his arms to steady her.

"Are you okay?" he said shakily as she echoed

the words at the same instant. She felt so good against him. Softer than she looked.

She nodded with a grin and made no effort to move. "You make a good landing pad."

He chuckled.

"What about you?" Andy asked.

"Pretty sure I'm as intact as I was a minute ago."

She started to laugh. Their eyes met. He swallowed hard and did what he had been wanting so badly to do: he folded his arms around her and touched his lips to hers...

THE FEEL OF his lips burned all the way through Andy, and she found herself responding with the same rush of heat she felt in him.

Reaction from the near fall. Relief that neither of us was injured.

As much as she tried to tell herself that, she knew it was something far stronger. He was awakening something she'd thought dead and gone.

Her body wasn't obeying her head. The whisper of his breath on her cheek, the warmth of his hazel eyes, the searching of his lips all blocked the part of her that wanted to deny it.

His lips explored hers, and her body ached with need.

Her arms went around him and she didn't feel so cold, so apart from everyone else. So alone. She found herself responding, her lips opening to him.

The air between them was magnetic, storm winds blowing temptation.

Wrong. It was wrong. Jared was dead!

She jerked away and stood. Trembling. "I... can't," she said.

He straightened. Leaned against the stove and his fingers soothed her hair. "It's okay. I'm...sorry. I..."

"Don't apologize," she said. "It's me. Not you. I'm just not ready." She looked up at him. "I don't know if I'll ever be ready."

He took a deep breath and simply nodded. "I don't usually come on so strong. You just...looked so damn pretty and felt...well, just right."

Just right. She couldn't stop the smile tugging at her lips. Not the most elegant compliment, but now it sounded like one of the nicest. She realized then why she felt so comfortable with him. There was no pretense about him. He was strong, capable, comfortable in his own skin. And sexy. Much too sexy.

"Food," he said, and she knew he was trying to cut the tension that the kiss had created.

She moved out of the way and picked up the unbroken bottle in her good hand. "You really think we should have wine?" she asked with a grin. "We're not doing very well without it."

"I think we can manage," he answered with a chuckle. "But I think I'll skip the ancient cheese with which I was going to tempt you and put the shepherd's pie on the table."

This time, he leaned against the kitchen shelves

as he uncorked the bottle. Then he took the shepherd's pie from the oven.

"The problem now, as I see it," Andy observed, "is getting it to the table without dropping it."

"Ye of little faith," he replied. "I considered the problem earlier. I have two plates here. I will load each with shepherd's pie and you can take one at a time to the table while I use the crutch." He looked very satisfied with himself and she couldn't help but smile.

She took the first plate, then the second, to the table while he limped over with the bottle of wine. He sat and watched as she took the first bite. Baked mashed potatoes covered with melted cheese topped a rich combination of beef, gravy, mushrooms and onions. Andy took a bite, then said, "Wow."

She took a sip of wine and leaned back. She couldn't recognize all the spices, but whatever they were, the shepherd's pie was one of the tastiest dishes she remembered eating. "That's not like any shepherd's pie I ever tasted," she said.

"It's my mom's own version. Ground sirloin, buttered mashed potatoes, onion, mushroom, several types of cheese and a bevy of spices known only to her. It's her favorite for everything from church socials to funerals."

"You should offer it at the inn," Andy said.

He looked thoughtful. "I haven't thought of that, but yes. I'll have to pry the recipe from her."

She changed the subject. "You said you had something you wanted to discuss with me."

He poured her another glass of wine. "The inn," he said. "You haven't seen it yet, but you came up with the Camel Trail Inn, and we're running with it. You know we're having a preview for some travel writers in seven weeks, and Josh and I were considering activities Covenant Falls could offer."

"And?" she asked.

"We thought of offering activities when they arrive—horseback riding, a Sunday brunch at the falls, fishing on the lake. A trip to an old abandoned gold mine. But we have women coming as well as men, and we need a theme, something to pull everything together."

Andy immediately knew what he meant. "You already have the theme," she said. "You have Angus and his story. Build entertainment around that. Songs from the time. Dances."

"You've seen excerpts from his journals," Nate said. "Maybe we can draw from them."

Andy went cold. "Al and Sara have been good to me. I'm not going to abuse their trust."

"I wouldn't ask you to. We don't want you to do anything you feel is wrong or unprincipled," he said. He drew a long breath. "Maybe it's just a dumb idea, Andy. Probably is. Josh and I were talking about what to do the night everyone arrives, and we were stymied."

She studied him for what seemed forever, then

said, "A play. A series of skits. Maybe even a pageant. I saw one in North Carolina when I was young. It was about the Cherokees being forced off their land. I still remember it. My da…"

Her voice faltered, then she said, "But it's not impossible. You already have enough legend here without the journals, but you need a writer. I was willing to try to write a brochure, but I'm not a scriptwriter. And seven weeks isn't very long…"

She watched the wheels spinning in his head, his brow furrowing with concentration. She liked watching him. More than she should.

"Maybe…" he started.

"Maybe?" she prompted.

"If we had a few scenes of Angus coming here, saving the chief and marrying the chief's sister, maybe the first birth in a new town. We could incorporate Western and folk songs in the telling. Most are out of copyright, so there should be no problem. We have a great drama and music teacher here. It could give students and recent grads an opportunity to show their talents."

"Would there be time?" she asked.

"I'll call Louisa, the drama teacher. Won't hurt to ask," he said. "She'll probably think I'm nuts, but hey, that's been said before. What's more, it could bring the town together."

"What tore it apart?"

"There's always been tension between Al and some of the other families. Some of it is just old-fashioned envy. Part of it was Al's dictatorial grasp on the town for years. Eve has made inroads, but it would be nice to put it to rest."

"A suggestion," she offered. "Ask for Al's thoughts, his help. Enlist his wife. She was an English teacher and she knows the history better than he does. She's read all the journals, has a deep interest in them."

"Okay, Eve first. She may think it's impossible. Or crazy. Or both."

"I should go," she said. "I think you have some work to do."

"I think I do," he said with a smile that warmed her down to her toes.

"That was a great dinner. Thank you."

It was polite. Nothing more.

It was all he could do to keep from grabbing her, holding her. But though she said she'd forgiven him, she was making it clear that she wasn't ready to go farther.

He watched as she walked down the porch steps and past the roses.

He wondered if he had completely destroyed any chance he had with her. Hell, he wasn't even sure he wanted one. A voice from within reminded him of his ex-wife, cautioning him he was a rotten judge of character.

He closed the door.

CHAPTER NINETEEN

ANDY CLOSED THE leather-bound journal as the door to the garden room opened and Sara appeared, followed by Elena carrying the tray of tea and small cakes. Sara had called her earlier in the day and asked whether she would like to read some more of the journals. Andy had grabbed at the chance. She had been far too occupied with thoughts of her dinner with Nate last night.

"I thought you might need a break," Sara said. "You've been reading for more than two hours, and it's not that easy to read."

Andy shoved back her chair. "I didn't realize... I'm sorry... I've just traveled a long way with Angus."

"He does bring you along, doesn't he," Sara said. "Where are you now?"

"Crossing the Mississippi. It took Angus and Liam two months to travel from New York to Hannibal by horseback."

"With only what they could carry in saddlebags," Sara said. "Their next stop is Independence, Missouri."

Elena poured tea into a cup and handed it to Andy, who thanked her.

Much to her surprise, she was beginning to prefer it to coffee. Suddenly, Al Monroe walked into the room. "Still poring over those old journals?"

"Have you read them?" she asked.

"Yes. Most of them. A long time ago."

"I want to ask you something."

"Nothing stopped you before," he said as his eyebrow arched.

"What would you think about an outdoor play about the founding of Covenant Falls?"

She waited for the fallout.

"That sounds like a lovely idea," Sara exclaimed eagerly.

Andy saw the denial in Al's eyes. It was there instantly, but then he looked at Sara. Her eyes were alive with interest. There was actual color in her cheeks. She looked like a different woman than the one Andy had met just days earlier. Still frail. Her face still had that unhealthy pallor. But there was life in her eyes, and Andy knew Al saw it, too.

"Who will write it?" he said.

"I think your wife should spearhead it," Andy replied.

Sara glanced at her husband.

He didn't react—at least he didn't say no.

"I think a play sounds like a wonderful idea," Sara said, "but me? It's been years since I've written anything…"

"I'm thinking a group effort," Andy said. "You know the history better than anyone. You've read the journals and you live here. You taught English. You love stories. And that's what this is, but it's better than fiction because it's true.

"I talked to Nate about it," she continued. "He thinks the high school's music and drama teacher could work on music and help with the script, but they need someone to put it all together."

"What about you?" Sara asked. "Aren't you writing a history of the town?"

"*Trying* is a better word for it," Andy replied.

Sara looked at her for a long moment, then asked, "Is there a deadline?"

"Seven weeks. Josh has some tourism officials and travel writers committed to be here then," she said as she glanced at Al's face.

"That's impossible," Al interjected. "Sara can't—"

"Sara's going to try," Sara interrupted her husband. "I used to think about writing Angus's story, and then Sam came to us." She looked at Al, challenging him.

"Then, do it," he said with a hint of a smile. He turned to Andy. "I expect Eve had something to do with this."

"I don't think so. I think it was all Nate Rowland this time."

He didn't look convinced.

"It may not happen," Andy said. "It's just in the idea stage, but I wanted Sara and you to know that the idea is being discussed. It's really essential that you two be part of it."

"If I know Nate and Eve, it's more or less certain," Al said with a strained smile.

"I don't think anyone wants to go ahead unless you approve," Andy said.

"It's not up to me to approve or disapprove. I'm not on the council now, and I couldn't stop you if I wanted. When does all this begin?"

"It has to be immediately if everyone agrees. In the meantime, I would love to read more of the journals."

"Come whenever you want," he said. He turned and left the room, leaving Andy to stare behind him.

"He's a proud man," Sara said softly. "What happened last fall, it hurt him. He loved Sam. I do, too, but I saw what was happening to him, and Al wouldn't let himself see it." She sighed. "He feels he hurt the town as well as the boy he thinks of as his son."

"How is Sam doing?"

"I think he's horrified at what he did," Sara said. "I don't know if you have heard the whole story, but one thing led to another and got out of control. I think Josh is the man Sam wanted to be and he…" Her voice broke.

After a few seconds, she said, "I visited him a few days ago, and he's doing well. He's taking several correspondence college courses and will be out in a year, thanks to Eve and Josh. It could have been a lot worse, but they spoke on his behalf."

Andy mentally added that piece of information to the puzzle that was Covenant Falls. Peaceful to the eye, but apparently there were ripples under the surface. She simply nodded. "Sometimes people just need a wake-up call."

Sara looked hopeful but diverted the subject. "What is the next step if you go ahead with the play?"

"Nate and Josh are trying to determine whether there's enough interest from the drama teacher and others in town to pull something like this together. I don't think they would try without you and Al. You're at the heart of the story. Because of the time element, there will be a meeting to toss around ideas. Can I tell them you and Al are in?"

Sara nodded. "Maybe a good place to start is with a narrator opening the first journal and reading an entry. Then the actors could dramatize it."

"I know nothing about plays," Andy said. "But it sounds good to me. The secret would be choosing the pertinent journal entries."

"I can certainly help there," Sara said.

Andy felt her excitement building. Sara's reaction was far more than she'd expected, and Al's more or less favorable attitude unexpected. She could hardly wait to tell Nate.

That sudden thought startled her. How could Nate become important so quickly? A lifeline? But she didn't want a lifeline. She didn't want a complication.

"Will you join us for dinner?" Sara asked.

"Thank you," she said, trying to keep her voice steady, "but I left Joseph home and he probably has to go outside."

"Please bring him next time," Sara said. "I truly enjoyed having him here."

"I'm sure and Stephanie could find one for you," Andy said.

"Al..."

"If I've noticed anything," Andy said, "it's how much your husband loves you. I fought the idea of getting Joseph. Too much trouble. I didn't want to be emotionally involved. I didn't want to lose someone again. Adopting Joseph is one of the best things I've ever done. And when I lose him— which I hope is many, many years away—I'll be pounding on the front door of the nearest shelter to get another."

Sara was staring at her, and Andy suddenly felt embarrassed about being so vehement. Dr. Payne would be proud.

"Have you ever told him you wanted a dog?" Andy asked in a gentler voice.

"No, but Sam did, and he refused to even talk about it, and he loved Sam."

"Maybe he didn't think Sam could take care of one."

"There's that," Sara admitted.

"Maybe he would like a well-disciplined dog,"

Andy ventured. "They adopt out retired military dogs."

Sara looked doubtful.

"I'd best be on my way," Andy said.

"Would you like to take one of the journals home?" Sara asked.

"I thought…"

"Al and I talked about it. We trust you…and we know you can't spend all your time here."

"You don't know me," Andy protested.

Sara smiled. "I think we do."

Andy was touched by Sara's words and felt unworthy. She had become involved to save herself, not anyone else. She stood. "I really should go."

Sara said, "Call me if you have any questions."

"Will I read about Chiweta?"

"Yes," she said with a smile. "And her brother."

"I'll call you when I hear from Nate about a meeting." Andy left quickly, the heavy journal in her hands. She felt as if she had a treasure chest in them. She also felt she'd made a friend in Sara, one of the few she'd had outside the military. Sara obviously ached from not having children and having so little purpose now.

That was why she'd suddenly decided that Sara, rather than the drama or English teacher at the school, should head the writing committee. If, indeed, there was one. She hoped she hadn't raised Sara's interest for nothing.

She also hoped that Nate and the others would

agree. There obviously were troubled waters between the Monroe family and the rest of town.

Had she overstepped?

Probably.

How had she ever become so involved?

Because she had nothing else.

How Jared would have hated that thought.

She arrived at the cabin, parked and hurried inside. Joseph ran in circles of joy as if she had been gone for weeks.

After a few minutes of affection, she hitched the leash to Joseph's collar. "Walk time."

Joseph patiently waited until she opened the door and they went outside.

They walked halfway up the trail, then turned back. She should call Nate, and yet she was avoiding doing that. She wondered whether he had talked to anyone, received any response. She feared returning to the nothingness she'd felt in the months following Jared's death, and yet she equally feared becoming so involved in other lives. She didn't want to care deeply again. It just plain hurt too much.

Joseph whined as if he could read her thoughts.

"You're different," she assured him.

Halfway back, she saw Nate. He was sitting cross-legged on her dock.

There was no mistaking his lanky form. His hair fell over his forehead and he looked so darn comfortable with himself. He rose slowly as she approached and limped toward her. "Hi," he said as he reached down and ran his fingers through Joseph's fur. The dog actually grinned.

"You should be using crutches," she scolded.

He shrugged. "Too much trouble."

"Too much macho," she retorted.

"I have news, and you didn't answer the phone." His grin was downright irresistible.

"I do, too."

"You go first, then."

"Sara Monroe," she said. "She's excited about a play and I suggested she head the writing committee."

"Writing committee?"

She shrugged. "She's really excited about participating." She paused, then asked, "Do you think I overstepped by asking her to head the committee?"

He stared at her, then threw his arms around her and swung her around. When he set her down, she tried to scowl at him. "Your ankle," she protested.

"To hell with my ankle. You've just managed a miracle. Does Al approve?"

"Let's say he doesn't disapprove."

He leaned down and kissed her on the cheek. Spontaneous and quick, but it sent quivers down her back. He straightened quickly and his face lost its exuberance. "I'm sorry," he said. "But you're a wonder. And hell no, I'm not sorry."

She stood there, stunned, both by his action and her body's response.

He straightened and looked rueful. "Can I come in and get the details?" he asked. "I promise to be good."

She smiled. "Of course." She started to lead the way to the cabin, but he caught up with her and they walked in companionable silence. Once inside, she turned to him. "Coffee?"

He nodded and she went straight to the kitchen and brewed coffee, but she was only too aware of his presence. Her body was, as well. She told it to behave. Nate was a friend. Nothing else. She certainly didn't want anything else.

After she brewed the coffee, Nate carried the cups outside. She avoided the double swing and sat in one of the two chairs. "You had something to tell me?" she said carefully in a cool voice.

"First," he said, "is that book on the table what I think it is?"

"It is."

"Did you steal it?" he asked conversationally.

"Nope."

"Find it?"

"Not that, either."

"I give up."

"Sara loaned it to me."

He looked at her in total disbelief. Then that slow smile spread over his face. "Can I read it?"

"Maybe. Now what is your news?"

"I'm embarrassed to mention it now."

She raised an eyebrow. "I won't belittle you."

"Oh, you're cocky," he said.

She laughed.

"I like that," he said, "and for that reason, I will tell you my good news. At least I thought it was until I heard yours. Anyway, the drama teacher thinks it's a great idea. Because of money shortages, they weren't planning a stage play this year. They will readily participate in ours. The principal gave his okay, as well. It helps that the drama teacher and principal are married. We can use their auditorium for rehearsals."

He leaned over and took her hand. "You said Sara Monroe wants to help write the play."

"She had this great idea." Andy related Sara's thought about a narrator reading directly from the journal.

"Are the journals that good?"

"I haven't read them all, but, yes, I think so. Your Angus was a good writer. Succinct, yet somehow he makes you feel you're there."

He stood. "Okay if I look at them now?"

"Sure. Just don't take the coffee anywhere near it."

"Right." He went inside, put his cup in the kitchen sink, then came back to the leather-bound volume. Andy knew from her own experience that he would become engrossed in it.

She fed Joseph, then poured herself another cup of coffee and sat in one of the big chairs and watched Nate. Joseph settled down next to her.

She noticed the bandage on his head was still there. He barely limped, although she knew how painful his ankle must be. He probably still had a headache, as well. He should be home in bed.

It felt pleasant having someone in the room with her. Nate was easy to be with.

She didn't know how long she sat there. An hour, maybe, before he lifted his head. "You're right. You're with him every mile. I see exactly what Sara has in mind." He reluctantly closed the book. "Have you had dinner?"

Andy shook her head. "I had a large lunch. I'm really not hungry."

She was. In fact, she was ravenous. But he was arousing feelings in her that frightened her. She wasn't ready for them. She didn't know what to do with them.

He gave her a lopsided smile. "Then I should go."

She swallowed. She didn't want him to go. But Jared intruded in her thoughts. He was standing there. Dominating the room.

Andy stood and walked to the door, leaving Nate to follow. When he opened it, he turned and looked at her. He started to touch her face, but she flinched and stepped backward.

She couldn't believe she was tempted, that she wanted his touch, wanted the tenderness that was in his smile.

But Jared was there, too, with his lopsided smile.

"Good night," she said, more curtly than she'd intended.

"If you need anything..." he said softly, then he left.

CHAPTER TWENTY

THE FIRST MEETING of the Covenant Falls Event Committee took place at 4:00 p.m. at the community center the next day. Maude sent sandwiches and drinks.

Bill was at the center when Andy and Sara arrived just minutes before the meeting. They'd spent the morning scanning and copying passages from the journals. They wanted everyone to get a feel for Angus's words.

Louisa and Ames Daniel arrived next and Bill introduced them to Andy. Louisa was the drama and music teacher and her husband principal of the school. Nate arrived next with Josh and Eve.

Louisa looked like a drama teacher. She had dark hair and vivid blue eyes and radiated energy. Ames had the look of an all-around good guy with a ready smile and hearty handshake. "Glad to have you in town," he said. "Covenant Falls has grown better with the arrival of each vet, and I hear you're no exception. Welcome."

Louisa leaned over and gave Andy a peck on the cheek, startling her. "Nate told us about your idea. It's an exciting one. I was planning a concert for the end of the year, but I'm really excited about the possibilities of an outdoor play. I think my kids will love it."

"It's sort of a joint idea with Nate," Andy said. "I really had very little to do with it…"

"More than a little," came a voice behind her, and she whirled around to face Nate. He'd offered to drive her to the meeting but she'd declined.

Josh and Eve arrived next, followed by Clint and Stephanie.

Josh grinned. "Clint just graduated from the police academy, and he and Stephanie are engaged. He told me I can tell everyone."

"I did no such thing," Clint said, but he grinned and put an arm around Stephanie. "She wasn't easy to persuade."

Stephanie smiled. "He's a hard guy to say no to, and if you're wondering why I am here, I'm told I'm the camel person."

Eyes widened around the circle.

"More about that later," Nate said. "In lieu of anyone else stepping up, I guess I'll call this little gathering to order, so to speak. I think everyone knows everyone now, but I want to explain why you in particular were invited.

"This started as a discussion about entertainment for the opening of what is now the Camel Trail Inn. We were able to get commitments for at least ten travel officials and/or writers, which was far more than I thought, and we were trying to come up with ways to entertain them.

"At the same time," he continued, "Sara Monroe was sharing Angus Monroe's journals with Andy Stuart, who recently came here. While talking about the entries, Andy came up with the idea of an outdoor play or pageant about the founding and early years of Covenant Falls.

"While it would benefit the inn, the idea grew. Covenant Falls has so much going for it—the lake, the mountains, the waterfall and its history—but no one knows about us. We are losing population and we are losing our young people. To be frank, we are dying out.

"I know there are some who don't want the town to change. I understand that, but with a healthy tourist industry, maybe we can maintain our town much as it is and develop enough jobs to keep our children here. I don't mean anything brassy or cheap, but activities based on outdoor adventure and historical interest. We have the falls, lake, streams, abandoned gold mines, even the remnants of a ghost town if you count one broken-down cabin.

"But we think the biggest draw is our falls and our history. We all know the legends, but it took a newcomer to believe that our history is something to be shared, because it's not only our history, but the history of Colorado and the West. The question then was how best to showcase it.

"So I called several people." He looked at Louisa. "First call was to Louisa to determine whether she thought it was feasible. I wasn't prepared for her enthusiasm.

"Sara Monroe offered to share the entries in Angus Monroe's journals, which would be the heart of any play or pageant, and she agreed to help write the play. If you are not aware, she has a degree in English and has a deep interest in history.

"Clint is here because he plays the guitar and has written several great songs. He could help develop the music with Louisa.

"Stephanie will work with any animals, including, as she said, maybe even a camel. Sara has agreed to work on a script. My mom has volunteered her sewing circle for costumes.

"Saying all that," Nate said, "This is obviously a wild idea, which will take a huge amount of work and might well bomb. I also might be volunteering some people who have not exactly agreed to any part in this harebrained scheme."

"Gee, you're convincing," Clint said, prompting chuckles.

Louisa raised her hand. "I, for one, like it. I've seen all my promising students leave town. This will give my seniors a project into which they can pour their hearts. I have a senior who can do anything with lighting and a young lady who is great in staging. This would give them great experience."

"Will they be willing to give up part of their summer for this?" Nate asked. "It will be all volunteers."

"Some will. It will give them experience if they try to find jobs in the entertainment field," Louisa said. "But the script will be the heart of this."

Nate broke in. "Andy will pass out copies of a few entries in Angus's journal, thanks to Mrs. Monroe."

After she passed out the copies, Andy watched the faces as the pages were circulated and read. She saw the growing interest in the room. The first excerpt was the opening entry in the first journal, when Angus prepared to leave Scotland. The second detailed finding his brother in New York, the third was an account of a raid on the wagon train they had joined, the fourth covered the death of Angus's brother and the last was on establishing the trading post on the lake.

Louisa's head was nodding as she glanced through the three pages. "This is good," she said.

"This is just a sampling," Andy said. "Mrs. Monroe—"

"Sara," corrected Sara Monroe. "It's Sara."

"Sara, then," Andy said. "She thought of having a narrator read passages from the journal, maybe in a study above the stage, and then the actors could enact the scene."

A smile spread across Louisa's face. "Or maybe Angus is writing the entry when he is older? And a younger Angus acts out the scene? I like it. I like it very much."

"Would you be interested in helping to write it with Sara?" Nate asked. "You know scripts and drama."

Louisa turned to Sara. "How do you feel about that?"

"I would like it very much," Sara said.

The drama teacher's gaze went to Andy. "And you?"

"I'm not a writer, but I'll do whatever I can to help. I'm good at research."

Nate turned to Daniel. "Can we use the school's facilities and equipment?"

"If it's a community-sponsored project."

"Is it?" Nate asked the group.

Andy was seeing another side of Nate. He was sharp, decisive and manipulative in a good way. A little like Eve but more laid-back.

"It is," Bill said. "We can coordinate it here at the community center, and the high school can be our partner."

"I'll run it by the school board, but I don't think there will be a problem," the principal said.

"We need a chair for the project," Nate said.

"I think we already have one," the principal said.

Nate looked questioning.

"What he means is you seem to be doing just fine," Clint said lazily.

"I agree," Louisa said.

"I do, as well," Sara added.

For a moment, Nate looked trapped, then shrugged. "Time is our biggest problem. We need a rough script in, what, three weeks?" He glanced at Sara, who looked at Louisa, who looked at Andy.

"We'll try," Louisa said.

"Clint, can you put together some possible songs from the mid-1840s? Maybe something original?"

Clint nodded. "The state song, for sure. And you and the vets can build the stage and help with the sets."

"Bill, can you work with Andy in combing through the stuff we have in the museum and come up with items we can use?" Nate asked.

Bill nodded.

"Susan, who is managing the inn, is really competent at advertising and public relations," Nate continued. "She can also design a program." He looked around the room. "Any questions or comments?" he finished.

"What's this about a camel?" Louisa asked.

"Ah, you didn't grow up here," Nate observed, "so you don't know about the camels."

"No, I'm an import. I'd heard you changed the name of the inn," she said. "I didn't know why."

Nate explained how Angus had bought the camels and how they'd made quite an impact on Covenant Falls.

Louisa laughed. "I love it, but are you really

going to try to get camels? I mean, should they be in the script?"

"That's kinda up to you three," Nate said.

"You're giving us that much power?" Louisa quipped.

"Hell, it seems I'm king of the world," Nate said, "and I have no idea how it happened."

Everyone laughed. Andy looked around and saw the obvious affection everyone had for him. And respect. It was the other side of the easygoing Nate she was getting to know.

Then Daniel asked the next question. "Are you proposing to do this one night, a weekend or a week?"

"Sorta depends on how well this goes," he said. "Ideally, I would like to see it be a weeklong annual affair, something entertaining enough to bring visitors from throughout Colorado and even farther. I've noticed that many towns have really revived after holding events for Western storytellers, rodeos or music festivals.

"We don't have much in rooms," he continued, "but maybe we can convince some residents to provide bed-and-breakfast rooms. We have some grand old homes here."

"What would Covenant Falls offer in addition to the play?" Daniel asked.

"Jeep trips up to the abandoned gold mine and ghost town. Horseback riding. Fishing. Swimming later in the summer. Hiking. Rafting down the river. We're planning a Maude-catered brunch at the waterfall, which could be an ongoing offering for tourists."

Heads nodded.

"I would love to see the other journals," Louisa said.

Sara piped up. "I've made a list of pivotal entries," she said, "and I suggest we start with those because time is so limited, but you can come over anytime and look at the journals."

"Why don't we meet Monday after school," Louisa said, "and you can show me the entries you think will work."

Sara nodded. "That will give me time to select, and copy, usable passages." She looked at Andy. "Four p.m. okay? You can have dinner with us."

Louisa nodded. "Daniel has a school board meeting that often runs late."

Andy nodded as well, but added, "I think I'm here under false pretenses. I'm not a writer." She had said that over and over again and no one paid any attention.

Sara smiled. "This was all your idea," she said.

Andy's instinct was to run away from home—or her temporary residence that was fast becoming home. What had she gotten herself into? What had she gotten Nate into? And Eve? What if it was a giant flop?

What if…?

The meeting broke up then. Sara left for home, but the rest stayed and ate Maude's sandwiches and coleslaw, then the others left as well, leaving Bill and Nate and Andy.

"How's your ankle?" she asked for lack of anything better to say when Bill disappeared to turn out lights everywhere.

"Better."

"You should stay off it, you know."

"Somehow that's difficult around you. You seem to stir things up." He grinned. "If you told me two weeks ago I would be chairing a committee to produce a pageant in seven weeks, I would have thought you were crazy," he said.

She stood and put the sandwich wrappings in a nearby trash can. "But you were good. Really good. Everyone seemed on board." She frowned as she said the last. "But can it really be done?"

He shrugged. "There's a lot of talent here, and the people usually rise to a challenge. The community center, for instance. No one believed it could be done. Still," he added, "I know it's a very short time, and a lot of people could be disappointed."

That was the Nate she liked. There were so many things to like, and she was finding more every day. He had a natural leadership. She hadn't noticed it until tonight. But then, she hadn't seen him in that role before. She had seen the sensitive guy who'd welcomed her and the relaxed one with his friends at

Eve's house and with Eve's son. There was the man who was fixing a home for an elderly friend and the one completely abashed by his fall and injuries.

She liked all of them.

"Did you walk?" he asked.

She nodded.

"Joseph?"

"I wasn't sure he would be welcomed by everyone. I noticed Josh didn't bring Amos." *Small talk. Keep talking and don't look into those warm hazel eyes and strong chin and a smile that would charm gargoyles.* "Do you always take charge like that?"

"No one else was going to do it," Nate replied.

"What about Josh?"

"He likes to be in the background."

"And you don't?"

He shrugged. "I grew up with most of these people. Josh is a newcomer."

Bill came in. "Closing up now," he said.

"It looks as if we're being run out," Nate said.

"No longer king of the world."

"A quick reign. All work. No respect. No glory."

"Poor baby," she observed.

"See, that's what I mean." He folded the last of the chairs and placed it against the wall. "Can I drive you home?"

Caution told her no. Fear told her no. Good sense told her no. She nodded.

"Good," he said and limped to the door. He

opened it for her and they walked together to his pickup.

"I can open the door myself," she said.

"Okay," he said to her surprise. "Heaven forbid that I don't respect that streak of independence."

But when he stepped inside and settled in the seat next to her, he took her hand for a minute. "Thank you," he said simply.

"Why?" she said. She was truly mystified.

"Because you, like Josh and then Clint, brought new life to this town, and you're dragging others along with you." He hesitated, then added, "Including me."

"I don't think I did much dragging tonight."

"Exactly. You drag them along without you, or them, knowing they're being dragged."

"I don't think so," she said slowly.

He chuckled. "It's not a bad thing. I bet you were at the head of your class," he said. "And not only that, I bet you helped everyone else along."

It was a nice compliment, made even nicer because he believed it. His hazel eyes had a glint in them and the air in the pickup was warm and growing warmer.

He inserted a key in the ignition and started the pickup and they rolled out of the parking lot. The silence during the very short drive to her cabin was heavy with sexual tension. She fastened her gaze on the road ahead, not on him.

But they arrived all too soon, and her body was alive with want as he gave her a long measuring glance, then stepped out of the truck. This time, she didn't jump out but let him go around to her side and open it. She didn't know why, except it was a courtesy she appreciated and missed, and she wanted to grasp that strong hand he held out to her.

He put his arm around her as they walked to the porch and then the front door. She was immediately greeted by an ecstatic Joseph, who after a moment of frenetic tail wagging turned a quizzical eye on Nate.

"Do you think he questions my motives?" Nate said.

"Should he?"

"Yep."

"Want a cup of coffee?" she asked.

"Yes."

He limped with her to the kitchen and she sensed he was watching her every movement, just as she was aware of his. She was asking for trouble by inviting him in, and yet she had questions. And she didn't want him to leave. She didn't want to be alone.

She'd already noted that he took his coffee black, as she did. It was an army thing where sometimes the niceties of cream and sugar were not immediately available and you got used to whatever kept you going.

When the coffee was ready, she handed him a

cup and led them out the back door to the deck chairs. Joseph came with them and sat next to her.

The sky was alive with color, a palette of scarlet and gold and crimson colliding in an explosion of hues. Nate's hand found hers, and her fingers tightened around his. She knew she shouldn't. She knew where it could lead. But tonight she needed the companionship of someone who had been where she had been.

"Were you career army when you were in Iraq?" she asked.

"No," he said. "Thought I would join, have an adventure, travel, earn educational credits, then come back, get married and go to college."

"You said you're divorced?"

He shrugged. "That's a long story."

It was obvious it was one he didn't want to tell. She digested that. She knew so little about him. News might move rapidly in Covenant Falls, but apparently not about Nate.

"How long were you in the army?" she asked.

"I reenlisted after four years. I was close to the guys in my unit. Didn't seem to be a reason to go home. I was accumulating education credits but not enough."

He was silent for a moment, then added, "Not that I regret it. I grew up. I had to. I learned a lot about myself, about loyalty and commitment and working with a team. I still keep in touch with members of my unit. But I don't want it to be the only choice. Louisa has told me how talented some of her kids are, and she tries to do what she can to develop that talent, but we just don't have the resources to showcase it." He paused, gave her a lopsided smile. "I didn't mean to get on my soapbox but I think…hope we can open some doors. Maybe this all is a dumb dream, but…"

If her heart fluttered before, it pounded now. She had been attracted to him from the beginning. She had fought it, thinking it a betrayal of Jared, but the more she saw him, the more she liked him, and the more she liked him, the more she trusted him, and the more she trusted him…

She shouldn't have invited him in, but there had been yet a new side to him today. Mischievous and self-deprecating when he'd said, "king of the world." She wanted more of that side. She wanted to smile again.

"What happened to the girl?" she asked.

"What girl?"

"The one that made you wary of women."

"That obvious?"

"Just hints here and there."

"The whole messy story?"

She nodded.

"Margaret was my high school sweetheart. She was Maggie then. Old story. She was a cheerleader, and I was on the football team. I wasn't the hero or good enough for a college scholarship, but I made my share of touchdowns. At the end of high school,

I wanted to study architecture. I was damn good at building blocks and forts as a kid and putting things together as I grew older. But that took money, and we didn't have much. My dad died when I was young, and I wasn't going to let Mom sign a college loan. I decided to join the army and earn education credits while in the service."

"And the girl didn't want to wait?" she guessed out loud.

"She said she did, but that lasted about two months after I was deployed to Iraq. I was one of many guys who got Dear John letters. When I came home on leave, I heard Maggie had married and moved to Chicago. I reenlisted. Three years later I was wounded, and I was in the hospital when my enlistment ended.

"I'd earned twenty credits online and I had money saved along with some educational credits earned while in the army. I went to the University of Colorado to study architecture. Maggie—she was Margaret now—showed up at the end of my third year and said her marriage had been a terrible mistake, that her husband had abused her.

"Long story short, we made love, or at least I thought it was love, and two months later she said she was pregnant.

"I married her and dropped out of school. I couldn't afford a wife and child and college expenses. She knew someone in Seattle, and I got a job in new home construction."

He looked at her. "Sure you want to hear this?"

She nodded.

"She miscarried in the fourth month, but I had already dropped out of college and I still had a wife to support. I stayed with the construction company and gradually became head of construction. I hated it. The builder wanted me to take shortcuts and the houses had no soul."

He hesitated, and she sensed how painful this was. She waited. She didn't want to push.

He continued after a moment. "End of story—she had an affair with my boss. I think that's how I got my job. They had an affair while he was married and I was more or less their cover. When his wife died, she wanted a divorce after we'd been married for five years.

"I knew it was not a good marriage, but commitment meant something to me. I thought we both wanted children but we were having bad luck. I later found out that she had lied about not taking birth control. I don't even think she was pregnant when she came to me for help. She spent every penny I made and piled up credit card debt in my name by forging my signature. It did a hell of a job in shattering my ability to trust."

"You didn't go back to school?"

"No heart for it. I'm a good craftsman and designer, but I wanted to come home. My brother moved to Chicago. Mom was alone and getting older, and I figured it was payback time. I loved growing up in Covenant Falls and its sense of community. I just didn't realize how much I did until I lived in a big city."

Andy reached out her hand to him. Regardless of his last comments, she sensed the wound in him.

"She's an idiot," Andy said.

"You think?"

"I know," she said with such emphasis that he leaned over and kissed her.

CHAPTER TWENTY-ONE

DAMN IF NATE knew why he was spilling his guts. She was just so easy to talk to. No judgment, no "you're an idiot." Just she was the idiot.

But the kiss was reward enough. His hand tightened over hers and he stood, guiding her to her feet. She leaned against him and their bodies gravitated toward each other. Her lips met his again, and his world exploded. Heat rushed through him.

So did the rush of other feelings, and they all had to do with the heart. They had been building since the days since they met. It seemed longer because they'd been thrown together so much...

He knew he was in deep trouble. He'd never believed in love at first sight, but basically that was what happened when he'd seen Andy summoning the courage to step out of her car and into a new life. He'd tried to deny it. Considered that it had been too long since he'd had any real feminine companionship. Or maybe an aberration that would disappear in the light of reason. Reason didn't seem to be working.

Her body felt just fine against his. Soft and supple and strong. The kiss deepened and ignited fireworks that radiated through every nerve in his body.

His heart thundered and his body shuddered as her arms went around his neck. She looked up at him with those large gray eyes. The void that was there the first day they met had been filled with an intensity and hunger that matched his own.

Then he felt her hesitation, and he stepped back, his hand catching hers. "I'll go slow, Andy, as slow as you want."

"I don't think I want you to go slow," she said. He heard the bewilderment in her voice. "How could I…feel this way…"

His fingers caressed the back of her neck. "I've felt as if I've been hit by a tornado since I first saw you. It's crazy, I know, but…" He looked down at those wide, confused eyes, and his heart melted from a different kind of heat than that which had rocked his body.

His fingers moved from her neck and traced the cheekbone. "You're so pretty."

"You're not bad, either," she admitted in a wry voice.

He chuckled at that. "You're not very good at compliments, are you?"

"I've been told that."

He realized they were standing there, lost in each other's gazes and making ridiculous small talk while her eyes were saying something else, and he imagined his were doing the same.

He reached out and took her right hand in his so she couldn't escape suddenly. Her fingers were soft, although he felt the strength in them. They would have to be strong and supple and efficient to work in an army hospital, especially a forward base. Casualties often came in multiples and they were usually critical.

Then he took her left one. The fingers were stiff and barely managed to curl slightly into his. She tried to pull her hand away but he took it up to his lips and caressed it.

"It's ugly," she said.

"I think it's beautiful. Just like everything about you."

She shook her head silently.

"I can't pretend to know how this is happening or why," he said, lifting her chin so she looked up at him, "but I'm sure as hell not going to question it."

She stood on tiptoes and kissed him thoroughly, and he felt as if he had arrived in some glorious place he hadn't known existed. The embers that had glowed between them flared, enveloping them in a circle of heat. Raw sexual hunger filled him and he feared it was very obvious. It was all he could do not to pick her up and carry her off to the bedroom.

Even the air around them was charged with electricity.

Not wise. Not yet. She was still fragile. Vulnerable. He wanted to make love to her, but he sure as hell didn't want her to have regret about it.

He drew back. "You don't know how much I hate saying this, but I should probably go."

"I...think I do know," she said with a rueful grin. "But I don't want you to."

He closed his eyes for a second to keep from grabbing her. She looked so...beguiling. And bewildered. The admission was obviously galling her.

He took her hand and they went inside, Joseph trying to get between them. "Do you think Joseph is trying to tell us something?" he said.

"Joseph?" she asked the dog.

Joseph barked.

"Do you think he approves, or what?" he asked.

"He likes you, so I think he approves."

"Let's see. One bark for approval," Nate said.

Joseph barked once.

"Great," Nate said.

"I think you rigged that," she said. Her gray eyes were alive but then he detected a shadow.

His fingers tightened around hers. He liked the quick comebacks. Her dry wit. Hell, he liked everything about her.

He led the way and they sat on the sofa. It was time, he thought, to address the third person with them. "Tell me about him," he said, knowing he risked losing her, but he also knew it was something she had to face before they made love, if, indeed, she wanted it as badly as he. He didn't want to be a substitute for someone else. He needed her to want Nate Rowland, not a ghost.

She didn't answer immediately, then slowly, hesitantly, she started to speak. "Jared and I worked together in Germany, then we were sent to Afghanistan. We were just colleagues then. He was a really fine surgeon and I was a surgical nurse, and there was a line I didn't want to cross. There was respect but distance."

Her fingers tightened around his as she took a deep breath, then continued. "Things changed when we went to Afghanistan. Our job was to keep our guys alive until they could reach Germany, and sometimes...we lost. We all grew close, especially as the danger increased. After one hellacious day and night when a ranger team was ambushed, we worked nonstop for eighteen hours and still lost three.

"I was exhausted, emotionally ripped to pieces. They were so young. It didn't matter that they were seasoned soldiers. They were little more than boys, and the wounds were so bad. They were depending on us and there was nothing...nothing we could do to save them.

"I was shaking when I left. Jared caught up with me. He took me to one of the storerooms to help me come down before I went to my quarters. He held me, as much for himself, I think, as for me, and suddenly we were tearing each other's clothes off." She looked up at him, tears in her eyes. "It was grasping for life. Trying to find something that wasn't blood and pain and...defeat because we couldn't save them. We made love that night," she said. "It seemed the last night in the world.

"That's how it started," she said. "Maybe it would have ended there except I saw a side of him he kept hidden. Unlike the emotionless, staid perfectionist he presented to everyone else, I came to know a man who hurt every bit as much as I did."

She looked up at him. "Everything was...intense. We took refuge in each other, but we knew we would be transferred if our superiors found out. Maybe the secrecy added to the...intensity. We fell in love, and when our deployment was coming to an end, he asked me to marry him. It didn't matter then if anyone knew. Neither of us were staying in the service."

She paused. "He was a great orthopedist, particularly with traumatic injuries, and he'd received a number of offers. He was considering job offers in Chicago and Richmond. We were going to be married. One week later, an Afghan orderly, a man Jared helped get the job and to whom I gave money for his family, charged into the operating room and shot everyone there. Jared stepped in front of me. He died. I lived. The others died, too. The anesthesiologist and two another nurses, as well as a soldier who was on guard outside the tent. All of them died...all of them except me."

Her face was rigid as she said the words, as if it were made of marble. All but her eyes, those big gray eyes, and they were misty with grief that was obviously still very raw inside her.

For a second he regretted asking the question, but then he realized he'd had so much bottled inside when he returned from Iraq that he'd been useless to himself or anyone else. It was like getting a two-ton truck off his back when he finally talked about it to someone who had been there, who understood. He hadn't experienced anything as rough as she had, but he'd seen some pretty bad stuff and had lost too many buddies. It still haunted him. *Why them? Why not me?*

"I'm so sorry," he said, knowing that the words meant little as he put an arm around her. "Maybe I shouldn't have asked..."

"Yes, you should have," she said. "I didn't *want* to talk about it, but I *had* to." She said it with such intense sadness that he felt it flow through him, as well.

Nate closed his eyes for a minute. He'd thought he had known what happened. He hadn't. No wonder she seemed so closed off, or why Josh's psychologist friend had recommended she come here. The mountains had a way of cleansing the mind and nourishing the soul, and Covenant Falls was a place where she could find others who'd gone through similar experiences, a place that would embrace her without asking questions.

But he *had* asked questions, and he wasn't sure she wasn't lying about needing to open up. Her fingers, which were entwined in his, had gone stiff, and he sensed she was barely holding herself together, and he…well, he had licentious thoughts.

He pushed them away. It wasn't what she needed now. She was already riddled with guilt that the man she loved had died protecting her. He knew he could take her to bed now. It would be for the same reason she went with the doctor that first time. Pain. She was still crying inside.

He leaned over and kissed her lightly. "Want to take a walk?"

"Your ankle…"

"To hell with my ankle."

The ankle was nothing compared to the ache in his lower region. His heart ached, as well. He had to get the hell out of this cabin.

He stood and guided her up. He put an arm around her shoulder and looked her in the eyes. "I want you as much as a man can want a woman," he said slowly. "And I'll wait as long as it takes for it to be right for you."

She looked at him with those haunted eyes. They were misted over. She visibly swallowed. "Did I tell you how much I like you?"

He noted the *like* instead of *love* but then, it was early. "Ditto," he said and grinned. "Let's go."

"I would like that," she said.

ANDY TOOK HIS HAND, and they walked to the door. She felt…drained down to her toes, but she needed the fresh air.

Nate limped slightly. It probably cost him pain, but she suspected he wasn't going to give in to it, no matter the cost. Joseph meandered along with them. He had obviously decided Nate was a trustworthy friend.

She still felt an emotional overload. She had relived what she had tried, unsuccessfully, to forget. She felt cleansed. The grief was no longer festering. She had said the words without going to pieces, without the terrible anger that had once sustained her, then eaten her up inside.

The moon was bright enough that they could follow the path up the mountain. They walked in silence but she felt his quiet understanding. Her hand in his, she moved closer to him, felt his warmth. He was a strong man. A good guy. She'd recognized it before but tried to ignore it.

But tonight proved what kind of man he was. She would have gone to bed with him. She'd wanted to. Her body had wanted it as well, and it had been evident that his did, too. But he'd sensed, more than she, that she wasn't ready.

They reached the lookout, and she was grateful there was no one else there. He was right about the night and the view and the peace this particular place fostered. She turned around and saw the snow-capped mountains rising ever higher as she looked west.

"It took me a long time to realize this is where I really wanted to be," he said softly.

"It's beautiful," Andy said.

"It is that. In the winter it glistens." Winter? Would she even be here then? Surely she should be vacating the cabin for someone else. The next vet.

She shivered. She didn't want to leave. Nate was behind her, and as if he sensed her mood—he was uncanny that way—he put both arms around her and she leaned back against him. He made her feel safe. And she would be kidding herself if she didn't know he made her feel other things, as well.

He touched her hair. "Your eyes... Damn, but they're dangerous. Sometimes I think I can see your world in them and then they're like the fog rolling in, and I'm losing my way."

New emotions flowed through her. With Jared, it had been all storm and fire and frantic love. Grabbed moments.

She felt something altogether different with Nate. It was almost as if she had found a sanctuary in his arms. She also wanted him. Wanted to sleep with him because she knew it would be achingly tender and yet tumultuous. She'd felt both in his earlier kiss.

It's too soon. You don't really know him.

Yet she did. More than she'd known Jared despite

the months they had worked so closely together. He'd always kept part of himself secret.

How can you even compare the two?

She swallowed hard, then moved away, but she couldn't help looking at him. He had long lashes. She hadn't really noticed that before, but now they swept down and half hid his eyes that always seemed to know too much about her.

"I…think we'd better go back before…" *Before I fall into your arms and sink to the ground and we make love right here and now.*

"Woof!" Joseph had looked asleep, but now he was on his feet. He nudged her. Apparently her words had awakened him.

She stooped down and gave him a hug. "Okay. Home it is."

Nate took her hand and they started down. About halfway down, his ankle apparently twisted slightly and he went down, taking her with him. She landed on top of him and she felt his body react. He felt good. So good.

She wanted to stay there, but Joseph wasn't having any part of it. Obviously concerned, he made distress noises and kept poking them with his nose.

Nate laughed, a fine rumbling sound that came from deep in his chest, and then she was laughing, too. Joseph barked. It was all too much for him.

She sat up, then stood and held her good hand down to him. He took it and slowly got to his feet. "You're strong," he said.

"I had army training, remember, and I carried my share of equipment."

"I bet you did, and we had better move, or Joseph will bring a rescue party or something."

He limped even more as they reached the Lake Road circle where the trail started and ended. "I'd better go home," he said, "before I get in more trouble with Joseph."

She nodded and he limped to his pickup. In the past few hours, he had given her a priceless gift. She was no longer alone. He understood. He accepted. She suspected he knew her in a way Jared never had.

"Come, Joseph," she said, "first a snack, and then I'm going to read more about Angus and Covenant Falls and maybe even the Rowland family."

CHAPTER TWENTY-TWO

April 7, 1849
*It is a sad day. My brother, Liam, died today
just days from the mountains he longed to see.*

*He drowned while crossing a stream swollen
by a storm. The wagon he was driving over-
turned, and his body was caught beneath it.*

*With a heavy heart, we gave him a Chris-
tian burial as the sun set. God give him rest.
I am now the only remaining member of my
family.*

*I will stay with the train until we reach the
mountains that are now in sight. Our scout
reports we will stop at a lake on the edge of
the mountains and stay there several nights
to rest and refill the water barrels before taking the southern route to California. He said
it would be a fine location for a trading post
since the Ute would willingly trade deer and
beaver skins for our goods.*

*I will make the decision when we arrive
there, but I am weary of travel and I wish to
be close to where my brother lies...*

From the Journal of Angus Monroe

ANDY REREAD SARA'S chosen selections in hard copy. She couldn't help but compare the experience to reading the same words in the journal.

It was different, reading it in faded handwriting, the ink blotted in one place. Was it a tear, or had Angus been as stoic as some of his writings indicated?

She'd gone back to reading Sara's selections after Nate left. She needed something to take her mind from the intimacy they'd shared. The next passage was her favorite.

July 15, 1849
We reached the loch our scout promised. We were nearly out of water and what little we had went to the animals. The loch is as deep and blue as the evening sky, as pure as those in my highlands. It lies at the foot of mountains that overlook the dry country through which we passed and is obviously fed by the snow that caps their tops. It is a beautiful, serene place, and I plan to stay and establish my trading post here.

There is a forest full of game and no one to say nay. I walked around the loch and felt as if I belonged. I am saddened my brother never saw it.

Andy put the selections aside and looked at her watch. It was past two in the morning. She stood and stretched. She had immersed herself in Angus's world to avoid thinking of Nate and the emotions he had aroused.

She ached inside as she remembered how her body felt next to his, how his lips caressed hers.

But she didn't believe in short romances. She'd seen too many of them happen to soldiers on leave, only to receive Dear John letters a few months later.

Her father had courted her mother for years before she agreed to marry him. Her sister had known her husband since grade school. She had known Jared several years before they'd fallen in love...

Or was she only making excuses? Was she simply frightened of love, of losing someone again?

To distract herself, she'd picked up the journal and read. Questions popped up in her mind. Had Angus been in love in Scotland? Had he left a sweetheart to find his brother? Had he found love in his wife or had she only been a convenience? Was the answer in one of the other journals?

In worrying about his problems, she'd put aside her own.

Joseph whined next to her. She opened the back door and let him out, but all she saw was the chair Nate had sat in.

The image hit her like a sledgehammer. Emotions roiled in her, just as they had a few hours earlier. The tenderness followed by sheer sexual need still sent tremors through her body.

Don't think about it. She tried again to think

about Angus. She had traveled with him from Scotland to New York and then halfway across a country new to him.

He hadn't let the death of his brother stop him, even though Liam had obviously been much loved.

His writing about his brother's death had been matter-of-fact, and yet she felt the pain in him. Maybe because her own loss still lingered.

She tried to put herself in his position. He had left everything familiar and risked everything he had to take care of his brother, the only close relative remaining to him. And then Liam had died.

He really was alone in the world. He didn't give up.

It was time she let go of her own losses. Maybe that was why she had been so intrigued by his story. He had handled it far better than she had.

She had been ready to give up until Dr. Payne had persuaded her to take a long drive to a place she'd never heard of.

Joseph trotted over to her, licked her hand and whined. She realized he had wanted something else.

"What is it?" she asked.

He went over to the chair where Nate had been sitting, put a paw on it and whined again.

"Oh, you like him, huh?"

Joseph whined.

"You approve?"

Another whine.

"You haven't been alone with him, have you?" she asked. "He didn't coach you?"

He looked at her quizzically.

"Not sure I believe you," she said. "Let's go inside. It's snack time."

At the word *snack*, he barked.

She followed Joseph into the cabin and gave him a biscuit. He led the way into the bedroom, neatly ate his treat beside the bed, then jumped up on it.

She pulled on her overlarge T-shirt and slipped into bed. She'd read longer than she intended, and she couldn't wait until she started the next journal.

Nor the next meeting with Nate.

She closed her eyes and for the first time in months she looked forward instead of back.

NATE SANG IN the shower. He never sang in the shower. But he felt happy, really happy, for the first time in years.

Oh, he'd had good days. Many of them. He liked working with Josh and would be eternally grateful to him for taking him on as a partner. It took a lot of faith.

He'd enjoyed transforming the old motel into the Camel Trail Inn, making something handsome out of an eyesore. He'd had a free hand, something he'd yearned to have in Seattle, and now he was totally into the plans to publicize it. No one knew more than he how much Covenant Falls needed to grow. Now he'd met a woman who turned him on in every possible way—emotionally, intellectually and sexually. Andy was smart as hell, and she had a way of relating to people. One reason he liked her so much was that she was totally unaware of the effect she had on others in the short time she'd been in Covenant Falls. He didn't think anyone else would have approached the Monroes, much less been welcomed into their home and invited to read what no one else had.

Nor, he thought, would anyone else have convinced them to take part in something like a pageant. Like Josh and Clint, she was making her own impact on Covenant Falls and on him.

And maybe it was time for him to get a dog. A friend for Joseph. He turned off the shower but not the song in his head.

ANDY SPENT SUNDAY morning at the community center. Bill had given her a key to the center and to the museum. She spent several hours prowling through the trunks and boxes. She found some dresses from the 1920s and packed them away. She read some more newspapers, but they had none of the drama of Angus's writings. She couldn't wait to read more about the Utes and Angus's marriage.

Another problem: she couldn't stop thinking about Nate and the emotions she'd experienced last night.

The cell phone rang. She looked at the caller ID. *Sara.*

"I hate to bother you more," Sara said. "But I'm trying to sort out the most important passages to give to the committee tomorrow afternoon. Can you help me?"

Andy looked at her watch. It was nearly 1:00 p.m. "I can be there in ten minutes, if you don't mind Joseph coming along."

"Good. I'll ask Elena to make lunch for us."

"Oh," she said, "I finished the journal you gave me. I'll bring it back."

Andy didn't waste time. She put everything back where she found it, and she and Joseph walked to the cabin. She retrieved the journal and drove the Bucket to the Monroe home.

When she arrived, Elena, as always, was at the door. "I'm glad you brought Joseph again. Miss Sara really enjoyed his visit last time."

She was shown to the garden room, where Sara greeted Joseph with joy. Joseph showed his usual enthusiasm with a few licks on the hand.

"I am going to get a dog," Sara said as she took the first journal Andy had brought and presented her with some of the selections she'd made along with another journal. "The journal you had was the first year. This is the second."

The first entry was dated April 3, 1850.

I have survived the first winter. It was hard and lonely but I now have a companion, a dog named Wallace that was left by a wagon train.

I have developed a wary relationship with the Ute. They bring me pelts for my goods, mostly knives and mirrors and beads with which they decorate their deerskin clothes. I fear, though, that there might be trouble coming with more and more pioneers and miners coming through.

Andy finished reading the passage. "I like this."

Two hours later they had picked five more passages to use as an outline.

The first told of a battle between the army and the Utes due to a misunderstanding. The second was about gold being found in California and rumors of it being in Colorado, as well. Angus decided to stay there.

As she finished reading the passage, Andy took a deep breath. "I think you should include all of these. They're short and each one has drama."

Sara smiled. "I'm so glad you agree. I was worried that maybe it was too much. I feel so close to Angus."

"I think everyone will love them as much as I do," she said.

Elena announced lunch then.

ANDY ARRIVED PROMPTLY at the meeting Monday afternoon after spending all Sunday reading the second journal Sara had loaned her.

Louisa was already there at 4:00 p.m. She had

the entries Sara had selected and looked delighted. "I see exactly what you meant by having a narrator. The trick will be putting that drama in action. I can't wait to tell Carl Bates about it." She looked toward Andy. "He's a history teacher and would be a great addition to this committee. He looks like Santa and has a deep, rich voice. He'll flip out when he reads these."

"Flip out?" Sara asked.

"Hey, I teach teenagers. I didn't want to talk to him or my kids," she continued, "until I saw more of the diary, but I'm ready now. I have a Ute friend who participates in traditional dance performances. Maybe they can include them."

"We can't pay much."

"They only take donations to help with travel, costumes and other expenses. They can stay with some of our families and expenses should be minuscule."

Sara's face glowed with the approval. "There's more," she said and gave them another sheet.

June 15, 1850
I have company at my cabin. Not completely welcome company. I believed him to be a Ute warrior. I found him at the foot of a great waterfall while I was hunting. He was grievously injured, bleeding from a gunshot wound, and his leg was bent unnaturally.

Before I left New York, I purchased opium,

knowing I was coming to the wilderness. I asked a physician friend and he recommended some books and instruments. I have alcohol for wounds.

But should I interfere? I hesitated, then he moved and his eyes opened and fastened on me. They were full of pain but his lips tightened. He was not going to ask for help.

I hesitated no longer. I tore a sleeve from my shirt and pressed it hard against a wicked wound on his chest that bled.

Then I brought my horse to his side, helped him on and tied him so he would not fall. He fought the rope, then fell unconscious again. I led the horse and Wallace followed. It was a long trip, five hours at least. Our guest woke several times then lapsed back into unconsciousness. I wondered all the way whether I was making a terrible mistake.

We arrived at the cabin. I carried him inside and put him on the bed. I treated the wound in his side by digging out the bullet. I was grateful he was unconscious. Then I left Wallace at his side while I found a suitable piece of wood to make a splint.

When I returned, the man was trying to rise. I shook my head. He tried again and fell when he put weight on the leg and the splint broke. "No," I said, and poured water into a cup and handed it to him.

He drank it rapidly, then looked at me. "Why?" he said. "Why do you do this?"

He spoke English, which surprised me, but he waited for an answer. "It would not be Christian to leave you there," I replied. I told him he would not be able to walk for several weeks and he could stay with me. I would not hurt him.

"Who shot you?" I asked.

He did not answer. He closed his eyes.

The excerpt ended there.

There was a silence around the table as each person waited for all of them to finish.

"Is the rest this dramatic?" Louisa said.

"There *are* moments," Sara said.

"What about the Ute princess?"

"That comes next," Sara said with mischief in her eyes.

"I'm sold," Louisa said.

"Can we do it in six weeks?" Andy asked.

"I think so," Louisa said. "My kids wanted to do a play this year. I think this sounds perfect for them. It's a terrific history lesson, not only for the kids but the community, and even farther."

"That's what I've been thinking about," Andy said. "It's important to have a big crowd, and not only residents of Covenant Falls. If we are going to do this, we have to start marketing to towns around us."

Louisa agreed. "Any ideas?"

"Why don't we divide tasks? We have marketing, writing, sets and lights, costumes. There's probably others that will come along. But why not recruit people to lead those things and they can appoint whoever they might need? Then the chairs of each group can meet every week to exchange progress, ask questions, make suggestions."

"I like that," Louisa said. "But there should be someone coordinating everything." She looked at Andy.

"Oh, no," Andy exclaimed, shaking her head. "I don't really live here. I probably won't even be here in six weeks."

Faces fell. "But you have to stay," Sara said. "You started this and..."

Her voice tapered off.

Louisa nodded, and they both stared at her with betrayal in their eyes.

"Isn't Nate doing that?"

"He's overall chair," Louisa said. "But he has his own business and the inn to look after. I don't think he has time to keep up with everyone involved in every project and what's going on every day and transmit it to the others." She looked expectant.

How could she even be thinking about it? It was

idiotic. She knew nothing about plays. Organization, yes. She was very good at organizing operating rooms in godforsaken places. But...

More time with Nate. Wise? No. Oh, what the heck! She nodded.

CHAPTER TWENTY-THREE

ANDY DROVE HOME after having dinner with the Monroes and Louise.

It was too late to attend the vets' meeting, and she was tired. She'd had little sleep last night and today, well, today had been busy.

Al had been gracious. He asked questions that indicated he had some doubt about the project, but he hadn't opposed it...

She was still in shock at Sara's suggestion that she coordinate a mammoth project after being in town for such a short time.

It was as if a group of fairies or gnomes or other magical creatures had taken over her life.

Still, she knew her back was straighter, her mind clearer, her heart more open. She had a purpose. She had people depending on her, and she wasn't running from it.

"We are going to celebrate," she told Joseph as she reached the cabin and viewed it with new appreciation. It was no longer just a haven. It was becoming home.

But it *wasn't* her home. She had to remember that. She only had it on loan.

Some of her enthusiasm drained away. Then where would she go?

Her phone rang.

She sensed who it was before she answered.

"Hi," Nate said. "We missed you at the vets meeting, but I hear you're taking over the pageant."

"Under you," she said, "and I really don't know how it happened."

"I do. Everyone likes you. Not everyone here likes everyone else."

"I haven't noticed," she said.

"You will." He paused, then said, "Would you like to have our first business dinner tomorrow night?"

"At Maude's?"

"Nope. At the inn. You haven't even seen the place you named. We're testing out menus."

"I'm now a taster as well as errand person?"

"A taster, yes, an errand person, no. Sara is so elated she called me and raved about you. You know how to listen," he continued. "It's a rare talent to listen and hear and understand. Sara's become a different person since you got her involved."

Andy didn't know how to take that. She'd been trained to listen. To doctors. To patients. To other members of a medical team. It wasn't anything special, but pleasure still flooded through her.

"I would really like to see the inn. I drove by it but haven't seen the inside. I feel a kinship since I named it."

"And so you should. Is seven okay? I'll pick you up."

"Sounds good."

"I'll see you then," he said and hung up.

Andy held the phone for a moment. What was she doing? Yet she'd found herself saying yes. And worse, it hadn't even occurred to her to say no.

She reminded herself she was here for weeks, not months.

She could handle it, she reassured herself. It was only dinner. She went back to the second journal. Would it tell her if Angus had fallen in love with his Ute wife?

She read again until she fell asleep on the sofa with Joseph curled up next to her...

TUESDAY SPED BY. She met again with Louisa and Sara, and the three of them selected more excerpts.

More and more people called to say they'd heard about the pageant, and Andy started a list.

She had lunch with them, then went by the community center. Bill was busy looking through boxes. He, too, had been queried all day by residents. Wanting more information. Unfortunately, information was scarce.

Then it was six. She and Joseph returned to the cabin. She couldn't wait to tell Nate about the latest entries and Louisa's excitement.

She headed for the bedroom and her limited

wardrobe. Exactly what did one wear in Covenant Falls for a formal date, even to an empty inn?

She already felt a flutter deep in her stomach, the ache of anticipation. She opened her closet and stared at the few garments. *Dismal.*

She selected a pair of navy blue pants and a light blue fitted blouse she'd found at the general store and looked at herself. She really needed something else. She looked in the small velvet pouch in which she kept her few pieces of jewelry: a necklace she had found during a brief trip to Greece when stationed in Germany, a bracelet her mother had given her when she graduated from college and finally the ring Jared had given her but that she had never worn except the few times they were able to leave the base. She hadn't been able to look at it since the attack. With a new stab of anguish, she returned everything to the pouch. This was a business dinner.

But the bracelet reminded her she hadn't called home.

She picked up the phone and dialed her mother's number. She heard the tremulous voice. "Mom," she said.

"Andrea—" her mother's voice was worried "—are you…are you okay?"

"I'm fine," she said. "Everyone here is friendly, and I'm involved in a city project. I just wanted you to know I'm doing fine. I'm…happy."

The moment she said the word, she knew it was true. She *was* happy. Excited. She still had black moments, the sudden, unexpected assaults of grief, but they were coming less often.

"When are you coming home, baby?"

She felt as if she was ten years old again, loitering at the library when she knew she should be home. "Not for a while. I have to finish what I started. But I love you, Mom."

"Love you, too, baby."

Andy clicked the phone off and dressed, finally picking up the jewelry pouch again and taking out the necklace. She put it on, then applied some lipstick.

"What do you think?" she asked Joseph, who barked happily at the attention.

The doorbell rang. Joseph rushed to inspect the intruder, then wriggled with delight when he saw Nate.

Andy thought she might be doing the same. Her heart was bouncing wildly about.

She went to the door and opened it.

Nate looked great. He wore a pair of jeans that fit his tall, lean body as if designed just for him. A light tan suede jacket was worn over a dark brown shirt open at the neck. His hair was wet, as if he had just come out of a shower, and that sent sensual images through her mind.

It didn't help that his eyes, which always seemed to change color, looked at her with an intensity that sent her blood racing. They were a molten mix of light brown, gold and moss green.

"Hi, there," he said as he stooped down and made Joseph a very happy dog by rubbing his ears, then running his hand down his back. Staid Joseph made a spectacle of himself by twisting his body around in excitement, then plopping on the floor and raising all four feet in the air while Nate rubbed his belly.

"Now, that is just plain disgusting," she said. "He doesn't do that for me."

"It's male bonding," Nate said with a grin.

She laughed. She couldn't remember when she'd last laughed with spontaneity.

She reached for a folder of Angus's entries and started for the door.

"You might need a sweater," he said. "I heard a cold spell is coming. We get some of those in the spring."

"I'll be okay," she said. "I like cold."

He nodded. That was what she liked best about him. He never questioned. He reached out and took her hand. It was warm and strong without being controlling. She didn't object when he opened the door of the pickup for her. She put the folder on the floor and stepped inside.

He turned and looked at her. "You're damn pretty."

She didn't think she was. She'd been startled when Jared had fallen in love with her. Now she wondered whether it wasn't the danger and fear and emotion that brought them together.

Nate drove and she watched him. His ex-wife had to be one of the country's biggest fools.

They reached the inn. The sign wasn't up yet, but the exterior looked appealing. Rustic with a touch of elegance. It resembled a sprawling ranch house with an exterior of cedar siding. There was an archway that led inside.

As they entered the lobby, her gaze was drawn to a huge natural-rock fireplace that took up one side of the room. The smell of hickory came from a large burning log.

The room looked warm and welcoming with its leather chairs and sofas. The reception desk resembled an Old West saloon bar. A very large painting depicting the mountains hung over the fireplace, and several obviously well-used saddles were mounted along the wall.

"We're not quite finished yet," he said, "but what do you think?"

"I love it." And she did.

"I'm trying to find a painting of camels to go over the reception desk, but so far no luck. I was thinking about commissioning one if I can find the right artist at the right price."

"There has to be a starving artists' website," she said. "You can ask for samples and sketches. It probably won't be great art, but you don't need that. Just good art that attracts people."

"I knew I invited you here for a reason," he said

as he leaned down and kissed her. It was a light kiss but there was a promise in it.

"Hi, there" came a cheerful voice, and Andy forced her gaze away from Nate to a very pretty woman probably in her early forties who stood in the doorway off the reception desk. She wore a simple but tasteful white blouse with a black skirt that showed off very nice legs.

Andy noticed all this within a second of seeing the woman and resented the jealousy welling up inside.

Nate put an arm around her shoulder. "Andy, this is Susan Hall. She'll be managing the inn. Susan, this is Andy Stuart, the creator of the name the Camel Trail Inn."

"It's a great name," Susan said. "I love it, and it's attracting attention. We're already getting queries." She looked at Andy. "Like to see the website? It's pretty basic right now." Andy nodded, and Susan went to the registration desk computer. The background of the home page was a photo of the waterfall with a rainbow just above.

There was also a sketch of the front of the inn. Opposite the photo were two sentences in a rustic typeface: Opening Soon. The Camel Trail Inn in historic Covenant Falls, Colorado.

At the bottom of the page she read, "Visit our historical falls, our national forest and old mining towns. Make reservations now." A phone number was listed and there was a link to a registration form.

"Right now I'm trying to pique interest, but we need copy about the town and the falls and Angus. Not much, but some," Susan said.

Andy suddenly realized that was her main job here: a short history. She'd become so involved with the play that her original job had flown out of her head.

She looked up at Nate. "I forgot…"

"You're steeping yourself in the history of the town, and I think you have far more to do than you ever imagined. Than I ever imagined. Susan thinks the pageant is a terrific idea."

Susan nodded. She looked at Nate and then Andy. "I'm heading home. Ethel has dinner ready for you. It's one of the options on the menu, so you two can taste test it for us." She grabbed a purse from behind the registration desk and started for the door, then turned back. "I'm so pleased to meet you, Andy. I've heard a lot about you. Welcome to Covenant Falls."

Andy watched her go, envious of the way she wore her clothes and her stylish haircut.

Nate caught her hand. "You haven't seen it all yet," he said. "But first, the dining room."

The moment she stepped in the dining room, her mouth watered.

"Homemade bread and rolls," he said.

The room was not large. Three sides were paneled and the last was a wall of windows that faced the mountains. The tables and chairs were oak. Small, intimate tables, but they were square so they could be moved together to seat large parties. Fixtures looking like Tiffany gas lamps were mounted along the two sides of the room as well as smaller ones on each table. A chandelier hung from the ceiling. It was simple, uncluttered. She turned to him. "It's wonderful."

He grinned. "Well, we knew what we wanted." He reached out his hand. "May I escort you to our table?"

"You may," she said. His hand felt comfortable in hers. Natural. He led her to a table in front of the window. It was already set for two with wineglasses and an open bottle of wine in the center.

As they sat, a buxom woman hurried in with a basket of rolls and a dish with butter.

"Mr. Nate, are you ready for me to bring in the food?"

"Where did the mister come from?" he asked.

"Well, since I'm working for you…"

"One more mister and I'll fire you. Josh will feel the same. You're family, Ethel." He turned to Andy. "Meet Ethel Jones. She used to babysit me. I loved it, because she always brought something tasty with her.

"And this is Andy," he told the woman.

Ethel beamed. "I've been hearing fine things

about you. It's a pleasure." Then she hurried out before Andy could answer.

Nate poured the wine. "No liquor license yet," he said, "so don't tell anyone."

"Lawless, huh?"

"Yes, especially when I have a pretty woman with me."

"Susan is attractive." She knew she sounded jealous but she couldn't stop the words from coming out.

"Yeah, and she also used to babysit me when I was young. Of course, she was young then, too." His eyes met hers. "We're friends, and that's all. We were lucky to get her. How is the wine?"

She took a sip. It was a white. Crisp and cold. "I like it."

His eyes caught hers. They were intense, the green in them more pronounced. He hesitated, then words seemed to explode from him, "I know this probably isn't the time, but damn, I can't help but saying it. I like *you*. A lot." He hesitated. "I know you're still…raw, and I never believed in, well, instant attraction, and it's probably too fast…" He stopped, then continued, "Hell, I'm rambling and you probably want to run out the door."

"No," she said slowly. "That's the last thing I want to do."

"That's good enough for me," he said.

Ethel returned with two steaming plates. They both had rainbow trout—whole, with the exception of the heads—and the tender white meat had been loosened around the bones. A mound of mashed potatoes with a puddle of butter in the middle and a medley of vegetables completed the meal.

She took a bite of trout. She identified garlic but there were other spices in a butter-lemon sauce. The potatoes also had spices, including a touch of pepper and cheese. The vegetables were fresh and slightly seared. "It's wonderful," she said.

"We want to keep it simple."

"You've sold me. Can I move in?"

"You haven't seen the bedrooms yet."

"No," she said as she took the last bite of mashed potatoes. "And I think I should finish the inspection…"

They took about two bites of the apple pie Ethel brought.

"I can't eat another thing," she said. "It was really, really good. I would come back just for the pie."

He stood and went to the kitchen, came out with two boxes and they put the rest of the pie in them. "I told Ethel it was beyond expectations, and that she could go home. I said I would clear up the dishes."

"She didn't question that?"

"Well, I think she kinda figured we might like to be alone."

"The whole town will know tomorrow."

"With most people, yes. I don't think so with Ethel. Do you care?"

She did. She didn't.

She stood and took his hand to see the rest of the Camel Trail Inn.

CHAPTER TWENTY-FOUR

NATE WONDERED HOW wise he was to show her the rest of the inn. Flames had ignited between them at dinner. They had been building, slowly but surely, from the moment they met.

He'd never felt this way before, not even with Margaret. Maybe especially with Margaret. With her, it had been teenage hormones, then trying to hang on to something when he was sent overseas, then a stupid one-night stand that had ended in disaster.

He hadn't thought magic, the kind Clint and Josh had found, existed for him. He certainly hadn't believed in love at first sight.

He took her good hand and her fingers closed around his. He led her out of the dining room to the hall that ran the length of the building. The air between them was fraught with tension and heat and emotion. He felt it in the way her fingers tightened against his. She stopped, looked up at him. Her gray eyes were smoky and wondering, and he sensed the same emotions that were running through him.

He leaned down and his lips brushed hers. Her

mouth opened to him with uncertainty, then a need that echoed his. He knew her well enough now to understand that survivor's guilt was still like a knife in her.

As much as he wanted to pursue the kiss, he gently withdrew and put his arm around her. "Come see the rest," he said in a voice he hoped was companionable rather than thick with wanting.

He tried not to notice the clean fresh scent of fawn-colored hair, which seemed to glow in the bright hall light, or the warmth of her body as he led her to the first room in the hall and put a key in the lock.

"No key card?" she asked.

"We decided on old-fashioned keys," he said. "Less convenient, but they seemed more in keeping with the atmosphere."

She stepped inside and was instantly charmed. It was obvious from the substantial oak furniture, rich tan drapes that were open to views of the mountains and the high headboard banked with pillows that it was designed for both comfort and the Western aesthetic. A large painting of the mountains hung over a desk. A horseshoe was nailed above the door and the lamps were of the same Tiffany style as in the dining room.

She turned to him. "Did you design it?"

"With Clint's help. He's a genius with computers. He found every wholesale outlet in the country. We kept looking until we found the look we wanted at a price we could afford."

"It looks like you," she said.

He looked at her questioningly.

"Strong, honest, comfortable."

"Sounds boring," he said.

"Nothing boring about it," she said, touching his face with her fingers. "It's rather rare, I think."

He wondered then about the man she'd lost. He wanted to ask more about him, but her gaze held a disquieting intensity, as if she could read *his* every emotion while deciding whether she could share her own. And then something changed in her face. An acknowledgment—maybe even acceptance— of what was passing between them.

Don't push. It was the hardest thing he'd ever done.

The room seemed to grow warmer.

He felt a tightening in his groin, but he had felt that far too often in the past few days. Now, however, all he wanted was to be next to her, to feel her relax against him, to know she trusted him.

He saw pain in those smoky eyes, pain and passion and guilt and need, and his heart ached for her. And for himself. But still, something subtle had changed between them tonight. The attraction between them was like a shifting river current.

Then her eyes lightened, as if some decision had been made. She reached up on her tiptoes and kissed him, this time without reservation.

The questions in his mind dissolved.

He smothered her lips with his, and his hands moved up and down her back. Her body shuddered, and his arms wrapped her close. Their lips parted. She rested against his heart. She must hear its quickened beating.

He was awash in need. He ached. He wanted her with every fiber of his being…

ANDY LOOKED UP at him. His eyes regarded her with so much tenderness her heart melted. How safe she felt with him! Not physical safety—she could take care of herself that way—but she knew to the depth of her soul that he would understand and protect who she was inside. In this short time, she sensed he knew her better than anyone had. Even Jared.

Everything with Jared seemed surreal now, an out-of-place time when emotions and feelings ran at warp speed.

This was real.

It's too soon to know that, the gremlin inside her whispered, but more powerful feelings were ruling her now.

For the first time in months, she felt like Andy Stuart, the girl who'd fought her way out of the West Virginia mountains and the woman who'd battled her way to one of the best surgical teams in the army. Without her realizing it, Nate had guided her out of the darkness that had enveloped her, had showed her that, crippled hand or not, she was of value.

"Thank you," she said.

"For what?"

"For knowing me better than I did," she said.

The corner of his mouth turned up in a smile. "I'm not sure that's true."

She touched his cheek, ran her fingers over the strong angles of his face, touched the thick eyebrows that framed his eyes and then moved down to his lips.

How could it become so familiar so quickly?

"It's fast, I know," Nate said, obviously reading her mind.

For the first time she didn't mind. It didn't feel like such a short time. She knew him better after a week than she had Jared after many months. The realization was like a kick to the stomach. How could she…?

She just looked at Nate. She knew he read the sudden dismay there. He leaned down and kissed her lightly. "I should take you home."

She didn't make a move and swallowed hard. "I don't want to go."

"You're arguing with yourself," he observed as one side of his lips quirked upward in a half smile. "I didn't believe anything could happen this fast, either," he added. "But I've taken a fierce fancy to you."

"Now, that sounds like something one of your

ancestors might say," she said, trying to lighten the tension. "In fact, I think you should portray Angus in the play." She took his hand in her good one, turned it faceup and studied it with her index finger, mainly because if she watched those lips much longer, she would collapse in his arms.

But looking at his hands didn't help. His fingers were long and the palms callused. She wanted to feel those fingers caressing her face again.

"I'm not an actor. I'm a backstage guy," he replied as he nuzzled her ear.

He was anything but. She'd watched him take charge of meetings and projects and now she'd just seen his talent at building and design. He led without anyone realizing it. It was a rare talent: to make everyone feel that what they were doing was their own idea.

He had done that with her.

His arms slipped around her, and her good fingers moved to the back of his neck. She stood on tiptoe and lifted her head so she could touch his lips with hers.

He kissed her again, long and tenderly, so tenderly she thought she couldn't bear it.

Then he backed away. "I want you more than I've ever wanted anyone," he said slowly. "But I didn't... I...didn't expect... Dammit, I've messed this up."

She had never seen him uncertain before. It endeared him even more to her. "Why?"

"I didn't bring any..."

He stopped, and she understood.

She remembered what he had said about his wife. About the baby that never was, the one that forced him into a marriage he didn't want.

She started to pull back. He held on to her. "It's not for me," he said. "It's you. I care too much to hurt you. I don't know how this happened, but I think I fell in love with you the moment you stepped out of your Bucket. It scared the hell out of me. It still does." He paused. "I want this to be right for you."

She touched his face. Ran her fingers over its angles, then through the thick chestnut hair. She wanted him. He made her feel safe and warm and wanted. And alive. She needed that.

She didn't want him to be right, but he was. It *was* too early to take chances. She couldn't trust her emotions now. She had been in a pain-filled world for months. She still heard Jared's voice, saw his face. Saw all the faces of those who were there that day, and then weren't.

She leaned her head against his heart. "He saved my life," she said. "He moved in front of me. He took the bullet meant for me. He died. I lived." She swallowed hard. "How could I forget..."

"You didn't forget. You will never forget," Nate said.

She wished she could feel that way. But she couldn't. Not yet. It still felt like betrayal.

Home. "I have to go," she said. "Joseph…"

She heard his cell phone chime.

He pulled it out his phone, looked at the caller, then answered. "Nate." He listened, then replied, "Okay, I'll head over there." He clicked off the phone as she looked at him.

"Something wrong?"

"Nothing I can't take care of. A truck carrying lumber for a construction job was hit by another vehicle. The boards are all over the road, and the truck is disabled. I have to round up a truck and a crew to get the boards before they are taken by the county as a road hazard."

He paused, then added, "We start the job this week, and we need the lumber at the project."

"Where's Josh?"

"He's on his way to talk to the police out there and figure out who was at fault. The last thing we need is a lawsuit."

She wanted to help, but she wouldn't be much use in carrying boards.

"I can walk home," she said.

"Hell, no," he said. "I can call some guys while I drive you home. It's only five minutes."

She didn't question him more. She knew she would only delay him if she argued. She grabbed her small purse from the bed where it had fallen and headed for the door. "Ready?"

He chuckled. "Now I know why I like you so

damn much." He followed her to his car even as he was calling around.

He ended the call as they reached the car. "Craig is getting some of the vets together." He sighed. "I hope none of the lumber was damaged."

He made another quick call, apparently to Josh, and she heard him explain he had a crew on the way. "I'll meet you there," he added. "It'll be about twenty minutes."

He replaced the phone in his pocket and opened the door on the passenger side.

Nate was all business now as he drove out of the parking lot. In minutes they were back at the cabin. "Don't get out," she said. "I can get into the cabin. I see Joseph at the window."

He just nodded. "I'm sorry. This is not how I wanted to end the evening."

"I had a lovely dinner and a great evening," she replied as reached over and gave him a quick kiss, then was out the door. She walked rapidly to the porch and opened the door, then watched him drive down to Lake Road.

She unlocked the door to the cabin and Joseph was ecstatic. He made little grunting noises of welcome, rubbed against her legs, then reached up and licked her hand.

She sat down on the floor, folding her legs beneath her, and hugged him. "I missed you, too," she said, ruffling his thick fur. "What did I almost do tonight?" she asked as much to herself as to him.

She closed her eyes. Remembering the sweetness of the kiss. The unexpected reaction of her body.

Images of Jared darted into her head. The last time they were together. Two nights before the attack.

She looked down at her hands. They were trembling.

She stood. Wobbly. But standing. She walked to the back door to let Joseph out, but he wouldn't go. He just stayed at her side. She took the step down. Joseph regarded her with a worried look, then did what he was supposed to do before going to bed.

The air was cool but fresh. She took a deep breath.

Why now?

Andy felt weak, hardly able to walk back into the bedroom. She stopped at her bed, took off her clothes and lay down. She looked at the medicine on the table beside her. It had helped in the hospital.

But she wasn't in the hospital. She was getting on with her life.

She sat on the bed, then stretched out. Joseph crawled up beside her and put his head on her chest. He stared at her with those wide, kind, unblinking eyes.

Think of tomorrow.

Maybe she could do that now.

CHAPTER TWENTY-FIVE

ANDY SPENT A restless night. As much as she tried to think ahead, the onslaught of the all-too-painful memories last night lingered. She'd feared having another recurring nightmare...

She worried about what had brought them about. The kiss? Her growing attachment to Nate? Guilt?

At first light, she gave up on sleep and brewed a pot of coffee. She filled a thermos, opened the door for Joseph and started up the path to the lookout on the mountain. She didn't bother with a leash. Joseph wasn't going to leave her side and she doubted she would see anyone this early.

Once there, she sat on the rock overlooking the town and watched as the sun filtered through scattered clouds and painted streaks of gold across the lake. She continued to watch as cars started to move through the streets.

Andy tried to pinpoint Nate's house from here, but she wasn't sure she found the right one. She looked for color; Nate had made light of the many roses in his yard, claimed that taking care of them was part of his rent, but she knew roses. Her mother grew them. They took time and tender loving care.

Another side of Nate. She was always finding new ones. He was far more complex than he'd appeared the first day they'd met.

She took a deep swallow of coffee. It was strong, the way they drank it in the army. She rested against the rock, listened to the birds trilling their morning song and put her hand on Joseph's thick fur. He looked up and gave her a big dog smile.

The leftover tension from last night's flashback gradually faded away as the sun burned off the early-morning dew and a fresh breeze stirred the tall pines. Darn if she wasn't falling in love with this place. And that wasn't a good thing.

Andy took a deep breath. She had to start thinking about the future, something she'd refused to do before coming to Covenant Falls. She hadn't wanted to think about a life without Jared, the army or nursing. But her stay here was temporary. The fact that she liked it more each day didn't change that.

She still had to get a paying job, visit her mother and sister and plot a new course. Covenant Falls was a temporary refuge, nothing more.

Joseph whined next to her. At least *he* was hers. She didn't know how she could have survived without him.

Activity increased in the town below her.

Toy cars were moving among toy houses. So untouched by violence. So different from the violence thousands of miles away. She tried to push the memories away, but they kept returning. Why Jared? April? Britt? They had been all about saving lives. It hadn't mattered whose.

Joseph uttered a low rumbling noise.

"No good answer, huh," she said. "Then, tell me this—what should I do about Nate?"

Joseph wagged his tail. It wasn't very helpful.

Every time she thought about last night, her body ached for something that went beyond a kiss. She'd felt alive last night, really alive, for the first time in months, and that felt like a betrayal to those who died.

And then there was his own past.

She knew from the way Nate touched her that he cared. But she couldn't help remembering the flatness with which he mentioned his ex-wife, the betrayal he'd felt. She wasn't sure she could love so strongly again, and to do less would be a disservice to him.

The brochure, Andy reminded herself. She had to get started on the town brochure. The event had taken over everything. She reluctantly stood and Joseph rose with her.

Back at the cabin, she made breakfast—toast and eggs and coffee—then she jotted down some notes for the brochure, picking out various phrases from the journal entries.

Her mind was not being cooperative. It kept skipping from the copy to her future to Nate.

He sneaked in her mind like a thief, stealing

all the common sense and reservations she had. Her heart warmed every time she thought of him, and yet there was caution, as well. She kept telling herself everything was too fast, yet she knew she wanted to see him. She wanted to finish what they had started. Then suddenly the scene in Afghanistan would flash through her head, and pain ripped through her again.

She was, quite simply, at war with herself.

She looked back at the first sheaf of papers that Sara had combined of the most important journal entries. *Tomorrow I leave my beloved Scotland.* She skipped ahead until she reached the entry with Angus's first impression of the place he would call eventually call Covenant Falls. She started writing.

"The loch is as deep and blue as the evening sky, as pure as those in my highlands. It lies at the foot of mountains that overlook the dry country through which we passed and is obviously fed by the snow that caps their tops. It is a beautiful, serene place, and I plan to stay and establish my trading post here."

Those were the words of Angus Monroe, who established one of the first trading posts in central Colorado. It went by the name Monroe until he saved the life of a Ute subchief during a time of friction between the American Indian tribes, the military and settlers. In appreciation, the Utes made a covenant with

Angus. They would protect Angus and every-one at the post. Angus was given the chief's sister as his wife.

Angus then named the post and the town he'd envisioned Covenant Falls.

Angus started a freight business, an extension of bringing in his own supplies. He bought camels from a circus, which had bought them from the US Army, to take supplies into mining camps. The camels made their way into the lore of Covenant Falls.

The Civil War tore the territory apart, and six of the men left to fight for the Union while one headed south to Texas. It was the beginning of a long tradition of service by the residents of Covenant Falls. Five of the seven did not come back.

Today, the town of Covenant Falls has grown from a one-man trading post to a town that boasts of warm hospitality, a spectacular waterfall and lake, a national forest and a living history...

She stood up and stretched. A start. It didn't sing, but she had something to work with. She looked at her watch. A little after 2:00 p.m. Where had the day gone?

The cell phone rang. Her heart raced as she saw Nate's name pop up. "Hi," she said. "Did you spring the lumber from police custody?"

"We did, thanks to Craig Stokes," he replied.

"I remember him," she said. "He helped me after your fall. He and his son."

"Well, I did well today, too. I went up the mountain path this morning, then worked on the brochure. It's not great, but I'm getting there."

"You might want to get together with Susan on the design," he said. "She has some photos, but you might want a few additional ones."

His voice was friendly. Businesslike. As if last night hadn't happened. As if flames hadn't flared between them.

"I'll do that tomorrow. I'm going over to Sara's tonight. The script committee is meeting again."

There was a silence, and she wondered whether he had been about to ask her out tonight.

"What time?"

"Seven."

Another silence. So that had been the plan. Regret flowed through her. Regret and maybe a little relief.

She wanted to see him. She wanted to be with him. She wanted to explore those feelings that aroused her. But she also knew it probably would mean making love. *Do I really want to go there?* "When do you start the addition?" she asked, trying to break the silence.

"Tomorrow morning at seven. We want to get it done so we can help with the pageant or whatever we're doing." He paused then added, "I'm beginning to wonder whether this was such a good idea after all."

"What particular thing?" she asked. "The play? Or…" She couldn't quite get the last word out.

He didn't answer that question. "I'll call you tomorrow," he said.

"Sounds good," she lied.

She put the phone down and stared at Joseph. She'd wanted more. The conversation had felt strained, but then why wouldn't it be? Neither of them was in a position to…have a relationship.

With a sigh, she turned back to the brochure.

CHAPTER TWENTY-SIX

LOUISA HAD SUPPLIED all the committee chairs with the proposal for the script. A narrator would read selections from the journal. Each selection would introduce a scene. It was agreed that the story should begin in Scotland, when Angus discovered his brother had left for America, and end with a celebration when Colorado became a state, a total of twenty-eight years.

She presented the group with the pages from Angus's journal concerning his wedding to Chiweta, the chief's sister, which would end the first half of the pageant. The second half would be about the Civil War and the fight for statehood.

Clint had agreed to work with Louisa on music for the production. Preliminary ideas included a hoedown with the wagon train segment. Perhaps a Scottish hymn at the death of the brother. A traditional Ute dance at one point was suggested by Louisa.

The meeting lasted nearly three hours, but they had a timeline, possible scenes and backgrounds. Craig would build the stage and work with kids from Louisa's drama class on props. Sets would include the shop in Scotland, the wagon train and the trading post and town.

Goal one belonged to the script committee—to write scenes that could be used to audition actors for the speaking parts.

When Andy arrived back at the cabin, her head was spinning. Three weeks ago, she had empty days and an empty life. Now she had had a schedule so full she had no idea how to get it all done.

It was a blessing. She had no time for memories. She fell asleep immediately Sunday night and slept until dawn. No nightmares.

When she appeared at the community center the next morning, Bill had already made a place for her. *His* place, really. He had surrendered his desk, provided her with one of the computers from the library and scrounged a file cabinet from somewhere.

"What about you?" she asked. "Where will you sit?"

"I don't need to be here," he said. "I basically open and close the place. I'm going to spend much of my time up in the museum. We really need to get that in order before we have those travel writers here, and I think you're going to be a little too busy to do it."

She wasn't sure she wanted to be the first person everyone saw when they came into community center, but he had gone to so much trouble she didn't have the heart to refuse. There was even a water dish for Joseph.

To her bemusement, volunteers appeared almost as soon as the center opened at 9:00 a.m. Word, apparently, had quickly spread that volunteers were needed. It seemed every resident in town wanted to participate, even though they knew few details about the project. They had all been sent to her.

As each volunteer appeared, she tried to discover their interests and talents and promised to turn their names over to the appropriate person.

With so many residents offering their help, Andy found herself liking Covenant Falls even more than she had. There was a spirit here that her town in West Virginia had lost. She spent more and more hours at either Sara's or the community center while Nate was busy sunrise to sunset at his construction site or the inn. Four days disappeared in in a flash.

And then they had five weeks until the pageant. After that, she should leave. She was healing. She had more confidence. The cabin should go to someone else.

She had to visit her mother. She had to find a future on her own.

That took her thoughts to Nate. She had not seen him since Tuesday night, although he had called each day. The conversation yesterday had been short and awkward. She knew he would be busy today, that there had been problems with the job, and that the construction business part of the partnership was paying some of the bills for the inn.

The phone rang and somehow she knew it was Nate. "I heard you're queen of the world," he said.

"More like the footman," she said.

He laughed. "What's happening there?"

"I'm being flooded with volunteers, most of whom are would-be actors and actresses. I'm trying to steer them to other committees."

"I can probably tell you exactly who they are," he replied and she heard the amusement in his voice.

"But I'm impressed how eager they are to do almost anything after I dash their hopes of stardom."

"Covenant Falls does that."

She changed the subject. "But I get failing marks on the copy for the brochure," she said. "I've been saturated with 'the event,' which everyone is calling it now."

"I have faith," he said. "I'm going to quit tonight around seven and try to make it to poker night. Will you be there?"

"Thought I would. I'm low on money."

She heard him chuckle. "Can I pick you up?" he asked.

"I'm just around the corner," she said before thinking, "and I expect both Joseph and I will need a walk after being inside all day."

"Okay," he replied. "It's just as well. I'm not sure when I can get there. If I'm running late, I probably won't have time to go home and change. I might be sweaty and uncouth."

"Already been there and done that, and I didn't even faint," she said. "I'm sure you've seen a group of rangers returning from three or four days in the field. I don't expect you'll be quite that uncouth."

"I'll try not to be." He hung up before she could reply, but her heart started humming. She suddenly realized that his offer to pick her up might have been an invitation, or a date, or something. She hadn't even thought of that until it was too late.

Would he expect to come to the cabin after the meeting? Should she ask him? Would they begin where they had left off before? Did she want to? *Yes!* She still ached inside whenever she thought of Saturday night. But did she really wish to start something that probably had no hope of a satisfactory ending?

She added up the reasons why she shouldn't. Her stay here was temporary. He was obviously wary of marriage. She was still too raw to make any kind of emotional commitment, and she had never just slept around.

A woman and toddler came in the door and headed straight for her. The woman introduced herself as Gail Simmons and said she'd had the lead in her senior play. Her son was a born ham, she added. She'd heard that they were looking for actors.

Mary was dark haired and slender and, if she could act, would probably be a good wife to Angus.

Andy took the name and contact number. "I'll call you about the auditions," she said, then added, "You know it's all volunteer?"

"Oh, yes," she said. "I just think it will be a great thing to bring more people to Covenant Falls. It's impossible to find a job here now." After she left, Andy looked into the top drawer of the desk. Maybe she would have a little time to cast a fresh look at the brochure copy. She took the several pages she'd written and photocopied them, then sat back down and tried to concentrate.

The front door opened and Stephanie stepped inside, a big dog with her. A pit bull, Andy thought.

"Hi," Stephanie said. "I came to see whether there was anything I could do and thought you might like to meet Braveheart. He's Clint's dog, formerly Eve's. We didn't bring him that first Saturday night you were here, but he's one of Eve's rescues and for some reason he really took to Clint, and Clint to him."

Joseph's tail wagged frantically when he saw Stephanie, but he looked more suspiciously at Stephanie's companion until he apparently decided the pit bull was on the approved list. Then he approached Braveheart, who trembled at first, but then let Joseph sniff him, and they sat down together.

Stephanie grinned. "You can't believe what Braveheart was like ten months ago. He was afraid of his shadow, and no wonder. He'd been used for dogfighting and thrown away when he didn't win. When Eve brought him to me, I didn't know if we could save him. Clint adopted him, and he's been staying with me while Clint has been taking the law enforcement program."

Andy leaned down and gently rubbed his ears. Braveheart's tail wagged.

"You're a friend now," Stephanie said approvingly. "I knew the dogs would get along. I came in to see whether there's anything I can do."

"I'm just a flunky here," Andy said.

"I don't think so. I hear you're rocking the world of Covenant Falls. Every place I go, I hear your name. No one else could have talked the Monroes into cooperating with this…"

"It didn't take much convincing. I think Sara Monroe was just waiting for an opportunity."

"But no one else recognized it."

Andy had no reply.

"Seriously," Stephanie said. "I really would like to help."

"Well," Andy said, "we might need Wallace, a dog," she said. "He seemed to be very important to Angus. And," she added with the slightest of smiles, "I think a camel or two has been mentioned."

"They spit," Stephanie said.

"I know. It's why the city passed a no-spitting ordinance."

"I remember," Stephanie said drily.

"Nick suggested it."

"Yes, he did," Stephanie said. Then she peered at Andy. "You're serious?"

"I really don't know if I am or not," she said. "Depends on the script and how far into Angus's life they want to go. But in the meantime, why don't you check on the availability of camels?"

"Okay," Stephanie said with a deadpan expression.

"But I'm leaving the final decision up to the scriptwriting committee. I've taken myself out of that activity. My job is to keep track of the committees and plain old pamphlet copy. Nate needs that soon."

"How is it coming?"

"The committees are great. They pretty much run themselves. But the brochure, not so well," Andy said. "A few paragraphs I've pretty much discarded. Volunteers for the pageant keep coming by, so I haven't been able to focus. I didn't know Covenant Falls was full of would-be actors and actresses."

"I could have warned you, but I've been told you're very diplomatic. I'm not good in that department."

"Everything *does* get around in Covenant Falls, doesn't it?"

Stephanie nodded. "Bothered the hell out of me in the beginning, but you get used to it. I had a problem last fall, an ex-husband from hell. You can't believe how protective this town was. Let me take care of it myself, but they had my back."

"That's good to know. But I don't have an ex-husband, and I don't plan to stay long. Just through the pageant. I don't want to take advantage of Josh's cabin."

"And then what?"

"I don't know."

"Have you thought about staying?"

"As I've learned, there's not many jobs around here, and I need one. I also should go home and see my family. I won't stay in West Virginia, though. Nothing there for a one-handed nurse."

"I don't know. You seem to do pretty well."

"The whole point of coming here was to get my act together," Andy said. "Thanks to all of you, I'm beginning to realize there *is* life after Afghanistan, but this is a bubble right now. I have to leave it sometime."

"You think?"

"You don't?" Andy retorted.

"I make a point of not giving advice," Stephanie said. "I'm too bad at taking it. So I'll shove off. I have some appointments this afternoon. Let me know if you need anything in addition to a dog and camels."

All the energy in the room seemed to leave with Stephanie.

At four, Andy realized she hadn't had lunch. She called Maude's and ordered a cheeseburger for herself and a hamburger, hold the bun, for Joseph. She would pick the order up. She really didn't want to run into anyone else and spend the rest of the afternoon answering questions. She just wanted to get away from everyone, eat in private, work on the brochure and get ready for the poker game.

When she reached Maude's, the order was ready.

Maude smiled, took her money and gave her a sack, then asked, "Say, you wouldn't have a cook in that play you're writing, would you?"

Andy groaned inwardly. "I'm not writing it," she said, "but why not? You might ask Eve."

A little bit of payback for Eve. She still didn't know how she had become so involved in the Covenant Falls, in the brochure, in the play. She suspected, though, that Eve was behind a lot of it.

ANDY LOOKED AT the clock. Ten to seven. Time to go.

She'd returned from Maude's, fed Joseph and herself and taken a long hot shower. She'd then listened to the news on a Denver television station. It was the first time she had consciously turned on the news since she'd arrived back in the United States.

After the shower, she dressed in blue jeans and her favorite shirt. Her heart pounded as she ran a brush through her short hair and added a touch of color to her lips.

"Come," she told Joseph, and he barked. Would she ever get used to the way he seemed to understand every word she said? He fetched his leash and waited patiently while she fastened it. He really didn't need one, but she was aware that other people might not know that. She walked at a fast pace to the community center and joined several of the guys who were also arriving.

"The card shark," said one of them, but there was no rancor or resentment behind the words. Good-natured teasing followed, and she relaxed. She was one of them. Rightfully here.

Josh was already there, along with Bill and Clint. The latter was getting his share of ribbing. "Out of school now?" someone asked.

"You bet, and you'd better watch your speeding in *my* town," Clint shot back with a big grin. "I'm going to be looking for you and that yellow pickup."

"Liked you better when you were a computer geek," said another.

They all made their way to the wastepaper basket full of ice and beer and grabbed one.

"Where's Nate?" Clint asked.

"He's finishing up at our work site," Josh said. "He and Craig said they would be a little late."

"No need to wait," Clint said. "I hear we have a ringer here. I want to see for myself."

All the guys looked at Andy and she gave them a mock salute.

"Always ready," she said.

Because Clint had missed a lot of meetings, he was given the honor of selecting the game. They were thirty minutes into the fourth hand when Nate and Craig arrived. Contrary to his warning, he'd obviously cleaned up. His hair was still damp and his jeans and T-shirt fresh. It was stretched against a very manly chest. Andy looked away.

It would have been a fine evening if she were not so aware of Nate sitting across from her, his gaze catching hers, his mouth laughing with hers at some terrible joke. The room seemed a lot warmer than it was when she'd first entered.

Her concentration was not the best, and although she won her share of hands, Craig was the big winner when the session broke up. Only then did she realize that the others were looking from Nate to her and back again.

Had she been so obvious? She was sure then that she was flushed.

As they gathered their nickels and cleared the table, an older vet looked at her. "What's all this talk about an outdoor show?"

She had no idea of what she should or should not say, so she reverted to the cliché that popped into her head. "If I told you, I would have to kill you."

Clint laughed and addressed the group. "What she's trying to say is no one in town, including those of us on the committee, knows exactly what we're doing. Right now, we're talking about an outdoor pageant based on Angus Monroe's founding of Covenant Falls. We're all operating on blind faith now, hoping everything will fall into place. Craig is asking for volunteers to build a stage and I want to talk to anyone who can play an instrument or sing. If any of your wives or kids or friends or neighbors are interested, there will be auditions next Saturday."

"It's really going to happen, then?"

"We hope," Clint said.

"Well, count me in," one of the vets said, and the others nodded their heads. They all piled their remaining nickels in their individual cans, packed them in a box and put it at the bottom of the bar. Covenant Falls was certainly the most trusting place she'd ever lived.

Several vets left and others stayed and helped clean up. Bill said he had to leave and asked Andy to lock up. She'd been given a key that morning, another case of blind faith. Covenant Falls seemed to thrive on it.

One by one the vets drifted out. Andy put the last chair to the side. She turned around. Nate was putting the remaining beers into the fridge. She realized she and Nate were the only two left. Well, two and a dog. Maybe that was what she'd wanted.

"Are we through?" she asked.

"Yeah, think so."

"Isn't the women's club going to be horrified to find beer in the fridge?"

"I think they are quite aware of the nefarious activities here on Monday nights," he said. "Would you and Joseph like a lift home?"

She should say no. She'd known what would happen if she lingered, but she'd lingered anyway.

"Just a ride," he said.

She nodded. "I think Joseph would approve of that."

He nodded. They left the room together and locked up. The park was empty tonight, the swings swaying slightly with the breeze coming from the lake.

The moon was almost full and the sky was filled with stars above the mountain peaks. Andy took a deep breath. The air was so clean, so fresh.

She closed her eyes with just the pure pleasure of it.

"This is one reason I came back," he said, and she knew he had read her thoughts. "I understand why Al wants to keep it this way. If it were possible, I would, as well. But we can't. We stay still, and we die."

"My town did," she said. "All that's left are people like my mother, who was born there and nearly everyone she loves is buried there. But unlike Covenant Falls, it has no chance of reviving. The mines ruined the beauty of the mountains. It won't come back."

"I'm sorry."

"Me, too. Not for my sake. But for the people trapped there." They walked to his pickup. Joseph jumped up and Nate held the door open while she stepped up into the passenger seat. Then he was next to her, and they were riding down Lake Road to the cabin.

CHAPTER TWENTY-SEVEN

ANDY HAD LEFT a light on in the cabin, and now it looked like a welcoming beacon. How quickly the cabin had become home.

She swallowed hard. Everything was happening so fast, and perhaps nothing as quickly as her feelings for Nate Rowland. She looked at him as he parked the car. Everything about him was relaxed. Easy. Comfortable.

Except...

Except for the way he made her feel inside. She was not comfortable at all with the way he made her blood warm and her heart beat faster.

Had Angus felt that way about Chiweta?

The thought was fleeting as Nate opened the passenger door and took her good hand to help her down.

He put his arm around her waist just as Jared had done when they were alone. She had relished the feeling she'd had when he did that, as if they belonged to each other...

"What is it?" he asked as she realized she'd come to a sudden halt.

"Nothing," she lied. But she fumbled with the

cabin key. He took it from her and turned it in the lock.

Then he stood there in the doorway, and she recalled his comment. *Just a ride.* She didn't want him to go and yet she felt guilt at that admission. Jared was still in her mind and heart. But so was Nate. New to it, but his presence was just as strong.

"Do you think Angus loved Chiweta?" she asked suddenly.

"Yes," he said. "He didn't have to marry her legally. According to lore, there was a Ute ceremony, and then three years later a traveling minister married them again legally. They had two daughters then. Isn't that in the journal?"

"I haven't read that part yet," she said. "I did read about the first wedding."

"The settlement was growing then," he said. "Chiweta was with child and I expect the newcomers had difficulty accepting a Ute woman whom they considered unmarried. A marriage was protection for them and their children. It still must have been difficult for both of them."

"I like him more and more," Andy said.

"From all the rumors over the years, he had a ruthless side," Nate said, "but I think almost anyone who succeeded out here in that time period was probably ruthless. There was a lot of land grabbing, and at one time the family owned a great deal of land around here."

"But he had his dream?" she said.

"I think that came later," Nate said thoughtfully. "From what I read in the excerpts, he didn't have many options after he sold everything in Scotland and traveled to save his brother. That was his original purpose, according to the journal. When his brother died, I rather imagine he wanted to build something that would be lasting, maybe for his brother, maybe for himself. Maybe for his children."

"Three, right? That's what is in his Bible. Could there have been more?"

Nate reached out and put his arms around her. "I doubt it. Never heard of any other." Nate studied her. "You're really becoming invested in him, aren't you?"

She nodded. "Reading the journal entries makes me feel as if I know him. He cared about people. He's beginning to feel very real."

"Remember, there could be warts there, too."

She looked up at him. "I sense ambivalence."

He leaned down and kissed her, almost reverently this time, and the sensations were warm and tender beyond anything she'd ever felt. She looked up into his eyes. Intense now. The green in them seemed even more pronounced. She lifted her good hand and traced his mouth with its wry smile and up to the faint lines around his eyes that told her his life had not always been easy.

Her arms went around his neck and his tightened around her shoulders, the warmth of them drifting through her body. Their bodies pressed together and she felt the restrained passion and strength in his. She trembled from its impact as they both stood there.

She wanted him. She needed him. She knew he wanted the same, and yet she knew he was restraining herself. "I said I was just driving you home," he whispered as if reading her mind.

"I know," she said, her innate honesty prompting the confession. "But we both knew…"

She didn't finish the sentence. His mouth came down on hers. His lips were smooth and strong and yet so very gentle. But then the gentleness turned into need that met her own.

His kiss deepened at her response and her body gravitated toward his. She felt him throb against her, and fires began to glow inside.

His body shuddered. He broke off the kiss. "Are you sure, Andy?"

"Yes," she said simply and knew she meant it.

"I do have protection this time."

"I thought you might," she replied. She might regret this tomorrow, but now it felt right. Very right.

Without any additional words, she led him into the bedroom, leaving Joseph outside as she closed the door. Nate slowly undressed her, then she slipped his shirt over his head. Her hands ran up and down his chest and lingered at the scar.

She leaned against him and memories were alive

between them. Still painful but somehow lessened in intensity by the sharing.

Then they were on the bed. She wasn't aware of which one of them had initiated the move. Or had it been in tandem?

He kissed her, so slowly, so tenderly she thought her heart would explode. "Sure?" he asked in a husky whisper.

"Oh, yes," she said, amazed at her answer and even more amazed that it was true.

He gave her that slow smile that always warmed her, then his hands caressed her body. Slow and seductive. He kissed her again, touching her lips with feather-like gentleness. His fingers cradled her breasts and moved downward, and she felt a warmth so sensual, so exquisite she could barely keep from crying out. He worked more magic as his hands moved down and touched the most intimate part of her body. The warm puddling inside turned into rivers of fire.

She was a mass of writhing nerve ends when he arched his body above and she pulled him down to her.

He entered her slowly, tentatively, and she moved shamelessly against him as she savored the feel of her body against his taut, hard one. He moved sensuously, slowly, like a dance building to a climax, each movement deepening the craving that was growing inside. Heat flooded her as his rhythm increased and he probed deeper and deeper until she thought he could go no farther, then bursts of pleasure rolled from her deepest core.

He collapsed on her and turned so they were side by side as echoes of sensations still rumbled through her.

He kissed her and she felt tears behind her eyes. She didn't know why. But then they started coming, trickling down her face.

"I haven't cried in a long time," she said.

"Are they good tears or sad ones?"

"Good, I think." Then in a stronger voice. "I know."

He smiled and it was one she thought she would always remember. "Then, cry," he said with a voice so tender it prompted more tears. He stroked her face while the tears came faster.

Nate just held her as they poured out for the first time since she'd woken up in the hospital after the attack. They came as she mourned Jared. She realized they were unlocking the grief and guilt bottled up inside.

Lying there, wrapped tightly in Nate's arms, she started to feel whole again. She would always have images of Jared, of the others, of that day in Afghanistan darting in and out of her head. She knew enough of PTSD to know that. But now maybe she could live with it. *Live.* Not just exist.

She held on to Nate while the tears dried. She stayed there when he stood. "Don't move," he said and left, returning quickly with a wet cloth and Joseph on his heels. Nate sat next to her, washed the tears from her face, then kissed her again. "You're beautiful, you know."

"I think my face is red, along with my eyes," she said critically.

"Doesn't matter," he said as she nestled in his ready embrace, resting her head against his chest. She ran her hands against his suntanned arms. There was so much strength in them, so much strength in him.

Nate looked down at her, concern in his eyes. Concern and a caring that made her heart melt. "I don't want you to regret anything."

She touched his face. Ran her fingers over the angles, then through the chestnut-colored hair. She wanted him again. He made her feel safe, and she'd needed that. But there was more. So much more.

Heat.

She'd had the latter with Jared. Lightning and thunder, too, but they'd never shared the easy companionship she'd felt with Nate since the day she'd arrived. There was the lightning, but there was also the soft evening sky.

Guilt struck her again like a rushing, swollen river. How could she…even think that?

Nate's arms tightened around her, and she realized he knew exactly what she was thinking. But then, he had since they first met.

She leaned her head against his heart. "I…"

"I know," he said softly.

"He saved my life," she said. "He moved in front of me."

He was silent for a moment, then his arms tightened around her. "For a reason," Nate said. "He wanted you to live. He'll always be a part of your heart. But there's room in there for others, as well."

"It's been so quick…"

"I've been told it happens that way some times," he said in a slow deep voice. "I saw it with Josh and Eve, then Clint and Stephanie. I didn't think it would happen to me. But the moment I saw you…"

"It took me a week," she said. "Almost."

He grinned. "There's them that are fast and them that are slow."

He stayed another hour, just holding her. He didn't promise anything.

She didn't want promises, and with that weird understanding of his, he seemed to recognize it. It was enough at the moment to talk of little things, the music they liked, the books they read and the dreams they'd had.

It was midnight when he finally dressed. They both had long days ahead, he with the construction job and she with meetings. She put on her long T-shirt she wore at night and walked him to the door.

"You think anyone…"

He reached down and kissed her. "I wouldn't lay odds against it," he said.

She felt her face flame.

"They'll pretend they don't," he added helpfully.

She shoved him playfully.

"I'll call you tomorrow when I finish up. Maybe we can have dinner at the Rusty Nail."

She nodded.

"No regrets?"

"No," she said and was startled that it was true.

ANDY WOKE AFTER a dreamless night. The sun was streaming through the window and she looked at the clock. Seven. Joseph looked up from his place at the end of the bed and crept closer, wanting a hug. "Ah, Joseph," she said, opening her arms as he inched into them.

She lay there for several more minutes, then rose. No nightmare. No dreams. She took a deep breath. What had happened last night? Magic? A huge mistake? Joseph gave her a big dog grin.

She quickly dressed in jeans and a shirt, fed Joseph, made coffee, then left for her morning walk up the mountain. Joseph gave up his usual dignified manner and ran in circles once they left the front door. They headed for the mountain trail. She would really love to go to the falls, but today was going to be busy. She had tonight to look forward to. Would the magic still be there?

The mountain had become her confessor, her comforter, her peace. It seemed especially beautiful this morning. The sky was bluer, the air fresher, the wildflowers brighter. Even Joseph seemed to have a special energy. Perhaps he had sensed that something had changed with her.

She didn't know whether it would last, whether something so fast could have staying power. Maybe it was like a display of fireworks. Spectacular but short-lived.

For a moment, grief struck her. "I won't forget you," she whispered into the air. "You were my first love." She remembered what Nate had said last night. Jared would always be a part of her. She took a deep breath.

A sudden breeze touched her face, ruffled her hair, but it didn't seem to rustle the trees. A bird sang a sweet note. She stood still.

Peace filled her. "You're here, aren't you," she said, and tears crept into her eyes.

Joseph whined next to her. She reached down and touched him. "It's okay," she said.

And it was. She looked down at the town. It looked different from the first time she'd glimpsed it. Then it was just a pretty town. Now she could pick out places that meant something to her, people who had befriended her in such a short time and the man who had given her a gift last night. They all had. They had believed in her when she didn't believe in herself.

"Goodbye, Jared."

She turned and left.

CHAPTER TWENTY-EIGHT

Two weeks passed in a blur. Andy didn't have time to think about the evening with Nate, nor did they have more than a few minutes together.

She missed the dinner at the Rusty Nail she and Nate had planned the night they'd made love in the cabin. The script committee meeting had lasted late into the night and she had to stay. It started a pattern that continued.

Time wasn't only *her* problem; it was also Nate's. He and Josh finished their construction job and immediately started building the sets for the pageant with Craig and other volunteers. They also had the inn and the tourism guests to consider.

Publicity for the pageant had already started. Reality struck everyone then. Covenant Falls was committed, and failure would really damage the effort to draw tourists or business to the town.

The pageant committee had originally planned to hold the pageant on Friday night to introduce Covenant Falls to the incoming tourism-related guests, but the committee had asked that it be changed to Saturday to draw a larger crowd and perhaps entice out-of-town people to come early and eat at Maude's or one of the saloons.

With the pageant moved one day later, Josh and Nate had to rearrange activities for their incoming guests. They decided to hold a dinner at the inn on Friday night. Entertainment would include Clint and members of the high school choir singing traditional American and Western songs.

Making things even more complicated, Nate and Josh decided to open the inn to the general public the week of the pageant. Requests for reservations had come in from people in outlying areas who'd heard about the pageant, checked the internet and found the Camel Trail Inn.

They dropped into the community center to tell her. "We decided it was better to have a packed inn than empty halls when the tourism folks arrive," Nate said when he and Josh dropped by the community center where Andy was stationed. "But it means additional work for Ethel and Susan, who are already shorthanded since nearly everyone in Covenant Falls is in the pageant or has some role in its production."

"I have faith," she said.

"I'll take some of it," he said.

"I also have news," she said. "Stephanie found two camels and decided to make them her contribution to the pageant. She either took us seriously or thought it a good joke on us. She swore, though, that they were gentle and would come with a handler. The script committee is, well, a bit puzzled about what to do with them."

The phone rang. Someone from the prop committee wanted to know about the weather next week.

"Should be good, according to the long-range weather report," she said. "I'm checking on it daily."

No sooner than she'd hung up, the phone rang again. She listened, then said, "I'll pass the suggestion on to the props committee. It's a good one, thank you." She sighed and looked up at Nate. "I seem to be the go-to person for everything between heaven and earth."

"What was that about the prop committee?" Nate said.

"The actor for the brother—Liam—wanted to make sure he would have a snake to bite him."

Nate started to laugh. "Since that's in the realm of my responsibility, I'll see what I can find in the way of deadly snakes. I do have some remarkably creative members of the high school drama club on my team."

"I think we can do without a real one," Josh said.

Nate grinned. "Josh has a reason for caution. He had a close encounter with a rattler at the cabin. It bit young Nick and Amos."

"The cabin? My— I mean, *your* cabin?" she asked Josh.

"Yeah, but not to worry," Josh said. "I think it had been hurt by an eagle or something and crawled under the porch. Eve shot it. No relatives that I could find."

"That's comforting," she said, but her tone wasn't quite as sure as the words.

"How are the programs coming?" Nate asked, changing the subject.

"Ah, the programs," she said. "I finished the copy with Susan's help. Eve approved it but you should take a look at it before we start printing them. Al's office staff will be printing them and handling the folding."

Josh shook his head. "I'll never understand how you charmed that old bas— I mean, pillar of the community."

Nate chuckled. "I think I know how. I ran into a few nurses in Iraq. You did *not* want to cross them," he said, then added, "I'll take a look at the copy, but if Eve approved, I'm sure I will. She's the boss on that aspect." He moved toward the door. "We have to go. We just wanted to make sure you weren't being overworked."

"I am," she said, "and the pay is really pitiful."

"But it put a sparkle in your eyes," Nate replied.

Josh raised one of his eyebrows. "I don't think it's the piles of paper that did it, my friend."

"Don't forget the snake," Andy said, smiling sweetly.

"Snakes and camels," Josh mumbled as the two men walked out. "They'll want pet vultures next."

"Great idea," Andy called from her desk.

After they left, she realized she was grinning like an idiot.

THE SCRIPT WAS still being written and rewritten. The first half was completed but no one could quite agree on dramatic elements in the second. Sara brought more entries from later journals. One mentioned Angus hiring a man to travel to Santa Fe, buy mules and bring back supplies. His name was Samuel Cates.

Sara said, "He didn't return from the second trip and everyone thought a gang of outlaws got him. It was sad. He had a wife and son. I think they left."

Andy decided to kill any mention of a mule train. "I really don't think Josh and Nate will go for it," she said. "Not with the camels munching their way through the streets."

Sara laughed. "I don't know how or where Stephanie found them, but they do add a certain..."

"Quirkiness?" Louisa, the drama teacher, offered.

"Welcomed or not," grumbled Al, who had wandered into the room. "Seems she should've asked."

"Kids will love it," Sara chided in a gentle voice.

They went onto another scene then, an emotional one in which Angus sends his daughters to school in the northeast, where there was less discrimination.

"Why not his son?" someone asked.

Sara shrugged. "From the photographs, he looked as if he could take care of himself. Maybe thought he could better handle it."

But he couldn't, and that was also included in the script.

At the end of the evening, they felt they had the last half of the pageant. There would be a lot of drama intertwined with the growth of the town, the coming of the Civil War and the loss of half the men who had lived in Covenant Falls and, finally, the fight for statehood.

After the meeting, Andy decided to stop by her "office" to run off copies of the script changes. The entire cast was meeting the next day. She glanced at her watch. It was nearly ten and the building was empty.

She was locking up when Nate drove up and stepped out of the car. His hair was rumpled. He wore jeans and a brown shirt with the sleeves rolled up. He looked so darn appealing she wanted to jump his bones right then and there.

But when she looked closer, she saw the lines in his face, particularly around his eyes. There was worry in them. She knew how much the upcoming weekend meant to him and Josh. They had bet everything on it, pouring even more money into production and promotion.

She stood up on tiptoes and kissed him.

"I have a bottle of wine," he said. "I've been driving around with it for the past few days."

Andy was tired, bone weary, but she nodded. She would much rather be with him than stay up reading until she fell asleep. That was what she had been doing to keep the old demons away. "I have the Bucket," she said. "I drove over from the Monroe house."

"I'll follow you," he said.

"You think people will notice?"

"I think they've already noticed."

She sighed. She knew all about the courtships of the previous occupants of the cabin. Why should she be any different?

Once at the cabin, Andy watched as he opened the bottle of wine. She took two glasses from the cabinet and then, without words, they walked to the sofa. He sat down, then pulled her down next to him. He put both arms around her and sighed, a long sigh. "You don't know how much I've wanted to do this," he said softly.

For a moment, she just closed her eyes and savored the comfort of his arms. They didn't need words. They had never needed words, she realized now.

She took a sip of wine, noting that it was very good. All the tension of the past few days faded away. She felt him relaxing, as well. "I know it's late," he said, "but I had this fierce need to see you. In fact, I've had it for several days, maybe even a week, and I restrained myself. It just quit today, that restraint."

"Good," she said as she ran her finger along the planes of his face. There was stubble there and it only added to his attraction.

"I didn't have time to shave," he said ruefully.

"I like it."

"Then, I'll let it grow. Look the part."

"There's not much time before the pageant," Andy said.

"You don't have to remind me. I feel like I'm on a runaway train."

"The play is good," she said. "Really good."

"I know. I attended the auditions. And the kids who are planning the props and sets are amazing. They're damned creative. They've begged a couple of covered wagons from a ranch that offers recreational wagon trail rides. They promised great publicity and huge crowds of covered wagon adventurers. One of the kids' fathers is a truck driver who has trucker friends, and they're going to bring them up here.

"And—" he grinned "—Stephanie's camels will arrive Thursday before the pageant. Temporary plans are to put them in Eve's corral and move her horses over to a neighbor's barn. Stephanie said the guy who's providing them is sending an attendant."

"Something tells me this is getting out of hand," Andy said after bursting out with laughter.

His arms tightened around her. "I could become addicted to that laugh."

"I think I'm addicted to *you*," she replied, startled by her admission. She kissed him. It wasn't a wildly passionate kiss like before. Instead, it was warm and tender and lingering.

"Then, it's a mutual addiction," he said when the kiss ended.

He rubbed her neck with his thumb and took a sip of wine.

Nate brought Andy's hand to his mouth and nuzzled it.

"Then what?" Andy asked.

She reached up and kissed him with a tenderness she didn't know was still in her.

"Wow," he said when she pulled back, then he studied her face. "Is it too early to say I'm falling in love with you?"

She looked up at him. "No. I think the same thing is happening to me. But I also think we should take it slow. I'm still raw. I'm better, but sometimes there's moments…"

"We'll go as slow as you want." He gave her the big grin she loved. "But then there's slow and then there's…maybe not so slow."

"I think there may be some leeway there," she replied after due consideration.

He led her into the bedroom. She trembled at the fierceness of her need. He undressed her, and she did the same to him, reveling in the hard, muscled body. She leaned against him and he kissed her with such tenderness her world shook. They sank down on the bed.

"I love you, Andy Stuart," he said as he took her slowly and with such care tears came to her eyes. But this time they were tears of wonder, not of pain.

CHAPTER TWENTY-NINE

IT WAS TWO days before the pageant.

Andy sat at her desk in the community center and planned her day, but Nate kept getting in the way.

Nearly two weeks had passed since she and Nate had made love, and he intruded into every thought.

He had stayed with her at the cabin until 2:00 that morning...

I love you.

She could barely wrap her mind around his words.

She tried to get back to business. The camels had arrived earlier today. They were accompanied by their handler, a wizened man named Murdoch.

She didn't have time to ponder the question of whether the camels were a good or bad idea. At any rate, they were written into the script. It was, Andy had to admit, one of the little historical oddities that brought added interest to Covenant Falls.

Word of the production had traveled by social media, thanks to Susan at the inn, and news releases went to newspapers around the state. The community center was flooded with calls asking about tickets. Andy finally recruited two women to answer and return those calls while she used her cell phone for other pageant business.

The sets were completed and their young creators were practicing moving them quickly. One set fell apart and she had to call Nate to repair it. Some of the costumes didn't fit, and the sewing-circle ladies were called in to make alterations. One actor sprained his ankle tripping over a prop. They were looking for a substitute.

It was midday when she received a frantic call from Maude. Camels were running down Main Street and residents were running for safety. The camels had apparently broken out of Eve's corral, and Murdoch had disappeared. Stephanie was in emergency surgery and couldn't be reached.

Andy sent someone to check the different bars and saloons in and around Covenant Falls. She couldn't think where else the man would go if he wasn't at Maude's. Then she headed for Stephanie's office, leaving Joseph in the care of a volunteer. She wasn't sure how he would react to camels.

There was a traffic jam on Main Street, probably, she thought, the first in history. One car had run into another while trying to avoid a camel. Maude hadn't been exactly right. The camels weren't running. At least not now. They were sauntering down the middle of the street, occasionally taking a bite off a tree. Two of the town's police officers were trying to lasso them, but the camels' heads were too high and the deputies didn't appear too competent at roping.

Andy hurried over to Stephanie's office. The tech met her. "Stephanie knows," her assistant told her, "but she's in the middle of removing a baby shoe from the stomach of a dog. She can't come now, but she said the camels' names are Martha and Sally, and they like bananas. She said if you offered them one, they will probably lower their heads so you can fasten a rope to their halter."

Muttering, "Thanks a lot," Andy left the office and met the officers who were looking baffled and holding useless ropes in their hands. "Have you tried going up to them?" she asked.

From the looks on their faces, apparently they had not. "I don't know if they bite," one officer said. "I don't know anything about camels."

"Go to the grocery store and get bananas," she told one of them.

"Bananas?" He looked at her as if she were crazy. "I didn't know camels liked bananas."

"Stephanie says these two like bananas, so they get bananas. Where's the chief?"

"Tom is rehearsing for that play. He said not to bother him no matter what."

Andy thought about countermanding that order, but Tom had one of the most important roles. And today was the dress rehearsal.

"You," she said to one of the officers. "Commandeer those bananas."

"How many?"

Patience. "A *big* bunch should do it."

He left while his partner stayed behind. Andy evaluated the camels. Did camels bite? She knew they spit. But these two elderly-looking ladies didn't look angry. Just kinda confused.

"Martha," she called. One of the camels turned around and stared at her. *What in the hell did you say to a camel?* Now she wished she had brought Joseph. He might have been able to herd them.

"Sally," she tried. The other camel turned around, looked at her, then came strolling over. The officer who'd stayed with her wore a look of total panic.

Sally looked at Andy with big camel eyes, then spit out some leaves, several of which landed on her right shoulder. Well, she'd had worse spit on her. Part of being a nurse. She just hadn't expected it to be part of being a coordinator or whatever she was now.

Undeterred, she caught the halter with her good hand and asked the officer to tie his rope to the halter. She hated to ask him, but her left hand just didn't have the dexterity to tie a knot. The camel didn't appear to object. In fact, she looked a little relieved.

Then she turned her attention to the other camel, who was staring at her.

This one didn't look as benevolent as the other. "Martha," she called again.

The camel lumbered toward her at the same time

the second officer returned bearing an armful of bananas. *Do they like them with the skin on or off?*

Just for safety's sake, she took two of the bananas, peeled off the skins and handed one each to the camels, who took them carefully between their almost prehensile lips. She held on to Martha's halter until the second rope was attached. She rubbed between Martha's eyes the way she rubbed Joseph's fur. The camel ducked her head for more.

She turned to the officers. "They're gentle as lambs, and they are all yours," she said. "Walk them back to Eve's ranch and stay with them until their keeper arrives. Tell him if he leaves again, you'll throw him in jail for creating a public nuisance."

"Yes, ma'am," one said.

Barely aware of the clapping behind her, Andy strolled back to the cabin, changed into an unsoiled blouse and returned to the community center, where she found herself confronted by two angry women.

The women of the Baptist church planned to sell hot dogs at the pageant to raise money for its missionary program. It seemed they had learned that the Methodist women were doing the same. They were told to come to her for a ruling. "I personally think popcorn would make you more money," she told the complaining party, a woman about her height and twice her girth. "Besides, it's a lot less trouble." They went away arguing over who would do popcorn.

She finally made it over to the high school auditorium and took a seat in the back. Joseph happily squeezed himself under it. The rehearsal was underway.

Today's rehearsal was a run-through of the play with costumes. Another would be held tomorrow at noon at the pageant site. The park would be roped off.

About ten minutes into the rehearsal, Nate slipped in beside her. "I hear you're now a camel whisperer."

"Things *do* get around in this town even faster than the speed of light," she said, giggling. She never giggled.

"You scared the hell out of the police officers. Jay and Leon were more afraid of you than the camels. They're in awe."

"That was my military nurse persona," she said. "You get pretty good at bossing even superior officers around."

He slipped his hand around hers as, on the stage, Clint joined members of the wagon train and started "Amazing Grace" while playing the guitar.

"He does have a fine voice," she said.

"You can hear him tomorrow night," he said. "He's going to be entertaining our guests at the inn. Some students, too. Will you go with me?"

"I would love it," she said, "but there seems to be

no end of emergencies and final details left. Maybe after…" Her voice trailed off.

Once the pageant was over, her reason for being in Covenant Falls was over. She had written the short history, helped with the pageant. She could function again. It would be time to turn the cabin over to someone else. Wasn't that the implied agreement?

"Okay," he said. "But we've been invited to Al's home Sunday night for a festive dinner, as he put it. He invited every committee chairman."

"I'm not a chair."

"You are the chair of the chairs," he said. "And if that's not good enough, chairs can bring a plus one."

"What if the pageant bombs?"

"Then we cry in our beer and wine at Al's expense, because we'll all be too poor to buy any."

The idea didn't seem to bother him. But then, nothing much seemed to unsettle Nate. "I accept," she said.

"That's great. I have to go. We've had some calls at the inn for reservations this weekend. We decided to book all but one room and save that one in case a last-minute tourist promoter appears. We have to finish up hanging paintings and a few final touches." His fingers tightened around hers, then he let go and left.

She watched him leave, then turned back to the stage. Maybe she was too close to it, but it was good. Really good. She checked her phone and found four frantic messages. She sighed and returned to the community center.

ANDY DIDN'T SEE Nate again that night, but he was at the noon dress rehearsal outside the community center at the picnic area.

The weather bureau promised sunny weather for the next three days, and the main set—the trading post facade—had been erected along with two large tents on each side. Two covered wagons were behind the community center, along with eight horses for the hitch. The camels were separated from them on the other side and secured to a post. Murdoch, having been threatened with bodily harm by Stephanie, stayed close to them.

Andy had bought a couple of bananas at the store and gave each camel the treat, then talked to them for a minute. They seemed attentive. Joseph had given her a new perspective on animals, both small and large.

She stood back and watched the play progress. She felt certain it was good, but then, she was prejudiced. The animals behaved toward the end. Louisa had indeed enticed the Ute dancing group to appear in the marriage scene between Angus and Chiweta.

All in all, it would be quite a spectacle if all went as planned.

If.

IT DID.

The pageant was better than any of them had expected. The churches had loaned them chairs, which filled up fast. Then a number of people brought blankets and settled down on the ground. There was hardly a vacant inch anywhere.

The sky was painted with a brilliant sunset as Clint strummed his guitar and sang a Scottish melody, "O'er the Sea," as the opening number.

Andy watched with a big grin as the camels appeared during a brief encounter between Angus and an outlaw who tried to steal them. The animals complained all the way, and Martha spit on Stephanie, who was leading the second camel. Much against her will, she was dressed as a camel driver with her hair piled under an old soiled cowboy hat. A duster hid her feminine body. Andy thought Stephanie would never, ever agree to anything civic again. If there was another pageant, Andy doubted it would include camels.

The choir's versions of "Wagon Wheels," "The Colorado Trail," "Oh Shenandoah" and "The Battle Hymn of the Republic" brought the audience to their feet, as did Clint's performance of "Amazing Grace" at the death of Angus's brother, and the state song, "Where the Columbines Grow," at the end.

The applause was thunderous when the pageant ended and even more when the cast was introduced and Sara Monroe brought on stage as author of the drama.

Sara looked beautiful. Her cheeks were flushed and her eyes sparkling as a member of the cast handed her a bouquet of roses. Andy watched as she walked off the stage and into the arms of her husband. Al Monroe beamed.

As Andy walked out, she saw a number of people heading for the donation boxes. A sense of pure joy and accomplishment flooded her as she watched happy people file out, all of them talking eagerly to each other. She suspected Maude was going to have a very good night.

She looked for Nate, wanting to share her excitement with him, then saw him. Dressed in Western casual, he was talking to a mixed group of men and women. When he saw her, he gestured for her to come over. She hesitated, aware of her ugly left hand and jeans. He gestured again and she went to him. "This," he said, "is the young woman who is the heart of this event. It never would have happened without her."

His eyes were warm with approval, with pride, and she felt as if she'd been handed the best present anyone could give her. She shook her head. "If there's ever been a community effort," she said, "this is it. I don't think there's one person in Covenant Falls that didn't have a part in this."

A tall, distinguished-looking man smiled. "I'm Neil Brock with the tourism bureau. I must confess, I'm astonished. Clint said you put it together in six weeks?"

"Nearly seven," she said. "The whole town put it together," she corrected.

"I'm certainly impressed," a woman chimed in. "I'm with a news syndicate, and I can't wait to tell this story. You *are* going to keep doing the pageant?"

Andy looked at Nate.

"We've been thinking of Saturday nights during the summer," he said.

"And you haven't seen our falls yet," Andy said. "They're pure magic."

"I'm certainly looking forward to it," broke in one of the men. "I had no idea you had waterfalls here. The entertainment last night was great, and the food... You really have a fine town."

Andy excused herself and left. Not knowing exactly what would happen tonight, she had left Joseph at the cabin. She was on the way out when Al Monroe stopped her and gave her a hug. "I didn't think it was possible," he said. "You gave my wife life again. Now she wants to write a book." He turned and looked at Sara with awe.

Andy finally arrived home at eleven. Joseph was there to greet her, rushing about as if she had been gone days rather than hours. "Everything will get back to normal," she said. Except that there was no normal. Not since she'd arrived in Covenant Falls.

It was too late, too dark, to go up on the mountain, but she took a lantern and went outside with

Joseph. She sat in one of the chairs and looked up at the sky. She couldn't remember seeing so many stars. Not even in Afghanistan, but perhaps then she'd been blinded by violence.

The pageant was over. She had done her part, what had been asked of her for use of the cabin. In doing so, she had found part of herself that had been lost.

It was time for her to leave. She had achieved her purpose. She would always have the horrendous images. She would most likely have nightmares and flashbacks. But now she thought she could manage them. She knew she could function again. The cabin should go to someone who needed it more than she did. She was sure Dr. Payne had another prospective guest. There was a lot of pain out there. A lot of injuries that couldn't be seen.

Reality hurt. She didn't want to leave Covenant Falls. She didn't want to leave Nate, but maybe she must if she planned to heal herself completely. Maybe she had just been in a bubble. She knew one thing. She had to get a job.

"What do you think, Joseph?" she said.

The dog made a sound like a plaintive cry.

"Can't say I disagree," she said. A decision was made.

THE DINNER AT Al Monroe's home was not what she'd thought it would be. She had expected a formal event and had not looked forward to it.

There wasn't champagne, but there was wine and beer. The menu included a large roast and roasted potatoes and grilled vegetables. But it wasn't the food that set the mood, it was Al himself.

He welcomed eighteen people with enthusiasm, thanking them for coming and congratulating them for what they had accomplished in the past weeks.

At the end of the dinner, he stood. "I was wrong," he said. "I was wrong in trying to keep everything as it was. Angus didn't do that. He invited people to his settlement. He was one of the first to call for statehood. He didn't fear change. He welcomed it."

He turned to Josh and Eve. "Thank you for bringing this town together in amazing ways." Then he turned to Andy and raised his glass. "I want to make a toast to the young woman who renewed the spirit of Covenant Falls, and that includes my family. Thank you."

The people in the large dining room exploded with applause.

Andy felt her face grow hot. And red. "It was a community effort," she protested.

"A young lady who invaded my office," Al continued, "and very nicely bullied me and encouraged my wife to do what she always wanted to do and I didn't know it, who stirred this entire town to work together for a common goal. It didn't happen until you came here, and I, for one, am grateful."

"Hear, hear," said Clint.

Everyone but Andy applauded. Her face just went rosier.

"So I wanted to do something for Covenant Falls. I want to keep Andy Stuart here. Eve and I joined forces, and we want to offer her a job as curator of our museum combined with executive director of our new chamber of commerce. The position of curator will be financed by the city and I'll pay for the chamber expenses. After looking at the museum, though, I wonder if she will accept."

Andy looked around, saw the smiling faces around and realized everyone else had known what was coming. She was speechless. She wasn't qualified. She was a one-handed nurse with PTSD.

At the same time, she started thinking of what she could do, the opportunities to build something. The museum was certainly a challenge. She'd always liked challenges.

"We won't put her on the spot," Al continued. "But the job is hers if she chooses to take it."

Clint stood up then. "I would like to make another announcement."

To Andy's relief, faces turned from her to Clint.

"Stephanie has finally agreed to a date. You're all invited to the wedding the first day of July."

A chorus of "about time" went around the table. Then they had strawberry shortcake with real whipped cream and, finally, champagne.

NATE DROVE ANDY HOME. She was still in a state of shock.

She'd made a decision earlier that day, and Al had just shoved a sword through it.

"What are you thinking?" he asked.

"I'm still too numb to think anything."

"It was Al's initiative," Nate said.

"You knew," she accused him.

"I did, but just since 2:00 p.m. today. I think Al and Eve were afraid you would leave before they could work something out."

"Did you know about Clint and Stephanie?"

"No. I don't think they planned to announce it yet. But I believe he knew you were uncomfortable and…"

Warmth filled her that someone would do that for her.

She liked Covenant Falls. She liked it very much.

When they reached the cabin, he walked her to the door. Joseph barked then wriggled all over when she and Nate entered. "I know you must be exhausted," he said.

"I have a call to make first," she said.

She dialed her mother's number. "Mom," she said when the phone was answered immediately. "I have a job. A great job, and I want you and my sisters to visit me. Maybe even, well… Covenant Falls is welcoming new people."

She answered the questions, then hung up and leaned against Nate.

She didn't have a decision to make now. She'd made it the minute Al mentioned the job. She didn't care what it paid. She wanted to stay here with people she liked and who liked her and thought her of worth. She loved her own personal mountain, and the people who had spent endless hours on a half-baked scheme. They'd made the impossible possible.

"I'm happy for Clint and Stephanie," she said.

"Me, too. Particularly for Clint. Stephanie was really gun-shy as far as marriage goes, but anyone who wasn't blind could see they were in love."

He took her in his arms.

"Maybe someday..." he said. She looked into those warm hazel eyes and understood exactly what he was saying.

She took his hand and led him into the bedroom. She knew, he knew, someday wasn't far away.

* * * * *

LARGER-PRINT BOOKS!

HARLEQUIN

Presents®

GET 2 FREE LARGER-PRINT NOVELS PLUS 2 FREE GIFTS!

PASSION
GUARANTEED
SEDUCTION

LARGER-PRINT BOOKS!
GET 2 FREE LARGER-PRINT NOVELS PLUS
2 FREE GIFTS!

H HARLEQUIN®

INTRIGUE
BREATHTAKING ROMANTIC SUSPENSE

REQUEST YOUR FREE BOOKS!
2 FREE NOVELS PLUS 2 FREE GIFTS!

Ⓗ HARLEQUIN®

ROMANTIC suspense

Sparked by danger, fueled by passion

YES! Please send me 2 FREE Harlequin® Romantic Suspense novels and my 2 FREE gifts (gifts are worth about $10). After receiving them, if I don't wish to receive any more books, I can return the shipping statement marked "cancel." If I don't cancel, I will receive 4 brand-new novels every month and be billed just $4.74 per book in the U.S. or $5.49 per book in Canada. That's a savings of at least 12% off the cover price! It's quite a bargain! Shipping and handling is just 50¢ per book in the U.S. and 75¢ per book in Canada.* I understand that accepting the 2 free books and gifts places me under no obligation to buy anything. I can always return a shipment and cancel at any time. Even if I never buy another book, the two free books and gifts are mine to keep forever.

240/340 HDN GH3P

Name	(PLEASE PRINT)

Address	Apt. #

City	State/Prov.	Zip/Postal Code

Signature (if under 18, a parent or guardian must sign)

Mail to the **Reader Service:**

IN U.S.A.: P.O. Box 1867, Buffalo, NY 14240-1867
IN CANADA: P.O. Box 609, Fort Erie, Ontario L2A 5X3

Want to try two free books from another line?
Call 1-800-873-8635 or visit www.ReaderService.com.

* Terms and prices subject to change without notice. Prices do not include applicable taxes. Sales tax applicable in N.Y. Canadian residents will be charged applicable taxes. Offer not valid in Quebec. This offer is limited to one order per household. Not valid for current subscribers to Harlequin Romantic Suspense books. All orders subject to credit approval. Credit or debit balances in a customer's account(s) may be offset by any other outstanding balance owed by or to the customer. Please allow 4 to 6 weeks for delivery. Offer available while quantities last.

Your Privacy—The Reader Service is committed to protecting your privacy. Our Privacy Policy is available online at www.ReaderService.com or upon request from the Reader Service.

We make a portion of our mailing list available to reputable third parties that offer products we believe may interest you. If you prefer that we not exchange your name with third parties, or if you wish to clarify or modify your communication preferences, please visit us at www.ReaderService.com/consumerschoice or write to us at Reader Service Preference Service, P.O. Box 9062, Buffalo, NY 14240-9062. Include your complete name and address.

HRS15